"Gerhardsen's masterful plotting takes us around multiple meta-phorical corners, possible killers, and surprise victims in her character- and emotion-driven saga. Maybe it's time to get back into Scandi noir—and you don't have to have read the previous books in the series to enjoy this one."

—*First Clue*

"Intricately plotted . . . Series fans will enjoy themselves."

—*Publisher's Weekly*

"A very exciting new voice from the north."

—**Ragnar Jónasson**

"Carin Gerhardsen writes so vividly, like she is painting with words, gripping your heart and soul in an ever-tightening tourniquet."

—**Peter James on *Black Ice***

"Plotted with the complexity of a 19th-century labyrinth."

—*The New York Times* **on *Black Ice***

"Complex, slow-burning thriller with a final twist that leaves no one unscathed."

—*Booklist* **on *Black Ice***

THE SAINT

THE
SAINT

CARIN GERHARDSEN
TRANSLATED BY PAUL NORLEN

THE MYSTERIOUS PRESS
NEW YORK

THE SAINT

Mysterious Press
An Imprint of Penzler Publishers
58 Warren Street
New York, N.Y. 10007

First American edition, 2024

Interior design by Maria Fernandez

Library of Congress Control Number: 2024941954

Paperback ISBN: 978-1-61316-555-3
eBook ISBN: 978-1-61316-563-8

10 9 8 7 6 5 4 3 2 1

Printed in the United States of America
Distributed by W. W. Norton & Company

LIST OF CHARACTERS

Hammarby Police—Violent Crime Unit
Detective Chief Inspector Conny Sjöberg
Police Inspector Jens Sandén
Police Inspector Hedvig (Walleye) Wallin
Police Assistant Odd (Cod) Andersson
Police Assistant Petra Westman
Police Assistant Jamal Hamad
Acting Police Commissioner Gunnar Malmberg
Police Commissioner Roland Brandt
Crime Technician Gabriella (Bella) Hansson
Forensic Physician Kaj Zetterström
Prosecutor Hadar Rosén

Deceased Friends and Family
Sven-Gunnar (Svempa) Erlandsson—deceased husband
Adrianti (Adri) Erlandsson—wife
Anna Erlandsson—daughter
Rasmus Erlandsson—son
Ida Erlandsson—daughter
Dewi Kusamasari—stepdaughter

Staffan Jenner—husband
Marie Jenner—deceased wife
Larissa (Lara) Sotnikova—Russian Summer Child

Lennart Wiklund—husband
Ingela Wiklund—ex-wife
Alexandra Wiklund—daughter
William Wiklund—son

Janne (Jan) Siem—husband
Katarina Siem—wife
Carolina Siem—daughter
Lovisa Siem—daughter
Josefin Siem—daughter

Kristina Wintherfalck—co-worker

Trailer Park Residents:
Gunilla Mäkinen
Svante Boberg
Roger Lindström
Rebecka Magnusson

AUGUST 2009, NIGHT BETWEEN SATURDAY AND SUNDAY

The air was still, as the thick scent and warmth of the summer night engulfed him. The moon, which a short time before was hanging big and yellow right above the treetops, was now almost gone. In among the trees a deer stood observing him with rigid neck and ears perked.

A doe, he thought. The correct name for a female deer was doe. At her side he could make out a fawn heedlessly rooting in the bushes for something edible, not showing him the slightest interest.

God is good, he observed. *Tonight God is holding His watchful hand over us.*

He was alone under the stars, alone on the walking path in the Herräng forest. One thought led to another, flowing through his consciousness without taking root. The schoolchildren, what were they up to on a warm, clear evening like this? No drunken teenagers had been seen since he left home. Perhaps these weeks without duties had taken their toll. Perhaps they'd had their fill of permissive socializing and freedom and were ready to return to the fold. And the homeless, what were they doing right now? Gathering strength before another merciless winter? Conditions had undeniably been the best this summer.

He felt fairly sure of what the soccer girls were up to: they were asleep, charging up for tomorrow's match. The progress they had made the past few weeks and the spirit the team showed during practice last Thursday convinced him it could only go one way: they would win. And it was well-deserved. All the hours that he and the girls had spent on that grass field had produced results.

What a summer. What an evening. Free and open exchange with the poker players at the Långbro Inn. Two kinds of herring, grilled to perfection, good things to drink and everyone there in the best of moods. Even Janne Siem, who drew the short straw when it came to paying the bill. But if you can't stand the heat . . . The fact was that the poker treasury should be used up every year and the one who lost the most naturally contributed the most. This year it happened to be Siem who didn't exactly have Lady Luck on his side, but he wasn't pouting because of it.

Even Staffan Jenner was in a better mood than usual. He had really livened up when he joined the poker club and had reason to forget the hardships of life for a few hours. *Poor Staffan, he should move out of that house, put all the bad times behind him and start over again.* Like Lennart had done after the divorce. When Lennart Wiklund's wife left him he picked himself up and went on, always in the same high spirits and a great asset in social contexts like this.

He took the cell phone out of his pocket, moved his index finger with a practiced hand over the display, and was just about to put the phone away again when he saw a movement in the corner of his eye. It was the deer, which seemed to have made a decision. Without forewarning she took an elegant leap in among the trees and was soon swallowed up by the darkness. He did not see the fawn, but presumably it went the same way. Now not a trace was seen of the August moon. He took a deep breath and his lungs filled with the damp late-summer air.

God is good, he observed again. *Tonight, God wishes us well.*

An overwhelming feeling of happiness, of gratitude, permeated him as he walked, alone under the stars in the Herräng forest.

The first shot struck him in the back and the second, after he'd fallen, struck with great precision in the neck.

—⁓⁓—

Possibly Sven-Gunnar Erlandsson's God did not have an ear for high-flown sentiments. He seemed to strike blindly, without considering the thoughts at the same time and in the near vicinity that were not quite so lofty and pure.

He knows about it, I'm sure he knows. For years he's known what I did and yet he keeps me under his wing . . .

And always with a smile. As if nothing had happened. First a slap, then a hug. And all will be forgotten. Although it's not, of course it can't be . . .

. . . not an honorable bone in his body, always these dirty tricks. Whether it's team rosters, referees' calls, or poker. And always with that sanctimonious smile . . .

I'll kill him, I can do it, I will kill. You'll all see, I can do it. I'll do it . . .

Two times, two goddamn times it's happened and he pretends not to know about it. Although he knows that I know he knows . . .

He rewrites the rules to suit his own needs, that fucking hypocrite . . .
It's like you're in a fox trap, I've got to be free from this yoke . . .
If he was gone, the pressure in my head would ease up and I could live my own life . . .
And we sit like driveling idiots all of us, puppets, and just go along . . .
I can, I should, breathe deep. One shot in the neck, clean and neat . . .

SUNDAY MORNING

Detective Chief Inspector Conny Sjöberg's summer had been intense: long days of work to finish the summer cabin and twilight nights with too much food and wine. Which unfortunately did not really cancel each other out. To the attentive, this was now noticeable on his no longer youthful body.

The Sjöberg family had moved back to town on Friday so the kids could start getting used to normal bedtimes before Monday's half-day start at daycare and school. Saturday had been spent at the Gröna Lund amusement park under chaotic conditions, with two adults and five children with five different preferences pulling in all directions. But the beauty of it was that now they could do this kind of thing together, all the children were big enough now that you could engage in activities somewhat more stimulating than crawling around on all fours or playing peekaboo. The twins had really filled out during the summer. And calmed down. This, in combination with the lovely summer place slowly taking shape in Bergslagen, a region north of Lake Mälaren, infused him with calm. A sense of liberation. Now the time was finally past when naps, strollers, binkies, baby food, and crying children ruled their existence.

Damned if he wasn't awakened at five thirty on Sunday morning. By the telephone this time, however.

———

Jens Sandén had put in a week of work after vacation and was already back on the grind. After his stroke two years earlier the now fifty-three-year-old police inspector, contrary to what anyone could have predicted, pulled himself together properly and lost no less than twenty-two kilos. He ate healthy, often took a long walk before breakfast, and played tennis with his old squire Conny Sjöberg every Friday morning. Generally he felt in brilliant condition, and the fact that his mildly mentally disabled daughter had her life under control nowadays didn't hurt. She too had returned to work—behind the reception counter at the police station—and quickly settled down again after the summer absence.

This morning Sandén woke up on his own at five fifteen, boiled an egg in the microwave recently purchased from Designtorget, and was now about to pull on his rainsuit and boots to go on a morning walk. But these plans were upset when the phone rang and he was asked to get in the car to go out to the Herräng forest. Oh well, he thought, the rain gear would come in handy there too.

———

It was pouring rain. After an amazing summer evening, during the wee hours storm clouds blew in from the Baltic and were now in the process of emptying over eastern Sweden.

Just to make things difficult for us crime technicians, thought Gabriella Hansson as she struggled with the cart in the mud on the fifth fairway at Nacka Golf Club.

Just to make things difficult for us golfers, thought Hedvig Wallin as she saw the ball come down and stop abruptly in the muck, approximately twenty meters before the green, after duffing a five-iron shot. She made a half-hearted attempt to dry off the slippery shaft of the club on a soaked towel and stuffed the club in the bag before she went and retrieved the not inconsiderable piece of turf she had sent off with the ball. With the back of her hand, Hedvig—for over a year now most often referred to as Walleye—wiped off the clay that had splashed up in her face with the half-unsuccessful stroke.

She was fifty-five years old, and after almost thirty years' absence from police work had returned to service, with the rank of inspector with the Hammarby police. Her late husband had been a UN official with the World Health Organization in Geneva until his death a few years earlier, and during that time she had been a housewife in the family villa in Soral. During the time left over when she was not devoting herself to her family and the household, she had improved herself, maintained her theoretical police knowledge, and earned a Swedish law degree at the doctoral level. And spent the occasional free hour on the golf course, which resulted in a handicap that vacillated between six and eight.

With her sixth stroke Hansson managed to get the ball up on the green, but it continued slowly past the flag. Wallin made the green with a nice chip shot not far from the hole and sank for par, even though her partner's cell phone rang just as she was about to putt.

"Hansson . . . Okay . . . Shall I bring Walleye along? We're at the golf course . . . It may take a while, we're as far from the parking lot as you can get . . . Forty-five minutes. An hour max . . . I'll tell the technicians to set up an investigation tent as soon as possible. And it would be nice if you made sure they don't tramp around the body too much."

"Game over?" Wallin asked.

Hansson nodded.

"For us, and for some poker player in Älvsjö. I'll putt out anyway," she said, and mildly sensationally but without great enthusiasm managed to sink her twenty-meter putt for a double bogey.

Like some kind of rash, a mild eczema; mostly you didn't think about it, but sometimes it itched like crazy. That's roughly the way thirty-one-year-old police assistant Petra Westman would summarize her emotional state during sleepless hours. It had been almost three years since that evening when she was drugged at Clarion's bar and then transported to a villa in Mälarhöjden where she was raped by two men. The one, senior physician Peder Fryhk, was now rattling the bars at the Norrtälje prison and hopefully would continue to do so for a few more years. With the help of prosecutor Hadar Rosén, she had managed to get Fryhk sentenced for several rapes without personally figuring in the investigation at all.

There were indications, however, that she was not as incognito as she had hoped, because pictures from the rape had shown up on several occasions in anything but agreeable contexts. Police Commissioner Roland Brandt received an invitation with attached images sent to him from her own email address. He took it quite seriously, tried to get her in bed, and when that didn't succeed fired her for misconduct instead. Which was called off only at the last minute by a resourceful Sjöberg. Then a video sequence from the same occasion had been sent out from Hamad's email address. Who knew how many people had seen that? And as if that wasn't enough, she had fallen right into the trap and almost broken with Hamad on top of it, even though he was one of those closest to her.

And all this had been orchestrated with a sure hand by the Other Man, as she referred to him. The one who held the camera. The one who zoomed in on painful penetrations of unconscious female bodies. The one who waited until the camera was turned off to commit his rapes. He who was so averse to light that the other exploited women presumably didn't even know of his existence. Who perhaps even worked in the police station at Östgötagatan 100 and was thus in her vicinity almost every day. Otherwise, how could he get hold of her pass card and have access to both her and Hamad's computers? No, it was beyond a doubt that the Other Man was in the building, but who was he? Petra Westman had absolutely no idea.

And that was what gnawed at her. The rape itself, at which she had barely been present mentally anyway, and the physical and mental aftereffects, she had to some degree been able to repress. But the fact that the Other Man lived and moved in their midst gave her chills. He had not bothered her for over a year, so it would be best to just swallow the indignity and move on. But it itched sometimes.

Like hell.

For that reason it didn't matter much that the phone rang right after five thirty in the morning, the last day of summer vacation.

—⁂—

It wasn't possible. It couldn't be true that the phone was ringing so early on a Sunday, and during vacation besides. He hadn't gotten up before nine a single time the whole summer, and he was no more eager when he heard the rain pattering against the window. He cast a glance over toward Mercury, but he was sleeping undisturbed, even though it must have rung at least three times. His six-year-old son had as usual kicked off the covers, which often ended up on the floor even before he fell asleep.

Odd Andersson was thirty-eight years old and had come from the city detective squad to the Hammarby police in October the previous year. With precise timing he'd made an entrance in the blue oval room only a few days after he failed, by a hairbreadth and before one and a half million TV viewers, to advance from a Friday final in *Idol 2008*. Like a considerable portion of the Swedish people, Conny Sjöberg and his subordinates quickly made a place in their hearts for the old rocker.

After having to go by the rather awkward nickname "Idol-Odd," Jens Sandén got tired of that and instead proposed "Cod." A cod, he said, was a popular fish with a big mouth. For that reason he thought it would suit Idol-Odd well, and he could also keep Walleye company in the aquarium—the big glass building on Östgötagatan 100. And in an effort at consistency, it didn't take long before little Mercury had become "Minnow" with the Hammarby police.

Before the phone emitted yet another ring, Odd picked up the receiver.

"Okay . . . Yes, it's probably best that way . . . I'll have to bring the boy along in that case, he's staying with me . . . Oh, I guess he can sit and chill in the car, it's cool."

As sleepy police assistant Jamal Hamad unwillingly performed his morning ablutions, his brain was still processing yesterday's impressions.

He had spent Saturday evening at the Pride festival, of all places. Not because he was particularly entertained by the phenomenon itself; he thought there was far too much focus on the sexual, the extreme. *With all due respect to tolerance and gay rights, but seriously—a dildo club? Did that sort of thing foster increased understanding for LGBT issues?* He suspected it was probably the other way around. In any event, it was not gimmicks or politics that lured him there; he was there for highly personal reasons.

In Tantolunden, in the immediate vicinity of a trailer where, if you were prepared to wait for thirty minutes, you could find out if you had HIV or chlamydia, a panel discussion was going on. A representative from RFSL, one from the National Board of Forensic Medicine, a researcher from the criminology department at Stockholm University, a few politicians from various parties, and a couple of police officers were talking about gender equality, gay rights, and hate crimes. The opening statement was given by no less than the acting police commissioner with the Hammarby Police Department, Gunnar Malmberg. Rapist Gunnar Malmberg.

Only Hamad knew that he was the Other Man.

From what Malmberg said during the ten minutes he spoke, a few things above all startled Hamad: "Credibility is of the greatest importance, especially within an organization like the police. In order for the equality process to have credibility, it is time to go from words to action.

"Empathy. We are all complicit in maintaining the gender power structure. Men ought to put themselves in women's situation. If men in general were to do so, we would not need equality enforcement.

"All experience indicates that equality is an unbelievably effective force against violence. There are no bad people—it is the silence of good people that I have a hard time with."

My God. A shiver passed through Hamad as he locked the door behind him to drive out to the crime scene in Älvsjö.

A tent had been set up over the body, but the dead man was a pitiful creature lying prostrate on his side. The clothes were completely soaked, and the rain had efficiently removed all the blood from the asphalt path he was lying on. The gaping holes in the neck and throat testified that there must have been a lot of blood. In addition, everything indicated that he had also been shot in the back.

He was properly dressed in suede loafers, beige trousers, light blue shirt, and navy blue jacket. An elegant watch could be glimpsed from under the sleeve and there was a gold ring on the ring finger of the left hand. The man's pockets had been emptied at an early stage to rescue as much as possible from the rain. His wallet had still been in the inside pocket of the jacket and it contained both cards and cash, which argued against a robbery gone bad. According to the driver's license, the victim was fifty-two years old and was named Sven-Gunnar Erlandsson.

Sjöberg, Hamad, Westman, and Andersson stood outside the investigation tent looking in to get a picture of the crime scene. Two technicians were working inside. It seemed to be a hopeless enterprise to sort out any traces whatsoever of the murderer from the pools of water on the asphalt.

"The weather was nice last night. Does anyone know when it started raining?" Sjöberg asked.

"I went to bed about twelve, it was nice then," Andersson replied.

"At a quarter to one when I came home it had clouded over a little," said Hamad.

"When I got up at four-fifteen it was raining buckets, and it has ever since," Hedvig Wallin attested, suddenly showing up with Bella Hansson, Sandén, and forensic physician Kaj Zetterström in tow.

"That's good, then we'll blame you, Walleye," said Sandén. "Nice seeing you all together, has the summer been good?"

"Hmm, until now anyway," Sjöberg answered. "Thanks for showing up."

He took a step to one side so that Hansson and Zetterström could enter the tent.

"I thought it would be good if everyone was here from the start, then we avoid going over everything again on Monday.

You'll get comp time on some other occasion, hope that's okay. If you'll take a look in there," Sjöberg continued, directing himself to Wallin and Sandén, "we'll take a stroll out here. I'm going to exchange a few words with the police officers who were first on the scene."

At the barricade tape a short distance away on the road stood two uniformed police officers, one male and one female, who seemed to be hoping for better times. One of them turned a face up to the sky, but it gave no indication of the weather breaking anytime in the immediate future, with its unchanging uniform gray.

"Who found the body?" asked Sjöberg.

"A jogger," answered the female police officer. "A young girl who lives here in the vicinity. We sent her home."

"Had she seen or heard anything?"

"Nothing. This was about five o'clock."

"Did she touch him?"

"She felt for a pulse, but it was obvious that he was dead, so she made no resuscitation attempts. Besides, she knew the victim."

"She knew him? How?"

"He was apparently her soccer coach," the other one explained. "She was extremely shaken. They probably had a match today, too."

"Good Lord. How old is she?"

"Thirteen. Her name is Josefin Siem. You'll get her information."

The male officer wriggled a notebook out from somewhere under his rainsuit, tore off a page, and gave it to Sjöberg, who nodded in thanks and went back to the investigation tent where the others were gathered.

"Nasty," said Sandén, shaking his head. "He looks like any old white-bread Svensson."

"They say he's a soccer coach," said Sjöberg. "According to the girl who found him."

"There were credit cards and money in his wallet," said Wallin. "Over a thousand kronor. So he doesn't appear to have been robbed."

"On the other hand he had no cell phone, and that must be considered rather unusual these days," Sandén said.

Sjöberg was doubtful.

"Cell phone thieves are usually young guys who use a knife at worst. I find it highly improbable that a gang of teenage boys would shoot someone's head off for a cell phone. Anything else you've noticed?"

Hansson looked out of the tent opening.

"I thought you'd want to know what we found on him. You know about the wallet. Sporty Seiko brand watch. Gold ring without inscription, apparently a wedding ring because it was on the left ring finger. And he had four playing cards in the breast pocket of his jacket."

"Aces?" asked Westman.

"Well, one of the cards was probably an ace, but not all."

"A cheater, maybe?" Hamad wondered. "According to time-honored tradition, you shoot cheaters in the head."

"What happened to tar and feathers?" Sandén sighed.

Zetterström appeared from inside the tent. "He wasn't shot in the head, but in the neck. At close range and with a large-bore weapon, I would guess. The bullet went right through the throat, so you'll probably find it hereabouts, I guess. I haven't found any exit hole from the first shot. Presumably the bullet hit the spine and changed direction, so it remained inside the body somewhere. I'll get back to that when I've gotten started on the autopsy."

The forensic doctor withdrew into the tent and Hansson picked up the thread again.

"We found a handwritten note in the same pocket as the playing cards, but it's so soggy from all the rain that the text can't be made out. It appears to be both numbers and letters, but it's extremely blurry."

"A telephone number maybe? Or an address?" Andersson suggested.

"Very possible. I'll do what I can to get it in legible shape. That was all."

"Thanks for that," said Sjöberg. "I'll find out where he lived, if he has any relatives, and whether he's been reported missing."

He took a look at his watch.

"It's not seven yet, so it's very possible that no one has missed him yet. He must have some family, judging by the ring. Let's go back to the cars."

Then Sjöberg dialed Lundin's number, whom he already knew was serving as on-duty commander at the station because he was the one who'd called and woken him up not that long ago. A short time later he learned that Sven-Gunnar Erlandsson had not been reported missing, that he lived at Vaktelsstigen 16 in Herrängen, and that his wife, Adrianti, was also registered there.

—⁓—

"Adrianti?" said Wallin as she and Sjöberg prepared to go and ring the Erlandsson family's doorbell. "What kind of name is that?"

They were in a pleasant area of single-family homes with mature gardens, right next to a patch of woods that effectively shielded the residents from two rather busy roads in the vicinity. Sven-Gunnar Erlandsson had been found in the same forest, although a few hundred meters from there. The house was painted a shade of green that might possibly be called olive, and in contrast to the surrounding villas it was reminiscent of a small-scale Victorian mansion.

The sky had lightened somewhat and what remained of the rain drizzled down on them as they went past the Audi in the driveway and up to the front stoop. Sjöberg pressed the button and a pleasing bell reverberated through the walls and out to them. It only took a few seconds before the door was opened by a middle-aged woman in a dressing gown and lambskin slippers. She stared at them with a hunted expression without saying a word. Sjöberg had his police ID ready and extended it toward her.

"My name is Conny Sjöberg and I'm a chief inspector with the Hammarby police. This is Police Inspector Hedvig Wallin."

"Has something happened?" the woman said. "Is it Svempa?" Sjöberg noticed a strong accent and presumed that she was of southeast Asian origin. The black hair was carelessly pulled into a ponytail that was coming undone. With her hunched shoulders and arms tightly crossed over her chest, she gave an impression of having just gotten out of bed. And that the wakening was not the best.

"Are you Adrianti? Sven-Gunnar Erlandsson's wife?" asked Sjöberg with a facial expression that he hoped did not reveal too much of their errand.

She nodded.

"We would like to come in and talk with you. Is that okay?"

She nodded again and took a step back to let them in. They were now in a small hallway with grooved panels on the walls and a rag rug on the floor. They stepped out of their muddy boots on the doormat and followed her into the house.

After passing a stairway that led up to the top floor and getting a glimpse of a comfortable living room with books on the shelves and an old piano against one wall, they ended up in the kitchen. It was a large country kitchen with room for ten people around a white-painted wooden table in peasant style, and here too there were rag rugs on the floor. The familiar aroma of curry reminded Sjöberg that he had not had any breakfast.

The woman pulled out a chair for herself and sat down with a sigh. Both police officers sat down across from her, and Sjöberg was about to speak when she anticipated him.

"He didn't come home last night. I went to bed at midnight and Svempa hadn't come home yet. And when I woke up, he had still not shown up. What has happened?"

She braided her fingers together in front of her mouth and tensed them with such force that the knuckles turned white.

"He was found dead a few hours ago," Sjöberg answered, right to the point. "Very close to here. On the walking path over there in the forest. I'm extremely sorry."

She stared at him with terror, incapable of saying anything.

He was letting the news sink in when suddenly creaking steps were heard on the stairs. A young woman walked through the doorway, barefoot and in pajamas. She appeared to be in her twenties and let her gaze wander in surprise from Sjöberg to Wallin before finally meeting her mother's. Or was it perhaps her stepmother? The blue eyes and blonde hair suggested that. A shimmer of worry crossed her face as she assured herself with a glance at the digital clock on the microwave that it really was as early as she thought.

"Has something happened?" she asked with a half-hearted attempt at a smile. "Is it Dad? Adri?"

The address convinced Sjöberg that he had guessed right. The stepmother could not get a word out, so Sjöberg answered in her stead.

"Sven-Gunnar Erlandsson, is that your dad?"

She nodded.

"I'm so sorry, but he was found dead earlier this morning."

Wallin got up and placed her arm around the girl, who was starting to cry—a quiet weeping—and then helped her sit down.

"What happened?" she asked weakly, with tears running down her cheeks.

"He was shot," Sjöberg answered. "A jogger found him about five o'clock on the forest path over there. Do you know where he'd been?"

"At Långbro Inn," Adrianti Erlandsson answered in a cracked voice.

She cleared her throat and continued.

"The poker club spends its treasury once a year. They eat and drink up all the money. It usually goes late, so I wasn't worried that he wasn't at home when I went to bed."

Then the tears came for her, too.

"Dear little lady," she said, pulling the girl to her. "Dear beloved Ida."

Then they sat quiet and composed and gave consolation and warmth to one another. Sjöberg thought the whole scene was marked by dignity. Quiet sorrow and love.

"Are there other children?" he asked carefully.

"Yes. I have to call Anna and Rasmus."

"We won't bother you with a lot of questions. But in order to go further with this, we still need to find out a few things right away. Then we'll get back to the rest on a later occasion. We need names and addresses or telephone numbers for those who were there last evening. Can you help us with that?"

Adrianti Erlandsson kissed the girl on the forehead, collected herself, and turned toward Sjöberg.

"Staffan," she said. "Staffan Jenner, Svempa's best friend. He doesn't live very far from here. On Blåklintsvägen. Lennart Wiklund. He lives over on Långbrokungens Väg nowadays. And then there was Janne Siem, who lives in Långbro."

Sjöberg was startled.

"Siem?" he repeated. "Does he happen to have a daughter named Josefin?"

She looked at him with surprise.

"Yes, she plays on the team that Svempa coaches. What about it?"

"She was the one who found him. When she was out jogging."

Ida looked up at him with troubled eyes and then gave her stepmother a look that was hard to interpret. The stepmother now looked even more overwrought, if possible.

"Poor child," she said, shaking her head. "I . . . don't know what I should say . . . I'll see if I have their number in my cell phone."

She got up with a heavy sigh and left the kitchen. Wallin took the opportunity to question the daughter.

"Ida, do you know if your dad left his cell phone at home last night?"

"No, he never would have done that," the girl answered, drawing her hand under her nose. "He always had his cell phone with him."

"What kind of phone did he have?"

"An iPhone, sixteen gigabytes. With a red case. Was he robbed?"

Wallin looked inquisitively at Sjöberg, leaving it to him to decide what ought to be said and what not.

"Maybe," he answered. "We haven't found any cell phone. On the other hand, his wallet was still there. Where did your dad work?"

"At SEB. Kungsträdgården."

"Do you know if he had any enemies?"

"Enemies?"

Ida Erlandsson seemed sincerely surprised.

"I have a hard time believing that. Everyone loves Dad. Loved Dad," she corrected herself.

Adrianti came back with her cell phone in hand. She had obviously also heard the question.

"Svempa had no enemies," she said. "I have never heard anyone say a bad word about him. Generous, helpful, appreciated at work, committed to the family. He helped homeless people and has been a soccer coach for many years. Volunteers."

New tears welled up in her eyes as she spoke, so she interrupted herself and sat down again at the table with her hands in front of her face. Sjöberg thought it was a bit much to ask more questions for now, so both police officers made sure to get the requested information and said their goodbyes.

SUNDAY MORNING

At nine o'clock, after everyone had managed to get something to eat, the forces gathered in the blue oval room at the police station. Sjöberg was able to reach Hansson as she was en route from the crime scene. So far, she did not think she had been able to produce anything new that might cast light on the case. For that reason she declined to be at the meeting and devoted herself instead to analyses in the lab.

The prosecutor, Hadar Rosén, drove in from his summer cabin in Roslagen just for this meeting, but judging by appearances had not considered it grounds for changing from recreational dress to a suit. An attitude he seemed to share with all those around the table, even if he was the only one who usually wore a suit every day.

Sjöberg opened the meeting with a brief account of known facts concerning the murder, primarily to acquaint the prosecutor with the case. He also summarized the short visit with the widow and daughter.

"There is naturally much more we want to talk with them about, but we'll let them be in peace today, then we'll make contact tomorrow."

"What did Erlandsson do for a living?" Rosén asked.

"His daughter said he was a banker, apparently worked at SEB."

"Was he murdered in the Herräng forest or somewhere else?"

"According to Bella, Sven-Gunnar Erlandsson was shot at the place where he was found," Sjöberg answered. "A lot of blood had been washed away by the rain, but under the body there was enough that you could draw the conclusion that it was there he was murdered. As I said, most everything suggests he was first wounded in the back and that the whole thing was concluded immediately thereafter with a shot to the neck."

"A regular execution," Wallin noted.

"Carried out by a cowardly bastard who didn't dare look the victim in the eyes," Sandén pointed out.

"I still believe he cheated at cards," said Hamad. "Can't see any other reason for there being playing cards in his pocket. If it had been a whole deck, that would be a different matter. And a shot in the head is actually what tradition decrees, even if it might seem like that belongs to a different time and a different place."

"But as we said, he wasn't shot in the head, but in the neck," Andersson pointed out.

"But that's splitting hairs . . . It's the same idea," Hamad said.

"We don't know how much money this concerned," said Sjöberg. "But from what I understood, these guys partied away the *whole* poker pot yesterday evening at Långbro Inn. Even if contrary to expectations it would be a single person who had to pay for the whole party, I have a hard time believing it would have involved enough money to be worth killing for. Three-course dinner and good wine, maybe even champagne and cognac for four people. I'll say ten thousand kronor, and then I'm overstating it. But it will be easy enough to find out."

"I agree with Conny," said Westman. "Ten thousand is way too little to get your head blown off."

"Neck . . ." Andersson tried again.

"Not if the guy has made a habit of it," Hamad persisted. "Maybe he's been cheating for years and finally it was the last straw for someone."

"Then it would be a matter of revenge," Westman continued. "And in that case, the shot would have been in the head. What kind of revenge is it if the victim doesn't even know what's happening? Besides, it seems to be the wrong time to get revenge when the bill is already paid."

"I'm still wary about that business with the cell phone," said Sandén. "Did you check if he left it at home?"

"He hadn't," Sjöberg answered. "According to the daughter he always had it with him."

"So we can say that the murderer robbed him of his cell phone, anyway," said Sandén. "What brand was it?"

"An iPhone," said Sjöberg. "With a red case."

"Sixteen gigabytes," Wallin clarified.

"One of those costs two or three hundred. But do any of us believe in a cell phone robber?"

Nothing but shaking heads. Sandén shrugged his shoulders, evidently not very convinced either.

"I think the fact that his wallet was still there means we can rule out robbery," said Andersson. "That he was shot in the back first seems to me that we're dealing with a cowardly wretch, just like Jens said. Maybe even a beginner. But in any event, an individual with the sole intention of killing Erlandsson. And who knows—maybe only to get at the cell phone. Maybe it contained important information. Something worth killing for."

"Interesting thought," said Sjöberg. "Or else he had it out and the murderer just couldn't resist. But let's do this: You, Cod, and Jens question Jan Siem and his daughter. I hardly need to point out that you may want to take it easy with the girl. Petra and Jamal will question the other two poker buddies, Lennart Wiklund and Staffan Jenner. Walleye can stay here and do research. Check the civil registration, the crime register, ISP, ASP, and so on for all persons involved. I'll contact Långbro Inn and then try to make contact with Erlandsson's coworkers, if that's even possible on a Sunday."

"Are you quite sure of that?" said Wallin incomprehensibly.

All eyes were turned toward her. Wallin was an odd duck that you couldn't really figure out. Presumably because she couldn't make up her mind whether she was a young woman or a middle-aged lady. The idea had struck Sjöberg that it could be as simple as they couldn't put a label on her, which gave rise to a certain degree of irritation. Except for Sandén of all people, who thought she was a "really damn nice type," as he put it. And Hansson of course, who spent a lot of time with her on the golf course, where Wallin evidently was a god.

"I'm not sure about anything," Sjöberg said drily. "What do you mean?"

"Are you sure it should be kid gloves for Josefin Siem? Why not a hard line?"

No one said anything for a few moments, but a broad grin spread over Sandén's face.

"She's only a child," said Sjöberg hesitantly. "Where are you headed?"

"I just think it's a peculiar coincidence that she, in particular, was the first one on the scene. As far as I'm concerned, she might well have carried out the murder."

"A thirteen-year-old . . . ?"

"They're precocious these days. Another alternative is that her father murdered Erlandsson and little Josefin helped him in some way. For example, by getting rid of the weapon. She's a soccer player, must be in iron shape, and could very well have run to Fittja and back."

Sjöberg nodded thoughtfully, forced to admit that she was right on that point. Far-fetched to be sure, but completely possible. The weapon had not been found, even though a rather large area around the murder scene had been fine-combed.

"Oh well, that was only a thought. Just so you keep your eyes open, boys," she concluded, firing off a smile at Sandén and Andersson.

At the same moment the door opened and Gunnar Malmberg walked in. As usual, impeccably dressed, today in jeans and piqué sweater, with a becoming suntan and a hairstyle that had clearly not been subjected to the morning storm.

"Jeepers creepers," Sandén exclaimed, "isn't it Sunday today?"

"And vacation besides?" Wallin added, who like Sandén did not concern herself much about her position in the hierarchy, but instead addressed the acting police commissioner as if he were just anyone.

"I have some piles of paper I have to plow through over the weekend," Malmberg answered guardedly, but changed the topic of conversation at once. "I heard from Lundin that you're investigating that Älvsjö murder, is that right? Was his name Erlandsson?"

"That's right," Sjöberg confirmed.

"I had a strange call just now." He glanced at the clock, which was at twenty minutes to ten. "About five minutes ago. He called me because I was the police chief, as he put it, and said he had information concerning the murder. I didn't know anything about it, but I got ready to take notes. Unfortunately he didn't say anything other than that we would never catch the murderer, and then he hung up."

"I'll be damned," said Sjöberg. "And it was a man, you're sure of that?"

"Absolutely. Rather young, I believe."

"Did he have an accent?"

"I didn't think about that."

"Age?"

"No idea. It was pretty noisy in the background, too."

"Voice distortion?" Wallin proposed, without anyone really knowing whether she was joking or serious.

"Well, that's possible of course," Malmberg replied, who seemed to take the question seriously in any event. "It's pretty hard to determine that these days, isn't it?"

"Would you be able to reproduce that conversation more or less word for word?" Sjöberg asked.

"Sure," said Malmberg, pulling a handwritten note from his back pocket. "I wrote down what I recalled. With reservation for minor inaccuracies: 'Are you the police chief for real or what?' 'Yes, you could say that. Acting police commissioner is the correct designation.' 'I have interesting information about the murder of Erlandsson.' 'Okay, let's hear it.' 'Then I can say that him who shot him you're never going to find. Fucking losers.' That was it."

"Well, he has no regrets, anyway, so now we know that," Sandén observed.

"Doubtful grammar," noted Wallin, without anyone attaching any great importance to it.

"Did you get the call on your cell or through the switchboard?" Hamad asked, who carefully noted everything Malmberg had told them.

"On the cell to be sure, but through the switchboard. It's the only way for an outsider to get in contact with me by phone. My cell number is obviously secret, but I forward all calls to the cell."

"You mentioned something about noise," said Rosén. "Could you make out what kind of noise it was?"

"Voices? Engine noise? Music?" Sjöberg suggested.

"I would probably say it was traffic noise. It went so fast, I hardly had time to react before it was over."

"I can get to work on that," said Hamad. "I'll get Telia moving so we'll find out what number the call was made from and where. I can request Erlandsson's phone lists too, since I'll already be at it."

Sjöberg started gathering his papers.

"Good, Jamal," he said. "We'll have to see how fast they are on a Sunday during vacation. And thanks for the information, Gunnar. I think we'll break here. Then we'll have another meeting tomorrow morning at nine."

—◠◠◠—

Sandén and Andersson picked up Mercury in Lundin's office, where he was sitting and drawing after, according to reports, teaching the on-duty commander two guitar chords. Then they took off in Andersson's car to the Siem family's residence on Vivelvägen in Långbro, while the six-year-old let loose on the guitar at full volume in the back seat. They were met by Mrs. Siem with the news that neither Josefin nor her father were at home; despite what had happened, they had gone off to play the planned away match in Södertälje.

"But was the girl really in any condition to play soccer after what she's been through?" Sandén asked with some skepticism.

"We made the judgment that it was good for her to get out and see people," the woman answered. "Think about other things."

She was somewhere between forty and forty-five and looked good, even if in Sandén's way of thinking she had a trifle too much makeup on her face for a Sunday morning at home.

"But as far as I understand, Sven-Gunnar Erlandsson was their coach. How do they resolve that?"

"Janne had to fill in. He's coach for another team and knows all the girls, so it's no problem," she answered unconcerned.

"But if the coach has been murdered . . . Isn't that a reason to cancel the match?" Andersson wondered. "Call a forfeit? All the girls must be upset, have a hard time focusing on the task?"

"We made the judgment," she said again, "that they didn't need to know anything yet. It hasn't come out, and—"

"And?"

She pulled herself together in a way that did not escape the police officers' notice.

"It was an important match."

Sandén had to exert himself to hide what he was thinking.

"And it's hardly our duty to inform them about what happened," she established.

Sandén was inclined to agree, but asked out of pure fascination with her manner of tackling the situation.

"So whose duty is it?"

She shrugged her shoulders.

"The club's. The police. The parents."

"Did you have anything against Sven-Gunnar Erlandsson?" Andersson ventured to ask, and her face now suddenly assumed a completely different expression.

"Not at all," she answered with a sorrowful smile that might well be genuine. "On the contrary. He was an amazing person. We're going to miss him."

"Amazing—in what way?" Sandén asked.

She appeared to think for a moment before she answered, moving her body weight to the other leg and seeming to seek guidance somewhere among the clouds.

"He was good."

A pause for effect.

"He had a good heart. Helpful, considerate. He devoted as much time as it took to those girls and their soccer. A wonderful dad. Yes, that was how he ended up in this business with soccer. And then, on top of it all, all the charitable work."

"Charity?"

"Yes, he devoted himself quite a lot to the homeless. We're going to miss him," she repeated, now with eyes that made Sandén wonder whether they weren't on the verge of blank.

"Did you socialize privately?" Andersson asked.

She shook her head.

"Not as a family, but Janne and Svempa socialized a bit. Partly through soccer, and they also played poker together."

"And they did that yesterday?"

"No, yesterday they just used up the money they had saved up. Yes, now, how that works, I don't know. But yesterday they were at Långbro Inn and had dinner."

"Do you have any idea how long they were there?" Andersson continued, without revealing what he was really after.

"According to what I heard, they were there until closing time. Janne was home about twelve-thirty, I would guess."

"It's time for us to go," Sandén concluded the conversation. "I'm sure we'll be in touch again."

—⁓—

"What a fucking robot." Andersson assessed as he closed the door and they went back to the car.

Sandén couldn't disagree.

"Either she didn't have all her chickens in the coop or else she's exactly the cold Stepford wife she appears to be."

"With strains of hypocrisy," Andersson filled in. "Whatever fits in from one moment to the next. A soccer mom in a Chanel outfit."

"Was she?" Sandén exclaimed in amazement. "Chanel outfit?"

"The hell I know? Do you think I know what that looks like? But I did notice she had something on, in any event." Then they started laughing. A raw, magnificent horselaugh.

—⁓—

Immediately after the meeting Hamad contacted Telia Telecommunications, commissioning them to get back to him as soon as possible with information about accounts from which calls had come into the police switchboard between 9:30 and 9:40 a.m. To be on the safe side, he asked them to do the same for Malmberg's direct number and cell phone. Besides this he put them on the somewhat lower priority job of generating a list of incoming and outgoing traffic for Sven-Gunnar Erlandsson's cell phone.

Then he left together with Westman to Blåklintsvägen in Herrängen.

—⁓—

Staffan Jenner was an odd character. Though he was only about fifty-five, he was stooped, gray, and shrunken, and his pants seemed to be held up thanks only to his belt. Hamad could not help thinking it was cancer, and then had noticeable problems during the interview dismissing the thought.

But Jenner met them in a friendly manner right from the start, invited them to sit down at the coffee table in the living room without first inquiring about their errand. He had a pleasant voice and a pair of intense blue eyes that now more than anything expressed curiosity.

"What were you doing yesterday evening?" Westman began, while Hamad took out his notebook.

"I had dinner at Långbro Inn with a few good friends," he answered straight out.

"What time did you get home?"

"At twelve thirty."

"How did you get home?"

"I walked, it was a fantastic summer night."

He smiled as he said that, a barely visible smile that could signify just about anything.

"So it wasn't raining then?"

"No, the rain must have come after I'd gone to bed. There were almost no clouds. We noticed that the August moon was enormous where it was hanging above the treetops."

"We?"

"Yes, to start with I was walking with a couple of the friends I'd spent the evening with."

Still no questions. Why didn't he wonder what they wanted?

"Was one of them possibly Sven-Gunnar Erlandsson?"

"Exactly," he nodded.

Westman struck while the iron was hot.

"What route did you take?"

He answered immediately, apparently didn't need to think about it.

"We took Bergtallsvägen and Stora Kvinns, and on the corner there by the old asylum we took the walking path down to Vantörsvägen, where we separated from Svempa. He crossed Vantörsvägen and went through the forest. There's a path there that leads all the way to his house. Lennart and I walked toward Långbrokungens Väg where he lives. Then I took Guldregnsbacken a short way, turned right at Nejlikevägen, then left on Isbergavägen and followed it all the way up to Blåklintsvägen."

Was this rehearsed? Or did the guy just have a good head on his shoulders? Hamad wrote so fast that the pen glowed.

"You've gone that way before," Westman observed with a dry laugh.

"Well, I don't know if I've done it that often. But I know the sur-roundings here, know what the streets are called. I've lived here for many years."

Still the same amiable tone of voice.

"Why are you asking all these questions?"

There it was.

"Because early yesterday morning Sven-Gunnar Erlandsson was found in that forest you mentioned," Petra said with a gaze that was clearly scrutinizing. "Murdered. Executed with a shot to the neck."

Staffan Jenner froze in his chair, taking a deep breath. Then he frowned. Both police officers studied his reactions, weighed them, analyzed. He let the air out of his lungs, moved his gaze worriedly from one to the other. Then he leaned across the table and put his face in his hands, while he repeatedly shook his head.

Hamad and Westman exchanged looks, without saying any-thing. The seconds ticked on.

Finally, he let his hands fall down on the table and leaned back in the armchair with a sigh.

"I am . . . crushed," he got out.

Was he really? Was he trying to convince himself that he was? Or did he want them to think he was?

"Sven-Gunnar . . . Why do I call him that? Svempa, my very best friend . . . What happens now? Maybe it's time to move at last . . . All the memories . . . Poor Adri, what will become of her? And the children—what will they think?"

Hamad cast a glance at Westman, but she didn't give herself time to meet it, she was completely occupied by Jenner. He did not seem to be addressing himself to them. Fragments of thoughts seemed to be coming out of his mouth without context. Hamad wanted to understand, was not content with half-sentences without substance. For that reason he resumed the dialogue.

"So Erlandsson was your best friend?" he asked. "Was that mutual?"

Jenner looked at him with an unexpectedly clear gaze.

"That's hard for me to answer, but I think so. I feel convinced of that. Was he robbed?"

"We don't know that," Hamad answered truthfully. "Did you socialize as a family?"

"Yes, we did at one time."

"At one time? When was that?"

The comfortable living room was full of framed photographs depicting children of all ages, so it was not a daring guess that Staffan Jenner had a family.

"The children moved out long ago. They are twenty-seven and twenty-five years old."

"And your wife?"

"I'm a widower. And not remarried," he added. "But to answer your question the children got along very well, they were more or less the same age. Well, except Ida of course, their youngest, but she kept up too. So we socialized frequently all together, we did."

Jenner seemed to have recovered somewhat, answered clearly and precisely even if his entire appearance gave a somewhat more tired impression. Which could be considered normal, Hamad was forced to admit to himself. But there was something not quite right about this man, he just couldn't put his finger on what it was. Was Jenner concealing something from them?

"Did he have any enemies, Erlandsson?" Westman asked.

Jenner shook his head.

"It's hard for me to believe that. He was extremely popular in all circles. At work—I've met a few of his coworkers—at the club, in the neighborhood. I wouldn't think anyone has a bad word to say about Svempa."

"And in the poker club?" Hamad added. "No discord there either?"

"Absolutely not. Good Lord, it's only a game."

"With a fair amount of money involved."

Jenner looked back at him with a suspicious frown.

"That's pushing it a little. We are four people who meet once or twice a month and play for a few hours. Mainly to socialize. No one wins any money, instead the money that anyone wins during the evening goes to the joint treasury. It's usually a matter of a thousand or two in the worst case. Or best," he added. "Depending on how you look at it."

"You say that no one wins any money," Westman said. "But those thousand kronor you're talking about someone must have lost, anyway, right?"

"Of course that's right, but most often it affects two or three people. As I said, it's not big money we're playing for."

"So how much money was it that you partied up yesterday evening?" Hamad wanted to know.

Jenner shook his head dejectedly and sighed.

"I think it was about seven and a half thousand. I assure you that no one—"

"And who paid the bill?" Hamad interrupted.

Staffan Jenner sighed again, but answered without grumbling.

"It was Janne who had contributed most this time. But last year—"

"And who contributed least?"

It was silent for a few moments before Jenner seemed to decide to stop complicating things.

"Svempa," he answered, looking down at his hands.

"Perhaps he cheated?" Westman suggested.

Staffan Jenner's mournful face cracked unexpectedly into a smile.

"Not a chance. That would be completely against his nature. Svempa was honesty itself. He was deeply religious besides."

"Active in the church?"

"No, but an active Christian."

"What do you mean?"

Staffan Jenner threw out his arms in a gesture that made him look like an evangelical preacher as he spoke.

"He had a big heart. Helped people around him. Was always there when you most needed it. For his family, his friends, and from what I understand the soccer club too. Handed out food and clothing to homeless people. Supported and encouraged. You could say that in everything he did, he lived by the golden rule. And all the other commandments too, for that matter," he added and fell silent.

Something caused Hamad to react. Exactly what it was he didn't have time to figure out. The golden rule was of course not one of the Ten Commandments, but it wasn't that. There was something that didn't seem healthy about this relationship, something about the way he talked that didn't add up. He portrayed his friend as a giant—did he diminish himself? See everything in black and white? Or was it perhaps how he suddenly stopped talking? Shame? Guilt? Skeletons in the closet? In his, or in Erlandsson's?

"You don't by chance own any firearms, do you?" Westman asked.

Staffan Jenner let his hands fall back down in his lap, looked her right in the eyes, and answered with a smile that contained everything but joy.

"No, I really don't. I'm against violence."

The last bit he said with completely unexpected emphasis, and Hamad could have sworn that Jenner was a hairbreadth from starting to cry. But the tears that might have appeared for a fraction of a second in Staffan Jenner's eyes immediately withdrew without him avoiding Westman's gaze. She studied him for a few seconds in silence before she asked the final question.

"Can you think of anyone in the circle around Sven-Gunnar Erlandsson who isn't? Lennart Wiklund? Janne Siem? Adrianti?"

His ice-blue eyes expressed nothing but conviction when he answered.

"Absolutely not. It must be a madman who's behind this."

Westman did not look equally convinced.

"This will have to do for the time being, and we will most likely be contacting you again," she concluded and got up. "We're sorry about what happened."

SUNDAY AFTERNOON

The match was in full swing when they arrived at the playing field in Södertälje, and Sandén could see right away that there had been significant progress since he played in his youth. Back then girls could not handle the ball, neither with their feet nor with any other part of their body, that's just how it was. But these girls appeared capable of taking a position on any school-yard team whatsoever, and that was heartening. Probably greatly thanks to enthusiasts like Erlandsson. And Gunnar Malmberg, he unwillingly had to admit. Not because he had anything against the acting police commissioner who had spoken so warmly in favor of equality issues, but the fact that Malmberg was acting police commissioner was enough to make him irritating.

At the far side there were two benches where substitutes and officials congregated, so Sandén and Andersson made their way around the field as Mercury ran around their legs with a soccer ball. Sandén zeroed in on the middle-aged man in a blue jogging suit who was standing on the sidelines and doling out orders in a loud voice to the girls on the field.

"Jan Siem—is that you?"

"That's right. Are you police officers?"

Sandén nodded with a gesture to take his ID out of his back pocket.

"Would you mind waiting ten minutes until the match is over?"

"If it's only a few minutes, that's no problem. We want to talk with your daughter, too."

"Sure, that can be arranged," Siem replied, returning to his loud order-giving. "Watch your back there, Sofi!"

Soon the match was over, and as the rest of the players and parents started moving toward the locker rooms, Siem and his daughter came up to the two policemen.

"How'd the match go, Josefin?" Sandén asked after they had greeted each other more formally.

"Uh, so-so," the girl answered, still out of breath after the exertions on the soccer field.

"Didn't you win?"

"Sure, but I didn't play very well."

"Not so strange perhaps, after what you've been through. Did you have a hard time concentrating?"

"Mm."

She took a few gulps from a water bottle. She was extremely pretty, with high cheekbones and coloring like her father, bronzed with blue eyes and thick dark hair tied up in a ponytail.

"Can you give an account of what happened this morning? I know you've already told it to the police officers who were first on the scene, but go over it one more time, please."

She cast a glance at her father, who nodded permission.

"I went out jogging at about four thirty. As a warm-up before the match, you might say."

"What route did you take?"

"I ran over to the Älvsjö forest and a little along the lake, then up through the houses all the way to the school. Well, Herrängen School, that is. And then a ways through the forest until . . . Well, until I caught sight of Svempa."

"And what did you do then?"

"First I called to him. Thought he was drunk maybe, because . . ."

"Because . . . ?" Sandén said encouragingly.

"Well, because I knew they'd been out partying. Dad was with them."

She looked a bit shamefaced at her father, who felt called upon to intervene.

"Yes, it wasn't really at that level, but Josie couldn't know that, of course. I mean, that he was dead was maybe not the first thing that—"

"Okay," Sandén continued. "So he didn't answer. What did you do then?"

"I caught sight of the blood and shook him a little."

"Like this?" Andersson asked, taking hold of Sandén's upper arm with both hands.

She nodded.

"And then I called home. But no one answered."

"I'd turned off my cell phone," Siem explained. "Didn't want to be woken up too early because . . . we'd been out rather late."

"And your mom?"

"She doesn't have her cell phone turned on at night, either."

"You don't have a landline?" Andersson wondered.

"No," the father confirmed. "The fixed network has played out its role and—"

He stopped himself in mid-sentence.

"Just costs a lot of money?" Andersson suggested.

"Exactly. But we had no idea Josefin would go out running so early. Then of course we would have left the phones on."

"And you called from your own cell phone?" Sandén continued, turning again to the girl.

"Yes."

"We'll have to check that."

He was directing himself now to Andersson, but was alert to the girl's reaction. She gave her father an anxious look, but that could be interpreted in various ways. For example, as a sign of worry at being revealed as a cell phone thief. Or as a natural reaction from someone whose credibility was suddenly being questioned.

"What did you do then?" Sandén continued.

"I called the police. They told me to stay there. Although . . . I walked a little farther away."

"Did you see anyone in the vicinity? In the forest or among the houses?"

"No. The weather was really bad."

"It must have been an extremely unpleasant situation."

She nodded, her gaze shifting a little.

"And yet you go and play soccer right afterward?"

"Dad thought that—"

"I judged that it was good for Josie to have something else to think about," Siem interrupted. "It was an important match. That she'd been looking forward to. And life isn't over just because . . ."

Then he stopped himself and let out a dejected sigh.

Sandén ignored the father's intervention, instead directing himself completely toward the daughter.

"What kind of relationship did you have with Sven-Gunnar Erlandsson? Were you close to one another?"

"He was . . . Well . . ."

Again she brought the bottle to her mouth and took another few gulps of water. Sandén did not turn his eyes away, did not want to miss the slightest nuance of her face.

"He was our coach. I thought he was good. Everyone liked him. He was really nice too. And helped out a lot."

"Helped out? With what?"

"With driving. With coaching us when the old coach quit. And then he helped homeless people and such."

It struck him that she apparently was only rattling off the sort of thing she'd heard the grown-ups say. How could he find out what she really thought? And the other girls on the team?

"Was he hard on you? Strict? Or was it mostly for fun?"

"We had to work hard at practices. But that's just the point. Thanks to him we started winning. But he joked around with us a lot too. He was a lot of fun, actually."

The last she said with a smile, and that could summarize her feelings for Erlandsson in Sandén's book.

"Now we would like to talk alone with your dad. Could you possibly teach this little guy something about playing soccer in the meantime?"

"Sure," Josefin Siem answered, turning toward Andersson and suddenly changing guise. "Could I get your autograph?" she asked with an almost coquettish smile that lacked any trace of the seriousness that had marked her behavior up to now.

Once again she was the carefree thirteen-year-old she perhaps usually was. Her father looked inquisitive as he mutely watched how without comment a smiling Odd Andersson wrote his signature on a blank page in the notepad, tore it loose and put it in the girl's hand, after which she happily ran back out on the field.

"What was that about?" he ventured to ask.

"Nothing serious," Sandén answered, giving his colleague a tender pat on the shoulder. "Andersson here has a past in the music industry. Now we'd like to hear a little more about yesterday evening."

Jan Siem took a deep breath and did as he was asked.

"The poker club used up the treasury in an evening at Långbro Inn. We started with herring and shots and continued with steak and red wine. Then we had dessert and coffee and cognac. We sat there till they closed at midnight, stood and chatted a while outside, and then each of us went home. I went in my direction and the other three in theirs. I'd say I was home by twelve-thirty."

"How much was the bill?" Andersson asked.

"About seven thousand, four hundred seventy-eight kronor."

"You kept pretty good tabs on that?"

"In principle, it was my money."

"Does that mean you're a worse poker player than the others?" Sandén interjected, in a conscious attempt to irritate.

"No, it means I wasn't as lucky during the past year. The year before, it looked different."

"I see, how did it go then?" Andersson asked.

"I contributed exactly nothing. It was likely Staffan and Lennart who divided it up then."

"My word. So Erlandsson got out of paying that time too?"

"Exactly."

"Is there anything in particular you'd like to say?" Andersson persisted. "Because if so, it would be best if it came out now."

"It's known that Sven-Gunnar Erlandsson was shot in the head," Sandén filled in. "An old proven method."

Andersson chose this time not to comment on the somewhat misleading description. But Siem had nothing to add.

"I'm only answering your questions. With no hidden subtexts, if that's what you're suggesting," he said simply.

"So you drank aquavit, wine, and cognac until midnight and then you got in the car at . . ."

Sandén took a look at his watch. It was almost one.

"About eight o'clock? Would you have passed a breath test?"

Siem sighed, crossed his arms across his chest and looked like a caricature of a Swedish soccer coach under fire. "We left at eight thirty. Besides, I didn't drink great quantities. I knew I would be driving in the morning. I had already planned earlier that I would drive Josie here."

"So you might say that the other three drank up your money?"

Jan Siem looked irritated, but whether the questions caught him off balance was not easy to say. He clenched his teeth so that the silhouette of his jaw was sharply marked in the backlight. He struck Sandén as a cartoon figure of some type. A first lover in the old Swedish comic, *Starlet*.

"As I said, I had my share too. But I wasn't exactly pouring it in."

"And Erlandsson?" Andersson added. "Wouldn't he be driving a car too?"

"No, he was going to ride with me."

"What was the mood like during the evening?" Sandén asked.

"Very good. As always."

"What did you talk about?"

Siem threw out his arms.

"Yes, what did we talk about? Everything under the sun. Not soccer so much, when Staffan's along. He's not involved in the club."

His arms were again in place, crossed over his chest.

"No? So how do you know one another actually?"

"You might say that Svempa is . . . was the hub. Lennart and I got to know him and each other through the club. Staffan is Svempa's buddy from the start. They probably met at one of those bicycle events."

Andersson looked bewildered, but Sandén, who was a home-owner, knew what this was about.

"You bicycle around the neighborhood and eat with each other to promote neighborhood harmony. But you all got along well?"

"Absolutely."

"Describe the other guys," Andersson asked. "Briefly."

Siem stamped a little in place.

"Lennart's a good guy, happy and positive. He works at the post office and is active in the club. Plays in the B league and coaches one of the boys' teams where his son plays. Before, he coached this team, but Svempa took over a year or so ago."

"I see. How did that happen?" Andersson asked.

"I don't know. It was just something they agreed on. But everyone seems content and it's going amazingly well for the girls now, so it was certainly the best for all concerned."

"Okay, anything more about Lennart Wiklund?"

"He got divorced a few years ago. It was probably the wife who ended the relationship. Why, I don't know. He has a certain appeal that women usually like, if I may say."

"Maybe that was the problem," Sandén interjected, but Siem did not let himself be disturbed.

"Staffan is almost the opposite. He's pleasant, but pretty quiet, a little gloomy. He doesn't seem to have been that way before his wife took her life."

Sandén and Andersson exchanged glances; this was new information.

"When was that?" Sandén asked.

"Six or seven years ago maybe. I didn't know him at that time. She took a bottle of pills and Staffan clearly took it extremely hard. Which is understandable, of course. He never talks about it, and you don't want to ask either."

"And then there was Erlandsson," said Sandén.

"Svempa was the one it all revolved around."

"In the poker club, you mean?"

"Yes, there too. But he was the kind of person that takes up a lot of room, who is seen and heard. He was extremely committed in everything he undertook. In the family, in the club's activity, in social life. Always helping children and young people. And then he did some kind of charity work for the homeless too. Exactly what he did I don't really know."

"Did he have any enemies?" Andersson asked.

"I can't imagine that. He was a gift to humanity. That type."

Sjöberg judged the project of contacting Erlandsson's colleagues at SEB too time-consuming on a Sunday, so he decided to let that stand until the next day. Instead, he got in his car and drove out to Långbro Inn.

Two of the staff who were there had also worked on Saturday evening and they contributed the following information: The group ate and drank a good deal, and they had been somewhat noisy but not in a disruptive way. The mood was cordial. Erlandsson was the one who talked the most and he was also the one who paid the bill. To be more precise, eight thousand kronor exactly with his own credit card. They unwillingly, but without causing any trouble, left the place at closing, that is at midnight, last of all the customers. Afterwards they stood and talked for an estimated fifteen minutes outside the inn and then departed. Who went in what direction the staff had not noticed. They did not have the impression that Erlandsson—or anyone else in the company, for that matter—had been in contact with any of the other customers. None of them stood out as conspicuously intoxicated.

Now Sjöberg was back at the police station, and on his way to the kitchen he passed Walleye's office without making himself known. He was not completely clear why, but on the other hand there were quite a few things he did not understand concerning his attitude toward Hedvig Wallin. And more than a few things he did not understand about her. For example, why one day she would have the hairstyle of an old lady while wearing the clothing of a teenage girl. And then the next day she'd arrive in a pleated skirt and pussy-bow blouse. Or a striped Marimekko dress out of the 1970s. As far as Sjöberg could determine, the woman had no taste whatsoever. As if that had any significance.

He had always taken great pains not to judge a book by its cover. But then, her entire being was a trifle . . . unpredictable. It was hard to know whether she was serious or joking. On the one hand, she might be quick to tease or be downright rude. On the other hand, with an intent that Sjöberg understood as serious, she was quick to see connections and events from more or less absurd perspectives. And then that blasted perm . . . It just didn't fit together.

Whatever the reason was, he harbored this irrational feeling of dislike. Wallin had done nothing wrong. She was a capable police officer, despite a lack of practical experience. In theoretical terms she was actually overqualified, but she never got up on a high horse or complained. She carried out the tasks she was assigned and more besides. And Sandén loved her. Which Sjöberg did not like at all. He did all he could to conceal it.

"Conny!" he heard her call from inside.

Of course he had meant to go into her office, he was only going to get something to drink first. But now he turned obediently and stepped inside. Cozy, with green plants in the window and photographs of children of various ages here and there on the shelves and on the desk. It smelled clean and fresh, with a trace of perfume.

"Walleye," he said, going up to the desk.

She waved him to her with one hand without looking up.

"Come here and take a look at something."

While he went around the desk and positioned himself behind her, she turned up the speaker and started a video that she had apparently found on the TV4 website. The scene was a forest glade in winter and at a distance a man was seen coming from among the trees with a stack of pizza boxes in his arms. He followed a small path and soon he was at an open area where a number of trailers were parked. He looked into the camera and started to speak:

"It started when I was on a business trip in Calcutta. You run into beggars and seriously ill people everywhere, and I was particularly moved by a little girl who perhaps was five years old and had an enormous tumor on her eyebrow. So large, that is, that it covered half her face and prevented her from seeing and functioning normally."

"It's Sven-Gunnar Erlandsson," Wallin whispered.

"Her life surely would have been different with simple intervention, but as it was now, she sat begging on a street corner. I was struck by a kind of powerlessness, hopelessness, and I didn't know what I should do. Should I help her? Take her to a hospital and see to it that she had an operation? But she wasn't the only one. I saw hundreds of children who were in just as great need of help. And women. Small, petite, undernourished people whose existence depended on a passerby giving them a coin. Naturally there were men, too, in misery, but the children and women were more vulnerable. At the time I couldn't do much more than throw them some small change.

"After that experience I started thinking, what can I do to help? To change someone's life, even if only a single one? When I came home, I decided to make an ever-so-little effort to help the homeless. They exist quite close to us here at home, but often we choose not to see them. So I go and visit a few of them sometimes, talk a while, show that I care.

"It's not much, but I think it's appreciated."

"And you bring food with you, I see," said someone who was not visible in the picture and who Sjöberg presumed was a female reporter.

"I usually bring a few pizzas or a grocery bag of food," Erlandsson replied. "You don't want to come empty-handed when you visit," he laughed.

"What a clown," Wallin said, shaking her head.

Sjöberg cast a bewildered look at her, but she was back to the video.

Erlandsson knocked on the trailer door and stepped in.

"Hello in there!" he called. "Anyone hungry?"

The film team also must have squeezed into the trailer, because then a sequence followed where greetings were exchanged, and pizzas unpacked. Besides the team and Erlandsson there were four individuals inside—two men, a woman, and a young girl with a pearl in her nose who was only seen for a few seconds before she seemed to disappear. The reporter asked a few questions while they ate, but Erlandsson was not in the picture and did not take part in the conversation any more until right at the end of the four-minute report.

"So you're a bit like one of the gang?" said the reporter, half in jest. "What do you talk about when you're here?"

"Everything under the sun," Erlandsson answered seriously. "Things that have happened or will happen. Everyday concerns. Respect. Vulnerability. Women's vulnerability. Even here. I think it's important that social hierarchies don't arise among the homeless either. Women tend to always end up lowest in such structures."

Erlandsson disappeared from the picture and the camera focused instead on the rest of the company. All three nodded in agreement. The feature was over.

"How about that?" Wallin said contentedly, turning off the screen.

"Amazing. How did you find this?"

"It showed up when I Googled. Pathetic, isn't it?"

"I don't really understand what you mean," said Sjöberg sincerely. "How could charity ever be pathetic?"

"If you're involved in it only for your own sake," Wallin answered simply.

"But where do you get that from? That he would be doing it for his own sake?"

"Don't you see it? How self-righteous he is when he comes tramping through the woods with those fucking pizza cartons? And starts talking about his commitment. As if he were the main person here."

"Maybe that was the idea. To encourage others to similar efforts. No, I don't agree with you. Not at all. I thought he made an extremely good impression."

"Respect, my ass," Wallin continued, apparently without having noted Sjöberg's remark. "He's the type who eats the homeless for breakfast. And what he said about social hierarchies—I'm ready to eat my hat if he's not at the top of the ladder in whatever social context he finds himself in."

Sjöberg cast an involuntary glance at the hat that did not exist, instead seeing only a blonde bird's nest with streaks of gray.

"I won't argue with you," Sjöberg muttered. "I'm sure you're right, but that the whole thing would just be for show seems to be going a step too far. Who has the energy to run around bringing pizza to the homeless just to look good?"

"We have no idea how often he was there. This may have been the first and last time."

"Oh well, that's pretty simple to find out. In any event I suggest we don't judge him before we have more meat on the bones, and work without bias instead. Okay?"

"I always work without bias," Wallin maintained. "For just that reason, I'm offering these viewpoints. Oh well. I thought I would wait with the civil registry until tomorrow, but I found some interesting information about one of the other guys. In GIR."

The General Investigation Registry was one of the police department's internal databases, where you could search for individuals in memoranda kept during previous investigations. An individual who appeared there and was of interest during an ongoing investigation to boot gave every reason to raise an eyebrow.

"The hell you say," said Sjöberg. "Who is it then?"

"Staffan Jenner," Wallin answered. "A really awful story."

Lennart Wiklund lived only a stone's throw from Långbro Inn, in an apartment on the third floor on Långbrokungens Väg. He let them in wearing only underwear, and he didn't need to be ashamed of himself. He was a tall man with ample muscles on his legs and upper body. His blond hair was cut in a boyish style that, to be sure, was now pointing in all directions, but which in Westman's eyes still revealed something about his personality. He looked half asleep, but brightened up when he found out who they were, and readily let them into the apartment.

"Was it a late one last night?" Westman asked as she sat down at the indicated kitchen chair.

Hamad took over another, but Wiklund remained standing in the middle of the room without any attempt to sit down at the table.

"Yes . . . No, I don't think so. It wasn't that late. Why—?"

"What time did you come home?"

He seemed irresolute and looked from the one police officer to the other.

"Hard to answer . . . Twelve? One? Two, maybe? Uh, I don't really know. What about it?"

"Do you remember *how* you got home?"

He hesitated a moment and then shook his head.

"I haven't had time to think it over. I was sleeping when you rang—"

"You had a few last night?"

He laughed. Not embarrassed in any way, more like at an amusing discovery.

"Yeah, I guess I did. But I don't understand—"

"Do you have *any* recollection of what you did yesterday evening?"

"Yes, but, seriously . . ."

He not only looked like a boy, he talked like one too. Both Westman and Hamad looked at him encouragingly. He took a deep breath and finally seemed to decide that he should sit down too.

"Three buddies and me were at the restaurant over here," he said, pulling an empty chair out with a strong hand. "We ate and drank and talked until it was time to go. Then we waved goodbye to our friend Janne Siem outside the inn and went home."

The sound of running water could be heard from somewhere in the apartment.

"I don't remember exactly what time it was, but maybe we can find out from the lady in the shower."

"Is it your wife?" asked Hamad. "Girlfriend?"

"She's a female acquaintance, if I may say so. What is this really about?"

"Sven-Gunnar Erlandsson was found dead in a patch of woods over here earlier this morning," Hamad explained with a gesture in the direction of the window. "You, Siem, and Jenner were the last ones who saw him alive."

"Dead?" Wiklund said, surprised.

"Murdered. Everything indicates that he was shot shortly after you separated."

"That's just terrible. Lotta!" he called toward the bathroom, but got no answer.

"Are you in possession of any firearms?" Hamad asked.

Lennart Wiklund's lightheartedness had now dispersed, and from here on he showed a meditative expression and seemed to weigh every word before he answered. Which made it extremely difficult to decide whether he spoke the truth.

"No. I've never done any shooting."

"How was the evening?" Westman asked.

"Pleasant. No disharmony. If you're wondering, I mean. Not because there usually is any—"

"Who paid the check?"

"Svempa. Erlandsson, that is. We ate up the poker treasury, and he was the one who took care of it."

"And you? Did you have any part in it?"

"Not much this year, I think. A few hundred maybe. It was probably Janne Siem who stood for most of it."

"No irregularities?" asked Hamad.

"How so?"

"Anyone who cheated?"

An uncertain smile quickly crossed Wiklund's face.

"No, it was only for fun. Not big money."

"So how big was the treasury?"

"Seven-and-a-half thousand approximately. For one year and four players. Not big money," he repeated.

"Did you socialize in any way other than at the poker table?" Westman asked.

"Staffan and Svempa socialized a great deal. They were close friends. Janne, Svempa, and I knew each other through soccer. My daughter plays on the same team as Janne's, but we don't socialize privately, so to speak."

"So you have children. Divorced?"

"Yes. That's why I'm living here in the divorcé dump."

"And the 'lady in the shower'?"

"A female acquaintance, as I said. Lotta!" he tried again.

And this time a barefoot beauty in a bathrobe that was much too large opened the kitchen door and looked at them with surprise. She appeared to be about twenty years younger than Lennart Wiklund.

"Do you know what time it was when I came home last night? It's important."

"No idea. But I think it was about one thirty when we turned off the lights."

"So was it quarter past one when he came home?" Westman interrupted. "Or maybe quarter past twelve? You must have some idea."

"I was already asleep," the woman answered frankly. "We fooled around for a while, but I don't know how long."

Westman felt how Hamad was seeking her gaze, but she controlled herself and simply repeated dryly the expression the woman had used.

"Fooled around. I see. So everything was as usual?"

"Nothing strange."

"Good. That's all we were wondering, so you don't need to stay."

Westman was alarmingly close to recommending instead that she swish back to the dance floor she came from, but restrained herself at the last moment.

"Can you think of anyone who had reason to want Erlandsson dead?" Hamad asked Wiklund.

He thought a moment before he answered.

"No, I don't think so. He had a dominant personality and filled up a room. We've had our clashes, but he was a damned upright and decent person actually. Didn't go around spreading a lot of shit. Even if he knew everything about everyone."

Something that seemed to be a surprisingly insightful analysis from a source least expected.

MONDAY MORNING

At nine o'clock on Monday morning everyone except Gabriella Hansson was gathered in the blue oval room to summarize yesterday's events. Wallin noted that even Gunnar Malmberg honored them with his presence, most likely because he felt important, having received the call from the possible murderer. Sjöberg hardly managed to open the meeting before the question came up.

"I've put Telia on the job," Hamad said, "but yesterday was Sunday and it's still vacation. There's a risk that what should normally happen in twenty-four hours will take a little longer right now. But they know it's high priority and I'll call to put the pressure on right after this meeting."

"Then we'll do a run-through of what came out during the interviews yesterday," Sjöberg continued. "We can start with the Siem family. Anything interesting to report?"

Andersson and Sandén summarized their impressions, followed by Westman's and Hamad's account of the visits with Lennart Wiklund and Staffan Jenner. Then Malmberg, who apparently had more important things to do, left the meeting. Which made

Wallin happy, because the really interesting bit of news had not yet come up.

"Everyone involved appears to have the impression that Sven-Gunnar Erlandsson devoted himself a great deal to charity," said Sjöberg. "Walleye has found a clip from a documentary on TV4 that supports this. Let's look at it," he said, starting the video on the computer that was connected to the SMART Board the conference room had recently been equipped with.

Westman was the first, four minutes later, to comment on the report.

"So yet another good person has gone to the happy hunting grounds," she sighed.

Sandén and Andersson agreed, and even Rosén nodded assent. Wallin noticed that Sjöberg was studying her for a moment. Not triumphantly, because that was not his style; more curiously, to see whether she was influenced by her colleagues. Which she was not. However, she did not intend to publicize her attitude.

"He can be as good as he wants," said Hamad. "I still think it has something to do with cheating at cards. All signs point to that. It was an evening in the company of his poker buddies, he had playing cards in his pocket and was shot in the head. Yes, Cod, I know it was in the neck, but the difference is marginal."

"He didn't cheat," said Westman dismissively. "Everyone says he was extremely generous, he unquestionably doled out food to the homeless, and, according to Staffan Jenner, was deeply religious besides. How does that fit with cheating at cards?"

"I agree with Petra," said Sjöberg. "Besides, I have additional info that supports that line of reasoning. Both Jenner and Wiklund say the bill at Långbro Inn was for seven and a half thousand.

The staff, on the other hand, assure me that the tab was for eight thousand kronor. It was Erlandsson who took care of the poker treasury and paid. So he threw in a good five hundred kronor out of his own pocket without anyone knowing about it. That's what I call genuine generosity, something you don't do just because it will look good."

When he said the last he turned to Wallin, who chose not to defend herself now, either, but Hamad was not finished.

"Generosity with all respect, but cheating isn't about that. I don't doubt for a moment that he was a pure marvel of generosity—where money was concerned. But in this case it's about winning, being the best. Top of the roost. Those are two different things."

Wallin agreed one hundred percent—in silence.

"Where did this poker talk come from actually?" she asked instead, to everyone's apparent surprise. "From the start, I mean."

Sjöberg looked at her with an almost regretful expression.

"It's been known the whole time that the *poker* club was drinking up the *poker* treasury," Hamad informed her.

"That hasn't been known the whole time. That came out with Conny's and my visit to the widow. When Bella and I were called to the crime scene, it was already said that a dead poker player had been found. I'm just wondering why."

"Maybe because he had playing cards in his breast pocket," Hamad said with poorly concealed sarcasm in his voice. "Easy to hide."

The part about being easy to hide she wanted to get to the bottom of. The only thing they had found out so far about those cards was that one of them was an ace. An easy-to-hide ace? Maybe.

But that was impossible to know until you had seen the rest of the deck. She decided not to make any more fuss about that right now.

"Four cards," she said instead. "In poker you have five cards in a hand."

"Now let's leave that," Sjöberg interrupted. "We have something much more interesting to talk about. Go over it now, Walleye."

"Okay. Eight years ago, the summer of 2001, that is, Staffan Jenner's family had a Russian summer child visiting. Are you familiar with the term 'summer child'?"

"Vaguely," Sandén answered. "But feel free to explain."

"It concerns an exchange between some Russian orphanages and a Swedish association that arranges for the orphans to come to Sweden during the summer. In certain cases over Christmas too. The purpose is that they will get to feel what it's like to live in a family and enjoy the Swedish summer. And welfare. The concept is very successful, and families often maintain contact with the children long after they've left the orphanage. It has even happened that families adopt their summer children."

"There you can talk about generous," said Hamad. "For real."

"Wait and you'll hear. This girl was eleven and was named Larissa Sotnikova. At the end of the summer, a week before she would be going home, she suddenly disappeared. Without a trace. There was a major effort, search parties and so on, and the whole neighborhood was involved. But she was never found. Staffan Jenner was naturally hard-pressed for a few months, but they were never able to prove he had anything to do with the disappearance. His version was that the girl was alive, that she had run away and was in hiding somewhere in the country. He said she was not very eager to go home and hadn't been during previous summers, either. Which certainly was true. Or that in the worst case she had run away and come to grief. Jenner consistently denied having been involved in any way. But the police didn't believe that. And not his wife either, one might suspect. Because she killed herself a year later.

"But Staffan Jenner's idea about what had happened was not completely improbable. It is a rather common occurrence that refugee children disappear of their own free will. Now this was a summer child and not a refugee child, but in any case. Who really cares? It's just a child from somewhere. Who doesn't leave a void behind them, whom nobody misses."

"That's just terrible," Andersson summarized what everyone was thinking.

"He was a little shady, that Jenner," said Hamad. "Sat there rambling to himself."

"An odd character," Westman attested.

"And I got a strong feeling he was withholding something," Hamad continued.

"This, no doubt," Sjöberg observed. "And that's not so strange. Regardless of whether it has anything to do with the case or not."

"Maybe Erlandsson had just found out what he'd done and threatened to expose him," Sandén suggested.

"It's conceivable. But you have to keep in mind that no body has ever been found. It's far from certain the girl is even dead," Wallin pointed out.

"I suggest in any event that Petra and Jamal work further with this lead," said Sjöberg. "Walleye and I will make contact with the Erlandsson family again, but first I'm going to visit the SEB office at Kungsträdgården. I'll arrange that myself, so you can devote yourselves to the civil registration and the crime register for the time being. And I'm a bit curious about those people in the trailer. Cod and Sandén will try to find them and see what they have to say."

Andersson had no objections.

"Pretty girl, the one there in the beginning. I'll take the ladies and you can take the toothless old men," he laughed, giving Sandén a thump on the back.

The meeting was over.

—⁓—

Sjöberg sat in a glass-enclosed conference room on the fourth floor in the SEB office building on Kungsträdgården. Across from him sat one of Sven-Gunnar Erlandsson's coworkers, who reportedly was named Kristina Wintherfalck. She did not look half as hoity-toity, however, as the name suggested, and he had to remind himself—how many times he didn't know—that most of the time people could not control what their name was. Like himself, for example.

She was about forty-five, tanned, and with long semi-blonde hair set up in a simple ponytail. She had hung up her black jacket at her workstation and was now reclining in the chair with legs crossed in a knee-length black skirt and white blouse. In her hand she had a sheaf of papers that she was mindlessly waving in front of her face. It was very warm in the glass cage, and there were no windows to open.

Kristina Wintherfalck and Erlandsson had worked side by side in the large trading room and spent the days buying and selling options, futures, currency, and other things the substance of which

Sjöberg barely understood. They had also done this in Singapore for a few years in the mid-nineties, which made her a particularly interesting person to question in this context.

"Good. A really good guy," she answered to Sjöberg's question about what Erlandsson was like as a person. "He was always available when you needed help. Would fill in when he was off if you were sick or forced to take time off. Treated everyone the same. That is, with respect. There can be a slight schoolboy atmosphere here sometimes, but he wasn't like that."

"I've gotten the impression that he was a rather dominant person. Do you agree with that?"

"Yes, sure. Although in a positive way. He was not afraid to say what he thought about things. But for the most part we were always in agreement, so that didn't disturb me in the least."

"And the others?"

"He was not especially controversial, so there were no problems. More the kind who said what everyone—or in any case the majority—thought."

"And the higher ups had no problem with that?"

"Not at all. Svempa was extremely diplomatic and could express himself in the right way."

"So he didn't have any direct enemies?"

"No, I would have a hard time imagining that," she answered with a sorrowful smile. "He was popular in all circles."

"And in Singapore," Sjöberg asked, "how was it there? Did anything special happen?"

With three fingers she brushed back a strand of hair that had escaped from the ponytail and thought for a few moments before she answered.

"Everything and nothing was special in Singapore. We worked the same way as here, doing the same things. But life 'outside of work' was different, of course. For Svempa, the biggest change was that he met his new wife there."

"Yes, can you tell me a little about that?"

"Haven't you talked with her?"

"Yes, but I would still like to hear your version."

A half-truth. True, he had spoken with Adrianti Erlandsson, but not about this.

"He was a rather recent widower when he jumped onto that Singapore job. His wife died from breast cancer about the same time that I and another friend from work moved to Singapore. He was probably a little inspired by that and thought the change of environment would do him and the children good. And I think it was the right decision, because the whole family did really well and the children learned to speak fluent English besides. In any event—the golfers used to go over to Indonesia sometimes, it took less than an hour by boat. Svempa didn't play golf, but he went along a few times anyway to try it out. During one of those trips he met Adri—I think she was a caddy for him, actually. And that's the way it was. He ended up going over there every weekend, with kids and all, and then they got married and moved back to Sweden."

"And what did the others think about that?" Sjöberg asked.

"We were happy for his sake. It was exactly what he and the children needed. And Adri of course. They don't have it so nice over there. Work their butts off for rich Singaporeans who go there and show off. Typical Svempa in some ways, to not just help himself but someone else too. It was a win-win situation. Clearly."

Sjöberg could not think of anything else to ask, so that concluded the conversation. The phrase "win-win situation" would linger in his mind during the entire investigation. Who had actually won what? In the end, everyone appeared to be losers.

———

After arguing with the management at TV4, they were finally put in contact with the reporter in the feature from the homeless people's trailer park. She was helpful and gave them the names she knew as well as directions to the forest glade in Huddinge where Andersson and Sandén now found themselves.

The place was not really the same. What had stood out in the TV images as a scrubby thicket, gray, gloomy, and unwelcoming, was now a moss-covered magic forest right out of a fairy tale. Damp Swedish summer aromas struck them as they got out of the car, and it was not hard to understand why this place had been chosen for their shabby trailer park.

There were people in motion around them; a few were hanging laundry on a line stretched between a trailer and a tree, someone was trying to saw through a metal pipe. A woman sat and smoked in a camping chair and a couple of guys were wandering around, not appearing to be occupied with anything in particular. The gazes that met the two policemen were curious, not suspicious, but no one said anything.

The trailer that primarily interested them was still in the same place as in the report, and the door was open. Sandén knocked a little carefully on the wall to the side of the doorway.

"Yes?" a woman's voice was heard from inside.

"May we come in?" he asked, sticking his head in the room. "We would like to ask a few questions."

"Are you from the city?"

"No, from the police."

"I see. Yes, come on in. We don't have any quarrel."

"I don't think so, either," Sandén laughed as he made his way into the trailer with Andersson right behind him.

The woman, who might've been in her fifties, was the same one as in the TV feature. She looked fresh, sitting with wet hair at the table and drinking tea. She was wearing a black T-shirt that was much too large, and under the table two bare legs in a pair of cut-off jean shorts could be glimpsed. It smelled of shampoo and cigarette smoke.

"Jens Sandén, Hammarby police. This is Odd Andersson. And you are Gunilla Mäkinen?"

She nodded in reply.

"We are also looking for Svante Boberg and Roger Lindström."

"And anyone else who knows Sven-Gunnar Erlandsson," Andersson filled in.

"It's probably just us who know him. Everyone knows who he is of course, but we're the ones he usually visits. Svante's in jail. For theft. Three months, he'll get out at the beginning of October."

"And Lindström?"

"Roger! There are some people here who want to talk with you!"

Andersson jumped. He had no idea another person could be in the little house trailer, and no signs of life had been either seen or heard from the sleeping alcove.

"He's not up yet," the woman explained with a smile that unfortunately revealed a row of teeth that lowered her overall impression considerably.

Now there was movement over in the bed and a grunting sound was heard.

"Would you like tea?" the woman asked.

Andersson's first reaction was to decline, but Sandén said yes and on second thought, drinking boiled water was just as good in a scrubby trailer home as anywhere else.

"Yes, thanks. A cup of tea for me too, please," he answered, looking around.

True, the trailer was worn and not very modern, but it seemed reasonably clean and the stuff that was there was not just piled up. Despite everything, it was someone's home. People lived their lives here, to the best of their ability.

A few minutes later order was somewhat restored and all four of them were sitting around the table drinking tea. Roger Lindström was reportedly several years younger than Gunilla Mäkinen, but not as well preserved. His mouth also exposed a gap or two among his teeth, and he was both wrinkled and scarred besides. It was not an unreasonable guess that he had a long-term mix of substance abuse behind him. He sat with his torso bare, revealing a few cheap, carelessly executed tattoos, but he had pulled on a pair of jogging pants.

"Excuse the abrupt wakening," said Sandén. "We have sad news and need to talk with you a little."

Gunilla Mäkinen's eyes became somewhat anxious and her shoulders hunched up as if to protect herself. Roger Lindström sprinkled fine-cut tobacco over a cigarette paper without looking up.

"Sven-Gunnar Erlandsson has passed away," Sandén said, getting to the point. "He was found yesterday morning, in a forested area not very far from here. Everything indicates that he was shot sometime during the night."

"And what does that have to do with us?" Lindström asked without tearing his gaze from what would become a cigarette. "Are we suspected in any way?"

"Do you have any firearms?" Andersson countered. "Or any motive?"

The man gave him a quick glance and then started rolling the tobacco in the paper with trembling hands.

"Neither nor," he answered.

"Why would we want Svempa dead?" the woman asked. "We like him. Don't we, Roger?"

"Of course, damn it. A little tedious, maybe. But he cares. Comes here with food and stuff."

"Takes time," the woman added. "Sits down and talks."

"How often did he usually come?" Sandén asked.

"Once or twice a month maybe. For the past year or two."

"Alone? Or did he have any social workers with him?"

"No, he came on his own. One time he had a buddy with him. That was a while ago, last winter, I think. But he wasn't all that amused. I don't remember what his name was."

"Were you the only ones Erlandsson visited? Not the neighbors?"

She shook her head.

"You could hardly expect him to support the whole camp. It was more than enough that he helped us."

"And how many are you?"

"You said it yourself. Roger, Svante, and me. Sometimes there are four of us, but the three of us have kept together for almost ten years."

"Are you a couple, the two of you?" Andersson ventured to ask. "Or maybe you and Svante?"

"Or Svante and Roger?" Sandén suggested.

"Haha. No, we keep together anyway," Lindström answered, moistening the edge of the paper with his tongue and stroking the now-ready cigarette with his finger.

"And the fourth person, who is that?" asked Andersson.

"There isn't *one* fourth person. But sometimes we let someone who needs a roof over their head live here a while."

"Any of them who knew Erlandsson?"

Roger Lindström put the cigarette in his mouth and lit it. Then he shook his head.

"I don't think you can say that. He did talk a little with everyone he met, but it was here in the trailer with us that he had long conversations."

"That girl in the TV feature, then?" said Andersson. "Young. Pretty."

"I don't know. We were the only ones in the story."

"She was seen passing by very quickly. I thought maybe she lived here too."

"Could that have been Rebecka?" said Gunilla Mäkinen. "She lived here awhile last winter, only a few weeks. She had run away from home. She was only fifteen. I ran into her in downtown Skärholmen. But it's true, Svempa talked with her a bit too. Tried to get her to change her mind, he thought she should move back home again."

"And did she?"

"Yes, I think so. I haven't heard anything else anyway."

Roger Lindström hadn't, either.

"How do we get hold of her?" Andersson asked. "Do you know what her last name is?"

Gunilla Mäkinen shrugged her shoulders and looked at Lindström, who was flicking ashes into a Coca-Cola can. He was amazingly shaky.

"Some -son name. Johansson. Larsson. No, I don't remember. But I have the idea she was from Norsborg. Sweet girl."

"You said he was a little tedious, Erlandsson," Sandén said to Lindström. "What did you mean by that?"

"Uh, I take that back. He was a fucking good type, actually. I probably meant he could be a little preachy. Overly serious."

"I would really like for you to expand on that."

Lindström took a couple of puffs on the cigarette, pondered. A note of disharmony, Andersson thought. Was it the case that the heavenly choir did not sing one hundred percent in unison? Siem had given Erlandsson nothing but praise with a single false chord. Bitterness? If so, only an ounce. Envy? Yes, probably. Hamad talked about power. He had used the expression "ruler of the roost" about Erlandsson. Was this perhaps simply the other side of the same coin? Had Erlandsson exploited his certified social position of power to do good? That is, in the best way he could.

Andersson had a feeling that Walleye did not harbor any great confidence in Erlandsson's celebrated generosity either, but then she was also a very contradictory woman. Considered it an honor to go against the current. Maybe it was also the case that she went in for critical thinking to a greater extent than the others, and that was what bothered him. Them. There it was again. Envy.

"We're sitting here in our trailer," said Roger Lindström. "And we're struggling with the weather, loneliness, making a living, health problems. Yeah, a lot of times for any justification for our existence at all. Some of us have drug problems on top of it all.

So you might think that equality isn't exactly at the top of the agenda."

Andersson started to open his mouth for an objection, but Lindström continued the line of reasoning.

"But then you're out in deep water, because it really is the case that we're in this shit together. Gunilla and Svante and me, for example. And like hell can she do our errands and help out with whatever just because she's a woman. It's enough as it is. So Svempa is right, damn it."

"But . . . ?" said Andersson.

"But we already know that. That's just how we live. Isn't it, Gunilla?"

She agreed convincingly.

"So then maybe we didn't need to go over that every fucking time. But it's clear, a good message bears repeating. Even if sometimes you got the feeling that Svempa was a little like a scratchy old LP record. You know, the arm keeps jumping back and the same section gets played over and over."

A metaphor that Andersson had no problem at all taking in.

—∿—

Wallin was sitting with her feet on the desk and the keyboard on her lap, knowing that this work position was devastating in more than one way. Sooner or later she would have back problems—if she didn't already. After sitting that way she invariably got a pain in her tailbone, a detail that did not however in any way overshadow the enjoyment the half-prone position gave her in terms of comfort. Visitors were always taken aback when they saw her like that; in some way it seemed undignified or possibly indecent. But this worried her even less than the ergonomic aspects.

She was well aware that for many people she was a hard-to-solve puzzle, where the pieces didn't really fit together. But that's just the way she was. She didn't intend to change, had no need to be loved by everyone. Hedvig Wallin congratulated those who liked her, and pitied the rest.

For example, Sjöberg, whom she respected for a number of different reasons. He led the colorful group of police officers with warmth in a discreet, intuitive manner. Discreet insofar as he got all of them to dance to his tune without making it obvious, intuitive in that he made use of each and every one's talents while being aware of their weaknesses. He was not afraid to delegate and was sensitive, always open to new ideas and approaches. Which could be thought to go directly counter to the reception he had given her own ideas most recently. But in reality he was simply of a different mindset, which he had every right to be.

Wallin was completely convinced that Erlandsson was a creep; she recognized an empty vessel when she saw one. After having been married to one for most of her adult life, and besides that living in a world that was populated for the most part by similar types, over the course of the years she had developed a kind of hypersensitivity to plastic facades. Sven-Gunnar Erlandsson at least appeared to be without a criminal record. Likewise his wife and the adult children. Nor had the Siem, Jenner, or Wiklund families been subject to any legal actions or even notices of nonpayment. The whole group was white as snow. On paper.

One piece of information from the civil registration, however, made her take both feet off the desk and straighten up.

—ᴡᴡ—

Immediately after the meeting Hamad called the police's contact person at Telia and applied pressure regarding the information about incoming calls to the police station switchboard and Malmberg's cell phone and direct line on Sunday morning. At Telia they were understaffed as expected, but he managed to get a promise that the list would be generated and delivered before the workday was over. After that he obtained log printouts from the switchboard itself and set off again with Westman to Älvsjö for a second conversation with Staffan Jenner.

It was Jenner who suggested they meet at his home again, and Hamad had nothing against leaving the city for a wooded suburb on a sunny morning like this one. Next time, however, it would probably be high time to call him into the police station. The institutional environment could have interesting effects on a conversation.

"So if you were to speculate, Staffan, what do you think was behind the execution of Sven-Gunnar Erlandsson?" Westman asked in a tone that Hamad recognized.

He sensed what was coming and his stomach fluttered. Westman opened with a shock. They were sitting as before in the living room, and Jenner looked at her with surprise with his almost unreal blue eyes. Just as he opened his mouth to answer, she struck.

"Money? Revenge? Love? Or Larissa Sotnikova?"

Hamad saw how Jenner froze to ice with his mouth wide open. And Westman sat leaning back in the chair with her arms resting on the arm support, studying him with a facial expression that was completely neutral. She was waiting him out. Not a word would be said before he answered the question. You could hear a pin drop.

"I have a hard time seeing that anyone would have a motive to murder Svempa," he answered at last.

Crystal clear. Expressionless.

"And I find it highly improbable that Lara would have anything to do with the case."

Westman did not take her eyes off him, wanted to get him to talk, give himself away, get off balance.

"As far as she is concerned, I have already had so many questions from the police, I have nothing more to add. But go right ahead. If you imagine that could have any relevance in this instance."

He hardened himself. Suddenly he could master his emotions. The situation was not new to him, he had experienced it before. Unlike the murder of Sven-Gunnar Erlandsson, whether he had committed it himself or not.

For Hamad, the moment was over. He realized that going forward, aggressive questions would get hardened answers.

"Lara—that's what you call Larissa?" he asked.

"Yes, that's what we all called her. What she was called there at home."

"What do you think happened to her?"

"I can't really think anything. I hope she's okay. That she ended up with someone who likes her."

"So you think she ran away so that she could stay in Sweden?"

"No. That's what I hope. I *think* she is no longer alive."

Hamad raised an eyebrow.

"Why do you think that?"

Jenner answered without averting his gaze.

"Because that seems the most probable. And because I don't feel her presence."

He was drying his hands on his pants. A sign, despite everything, that he was not comfortable with the situation.

"So it's not the case that you *know* she is dead?" Westman put in.

Jenner did not answer, only gave her a tired glance.

"In your most intimate circle, three people have died in recent years." Westman continued. "Don't you find that strange?"

He sighed.

"I presume that the third person would be Marie, then? She took her own life as a direct consequence of your work the last time."

"I'm sincerely sorry about that. But could you expand on that?"

For the first time he looked away, disappearing through the window with his gaze. But he answered the same way as before. Calmly, factually, and with a certain degree of resignation.

"When Lara disappeared, the whole family was put under enormous pressure. First from the sorrow and desperation that perhaps we had lost her. Then from the police's repeated interrogations and insinuations. Finally, by the wait-and-see attitude of those around us. Unstated suspicions. Rumors being spread. All the whispering."

"Lost her?" Hamad asked. "Did you think you owned her?"

Jenner looked at him with regret in his eyes. Or maybe it was indulgence?

"You can't own another human being," he answered. "But we were Lara's parents. When she was here. And we were in the process of adopting her."

"Could you adopt her?"

"Yes. We loved Lara. Her disappearance put a strain on all of us, but Marie took it the hardest. A year after we lost Lara, she gave up. To be honest, I think perhaps she took the suspicions against me harder than the loss of Lara itself. Because the sorrow you learn to live with, but not the shame."

"So it wasn't the case that Marie also suspected you?" Westman went on, but Jenner took the question with composure, still with his gaze lost somewhere outside the window.

"She was not unaffected by all the talk. But she knew me. She knew I wasn't capable of any such thing, and—"

"Of what exactly?" Hamad interrupted.

Jenner was back, looked him in the eyes when he answered.

"Of something criminal."

He didn't let himself lose control. Not this time.

"And there were others who were equally convinced that I was innocent. Everyone who knew me well. Svempa, for example. He's been there for me the whole time. So why would I want him dead?"

"Maybe because he changed his understanding," Hamad replied.

The words remained hanging in the air, in the room with all the photographs. No one said anything for a while. It was completely silent, no voices, no noise.

It must be so lonely to be Staffan Jenner, Hamad thought. Widower, children on their own. Life edged by sorrow and grief. Last one left in a house full of memories. What was it that kept him here?

Wasn't that exactly what Staffan Jenner had asked himself during his little breakdown the last time they saw him?

Finally Westman broke the silence. "Then may one assume that you will stand by Adrianti the same way?"

There was only a shift. Something uncertain that swept past his eyes, a slight trembling in his voice when he answered.

"Of course. Of course I will."

Hamad was struck by a sudden impulse to call in a K-9 handler. What if Staffan Jenner *couldn't* leave the house? If a sale of the property involved such great risks that it was inconceivable?

MONDAY AFTERNOON

Once again Sjöberg and Wallin found themselves in the Erlandsson family's comfortable kitchen. This time, besides Adrianti and Ida, the grown children were also sitting around the large table.

Rasmus was twenty-five and studying law at Uppsala University. Anna was two years younger and studying to be a doctor, also at Uppsala. They had arrived the day before and the family had had time together to process what had happened. Even though there were so many in the room, a stillness rested over the whole company that Sjöberg associated most closely with the Good Fridays of his childhood.

"I got a text message yesterday after you left," said Adrianti. "From Svempa. He sent it at 12:25 a.m."

"12:25?" Sjöberg repeated. "What did he want?"

"Just to say that he was on his way home. You can look at it yourself."

She pushed the cell phone to him with the message displayed. "Home soon. XOX S." Dated Sunday 12:24 a.m. He angled the phone so that Wallin who was sitting beside him could see too.

"But you didn't have your cell phone turned on?" Sjöberg asked.

"Yes, but it was out of power when I got up. The battery must have run out while I was sleeping. In the morning when I woke up and Svempa wasn't here, I plugged in the phone to charge it. That was right before you arrived. I only discovered the text message after you'd gone."

We really would have liked to have known that right away, thought Sjöberg, but refrained from criticizing the new widow. Erlandsson had consequently been alive right before 12:30 in any event. If he really was the one who sent the message. Just as he was about to ask, Wallin took command.

"Do you usually have the cell phone on at night?" she asked in a surprisingly authoritative tone.

Where is she headed?

Adrianti looked uncertainly from the one to the other.

"Or was there something special about just this occasion?"

"I always have it on."

"If something happens?"

"Yes."

"Was there any reason to think something would happen?"

Clever.

"No," Adrianti said with a smile, relieved now. "I didn't mean it that way. I would have it on in case Svempa called."

But Wallin did not give in. Struck like a barracuda.

"Would you have to answer then? Even if you were asleep?"

Unnecessary, that was enough now. Adrianti's smile disappeared just as quickly as it had come. Anna looked tense, Rasmus and Ida distressed. They felt sorry for their stepmother. It would have been better to handle this carefully.

"No, of course not. But maybe I wanted to answer."

"Are you sure it was your husband who wrote that message?" Sjöberg asked. "I'm asking, you understand, because we haven't found his cell phone."

"I'm sure," said Adrianti. "He always wrote like that."

A few seconds of silence, time for reflection. And then Walleye again, now in an unpredictable attempt to lighten the atmosphere.

"You have an extremely nice home here. I love this combination of classic country and modern. And everything in its place, that's not easy."

Sjöberg looked around with new eyes. Wallin was not off base; it was, when you looked more closely, really very well thought-out altogether. Old cupboard doors with charming knobs and an old wood stove. This in combination with a ceramic hearth from Gaggenau and a built-in coffeemaker. Discriminating with loose objects, apparently randomly thrown on the shelves. Well-polished copper and old Rörstrand flour and salt bins. Modern porcelain and designer glass in rustic white-stained glass cabinets. Everything pedantically arranged, which appealed to Sjöberg in every respect.

"But that takes the right person," Wallin continued. "It's hard to get it to all come together. I'm impressed."

Adrianti cracked a smile and the children could breathe out.

"Thanks," she said. "It's nice that you notice it. There is quite a bit of work behind it."

Fascinating to hear Wallin talk interior decoration. Right on target besides. With her clothing style, you might think she completely lacked a sense for such things.

"Do you work at home?" she asked.

Neat transition. But Sjöberg had no idea where she intended to go. Wallin was a mystery.

"I'm a housewife," Adrianti answered directly. "There aren't any jobs for someone like me in Sweden. And with all the children and then . . . Well, you know. It was best for us."

"Nice to have someone to come home to after school?" Sjöberg commented, wanting to bring the children into the conversation, and also realizing he had lost control and wanted to be included.

"Yes, there were always milk and sandwiches on the table," Rasmus said, placing his arm around his stepmother's shoulder.

She leaned her head against his, and it seemed undeniable that this family was well united.

"Tell us what happened when you met," Sjöberg asked. "You were living in Indonesia then, right?"

"Yes. On an island called Batam. It's pretty close to Singapore, where Svempa and the children were living. The Singaporeans come to Batam to play golf, and I worked at the club. One time I was caddy for Svempa and the following weekend he came back."

Adrianti Erlandsson's whole face was beaming. The children too were affected by the emotion in the story that changed their lives as well.

"Caddy," said Wallin, she too with a smile. "So are you a menace on the course?"

"A menace? No, I don't think so," Adrianti answered modestly.

"What's your handicap?"

"I haven't played golf since then. That was thirteen years ago. Then I had two, three something."

Sjöberg had no idea whether that was good or bad, but it irritated him that Wallin led the conversation onto a sidetrack.

"Why haven't you played since you came to Sweden?" she continued. "There are lots of nice golf courses around here."

That determined wrinkle between her eyes had returned. She was sincerely interested, the only question was why. Sjöberg concluded that it was because she was a golf nut. Like all other golfers.

"Oh, I didn't have time for that," Adrianti answered. "With the family and everything. None of the others played. It was soccer that ruled here, wasn't it, kids?"

They nodded in agreement.

"Yes, it was soccer all the way," said Ida. "We all played. And Adri cheered and washed team jerseys."

Adrianti laughed.

"Okay," said Sjöberg, who was starting to get extremely bored. "You carried . . . Svempa's clubs, and then?"

"Then he came back and back and always wanted to have me as a caddy. Otherwise he didn't play. He fell in love with me. And I fell in love with him. Then we got married and moved back here."

"And you're a Swedish citizen since . . . ?"

"Since 2000."

"Do you still have your Indonesian citizenship too?"

"Yes, you can have both."

"I'm sure that's right," Sjöberg managed to say before he was again interrupted by Wallin.

"And the children. How did it go with them? Did they all get along well together?"

Sjöberg saw it. It lasted only a fraction of a second, and he didn't understand what it was he saw, but he saw it. A shadow drew past Adrianti Erlandsson's face and she hesitated a moment too long with the answer. She cast a glance at Wallin and she was prepared for this, he realized, because her gaze was very sharp and her entire being was directed at decoding just this reaction. Sjöberg loved those moments, he lived for them. But right now he felt completely left hanging.

"They thought it was great," Adrianti replied, now without a trace of . . . whatever it was. "They loved each other from the first moment. Didn't you, honey?"

She stroked the oldest girl across the cheek; the question was obviously aimed especially at her. Anna nodded with a mournful expression in her eyes, a sorrow that in some way seemed to differ from the obvious. But Ida objected.

"Don't talk that way, Adri. Dewi is just as much my sister. And Rasmus."

She said it gently and kindly. Lovingly. In some way it was clear to Sjöberg that this was not an accusation, simply an appeal. The mood in the room was suddenly quite different. The loss had been there the whole time, but now it was . . . more painful? And at the same time shyer? A sorrow that did not have a name. In contrast to death.

"Dewi Kusamasari," said Wallin. "Is there any particular reason you haven't mentioned your daughter before?"

"She's not in Sweden," Adrianti answered. "She's out traveling. Besides, I talk about the children all the time and she's one of them."

"Tell us about Dewi."

Adrianti considered, did not know perhaps where she should begin. But when Ida opened her mouth, there was no stopping her.

"Dewi is amazing. When we first met her, we thought she was the cutest kid we'd ever seen. Me too, even though I'm three years younger. She was happy and positive, lively, adventurous, and capable at just about everything. Dewi was only ten years old then and didn't know a word of Swedish, but after just a month or two she kept up when we talked. She didn't know that much when she came here, because they don't have very good schools in Indonesia, so they put her in a class with children one year younger. By the next year she did so well she got to skip a grade and be in Anna's class. When she graduated from high school, she had 320 credits. Top grades in all subjects.

"Dewi had never played soccer, but she learned right away. And of course became the team's best player even though she had a very unique playing style. She was a real artist with the ball. And she was the best friend you can imagine. If you were sad, you could always go to her. She never quarreled with anyone. Mediated if the rest of us quarreled with each other.

"I really miss Dewi, I want her to come home."

Now the tears welled up in Ida's eyes and Adrianti too appeared ready to burst into tears at any moment. Rasmus and Anna sat unmoving and looked down at the table.

"So why isn't she here?" asked Sjöberg, who had managed to collect himself and wanted back in the game.

"She's on a long journey," Adrianti answered quietly, with her gaze directed at her hands, which were furiously massaging each other on the table before her. "Trip around the world. And Svempa isn't waking up in any case," she added with a catch in her throat.

"Where is she? When did she leave?"

"I don't know where she is right now. She's been all over. She's been gone for four years."

"For four years!" Sjöberg exclaimed. "You haven't seen her in four years? Anna?"

Anna shook her head without looking up.

"Why so long?"

"She's adventurous," Anna answered. "Like Ida said. She had no problems moving here. I guess it wasn't any harder to move away."

"Do you mean she's rootless?"

"On the contrary. Dewi can put down roots anywhere."

Sjöberg could not get this to fit together. A strong family where there was so much love and consideration—had something happened?

"But you're in contact?" Wallin asked.

"We send emails," Adrianti answered.

"Not very often, apparently, because you don't know where she is right now?"

"Often enough for me to know that she's okay."

"How was Svempa and Dewi's relationship?" Sjöberg asked, letting his gaze wander over all of them.

It was Rasmus who answered.

"It was good. Very good. Like Ida said, we all loved her from the first moment. Dad considered her one of his own."

There was no reason to doubt that. The remaining family members appeared to be of the same opinion.

"But he never adopted her?"

The question was placed to Adrianti, but Anna answered first.

"She didn't want to give up the hope that she would meet her real dad one day."

"And who is that? Her real dad?"

Everyone's eyes were now directed at Adrianti, who was squirming.

"A Singapore Chinese."

"A Singapore Chinese?" Sjöberg echoed, uncomprehending.

"A Chinese from Singapore," Rasmus answered in his mother's place. "That is, someone from Singapore who isn't Indian, Malay, or something else, but Chinese. There's no judgment in that, it's just a clarification."

"Okay. But he's still alive?"

"That I don't know," Adrianti answered. "We lived together for eight years. On the weekends. He lived in Singapore during the week. But then he got tired of it and we never saw him again."

"So you weren't married?"

"No."

"But he acknowledged the paternity?" Sjöberg asked, in an awkward attempt to put the pieces in place.

"Yes, of course. For me and Dewi and everyone in the village. We did live together in a house that he bought. But not officially. There are no papers."

"Why is that?"

Adrianti answered with a shrug of her shoulders. Sjöberg was presumably an idiot.

Indonesia and Sweden were two different matters, he understood that much in any event. He gave up.

"We talked about motives the last time we were here. Have you happened to think of anyone who might conceivably have a reason to want Sven-Gunnar Erlandsson dead?"

Nothing but shaking heads.

"Dad was extremely popular," Rasmus answered. "And not particularly controversial. He was a leadership figure, but not at the cost of others."

"Then I would like to hear your opinions concerning the people he was out with Saturday evening," said Sjöberg. "We'll start with Siem. What is there to tell about him?"

They looked doubtfully at each other. Shrugged their shoulders.

"The children don't know Janne Seim particularly well," Adrianti answered. "I don't either. Svempa thought he was a good fellow. But a little . . . looks out for number one? Can you say that?"

Sjöberg smiled and even Wallin cracked a smile.

"Oh yes," Sjöberg answered. "Someone who devotes a lot of energy to looking after his own interests. Do you know what your husband meant when he said this about Siem?"

"When you played poker, it was the rules' fault if Janne lost. If he won there was no problem. Wasn't there something about soccer too, Ida?"

"Yes," the girl confirmed. "I played on the same team as his oldest daughter. She wasn't a regular on the team and Dad was our coach. Apparently, Janne hinted that I ought to be the one sitting on the bench, that Dad favored me because I was his daughter."

"It wasn't like that?"

"Definitely not." Rasmus came to his sister's defense.

Loyalty? Or an objectively supported statement?

"And the thirteen-year-old?" Wallin broke in. "Josefin Siem?"

Ida looked uncertain, sought confirmation in her brother's eyes. Rasmus nodded.

"From the little I've seen, she doesn't give a particularly pleasant impression. Bitchy. Like her two sisters. I don't like anyone in that family. But Dad defended them. Dad liked everyone. Said that we all have little faults and deficiencies."

"Lennart Wiklund, then?" Sjöberg asked. "What's he like?"

It started to feel like they were indulging in pure gossip. But they were forced to ask these questions. How else could they understand the interplay between Sven-Gunnar Erlandsson and the people who last saw him alive? They had to start somewhere. Because somewhere, something had been smoldering. Enough to cause a substantial conflagration.

"He's nice," Adrianti answered. "Fun. Talks a lot."

"Bullshitter?" Wallin suggested.

Adrianti laughed. A wisp of black, shining hair fell down on her face and she pushed it back behind her ear.

"Yes, he's good at talking shit. Or do you mean where he talks shit about others? He doesn't do that. That's not his style."

"That was exactly what *he* said about Svempa, too," Wallin recalled from the morning meeting at the police station. "That he didn't spread a lot of shit about people."

Adrianti nodded.

"That's right. Svempa detested that sort of thing. Said there was something good in everyone."

"But that they'd had their clashes," Wallin continued. "What do you think Wiklund meant by that?"

"No idea. I haven't heard of any trouble between them. Svempa thought that Lennart was a cool character. Good to deal with."

Wallin did not give up.

"But he must have meant something. Could it have anything to do with poker? Or soccer?"

The children knew nothing. Looked attentively at their step-mother while she searched her memory.

"The only thing I can think of was when Svempa moved Lennart from coaching his daughter Alexandra's team to coaching his son's. William's. It was no big deal."

"Did Svempa say that?"

Adrianti nodded. Something ignited in Wallin's eyes.

"Maybe it was for Lennart Wiklund. Why was he moved?"

"Because some of the girls said he was looking at them. Or hit on them, maybe you could say."

"But Svempa brushed that aside?"

"No, he remedied it. So that everyone was content."

"Except Wiklund, apparently."

Sjöberg studied Wallin with a certain fascination. He imagined poor Adrianti Erlandsson as a lemon in her hands. That would be squeezed until every drop was out.

"He got a good deal. The girls and their parents were content and Lennart got to coach a different team instead. Svempa was diplomatic."

"Could you say that the matter was hushed up?"

"There was nothing to hush up. Svempa said that the girls were just messing with Lennart a little. That there was nothing to it. He took over the team himself and made sure there was no bullshit."

"I see, so it's that team. The team where Josefin Siem plays. Was she possibly one of the accusers?"

Adrianti looked down at her hands and pressed hard with one thumb on the palm of the other.

"Yes, it was her," she answered quietly. "But Svempa didn't want that to come out. For Lennart's sake. And Alexandra's."

"What a mess," Wallin noted with a smile that seemed both triumphant and bitter at the same time.

"May I say something?" Ida asked. "I haven't heard about this before, but I would guess that Dad was right. That Lennart was innocent. Now I don't know about Josefin Siem, but a lot of girls think Lennart is really good-looking. For example, her big sisters, who were slobbering after him and sucking up to him all the time. He probably *didn't* show those girls the interest they wanted and so they fabricated this story. That's what I think."

Sjöberg thought it was time to change tracks.

"And then there's Staffan Jenner. I understand that all of you know him well."

The children seemed indifferent. Adrianti exhaled deeply. Perhaps she had a feeling what was coming.

"A close friend of the family, isn't he?"

The children nodded. Adrianti swallowed.

"Any spontaneous comments?"

"I think . . ." Adrianti began.

She looked pale and hollow-eyed. Perhaps it was nervy to bring up this misery on top of everything else. But the subject had to be talked about, and there was no point in postponing it.

"I don't think I can bear to be interrogated any more now. Can we deal with this later?"

Rasmus and Anna exchanged glances. Ida looked resolute.

"I'm sorry," Sjöberg said gently, "but we have to ask these questions to go further. The sooner the better."

Ida was once again the one who was able to talk about what the other family members shied away from.

"We know where you're headed," she said cuttingly. "Lara—right? She was one year younger than me. We played almost all the time. I knew her better than anyone else. The way kids do. She loved the Jenner family. She loved Staffan. And they loved her. Staffan is a good person through and through. Kind, gentle, understanding, loving, a teacher. There's no way Staffan could have done her any harm. Do you get that? There's no way."

"So what do you think, Ida?" Sjöberg asked. "What was it that happened?"

"I think she ran away because she didn't want to go home. And met with an accident. Or a lunatic."

"I agree completely," said Rasmus. "Staffan had nothing to do with it. Can we leave that now?"

Sjöberg gave in. They could dig into the circumstances around the Russian summer child's disappearance themselves. In any case they now knew where the Erlandsson family stood.

"Okay," Sjöberg sighed. "But regardless of that, we want to know what the relationship between your families was and is. From what I've understood you have been pretty close to each other. Adrianti?"

Adrianti still looked almost terrified. Rasmus answered in her place.

"We were good friends, all of us. Anna, Dewi, and I played a lot with their kids. Ida was a little too small, for that reason it was extra fun for her with Lara. Staffan's wife and Adri got along extremely well. Marie was invaluable when Adri was new to the country, helped her find her footing, you might say. Wasn't that so?"

Adrianti nodded, but her gaze revealed that she was somewhere else in her thoughts. Tears welled up in her eyes. They were dangerously near the edge of what she could handle now. It was time to leave the Erlandsson family in peace.

"And Dad was strong as a rock when . . . when it happened," Rasmus continued. "Stood up for Staffan through thick and thin. They relied unconditionally on each other and were extremely alike in their way of looking at things, even if outwardly they were very different. If you're looking for a crack between them, you're searching in vain. Staffan Jenner did not murder Dad."

The last he said with emphasis. Adrianti Erlandsson pulled on her little finger so that it cracked. Her tears flooded over. The limit was passed.

Or perhaps she was not equally convinced.

———

Sven-Gunnar Erlandsson's life was a mosaic of happenings and people. At the moment they were rooting amongst the central aspects of his everyday life with a starting point in the present. But he was fifty-two years old when he died and had moved in wide circles over large areas for a long time. Even though a good deal of interesting information had emerged, there was really nothing that said that the murderer was among those whom they had questioned or even heard about. Even if Hamad himself thought that a missing Russian girl and a suicide were sufficient for a little extra digging in the Jenner family's backyard.

On the other hand, he was not quite prepared to give up the poker lead. The cards in the pocket, the fact that in some sense this was a poker evening plus the fatal shot in the head, spoke for themselves. It was irresponsible to overlook these indications, even if it might well be a smokescreen.

He did not believe for a moment that Lennart Wiklund would have shot Erlandsson. The guy was a good-time Charlie and apparently a lecher too, but Hamad did not believe he was a murderer. He did not think much of Wallin's idea about Josefin Siem's involvement in the murder, either. Jan Siem might very well have had something to do with it, but that he would subject his thirteen-year-old daughter to something as horrid as finding the corpse seemed unlikely. Perhaps this happened by accident, but in that case it was also a large coincidence and he did not believe much in coincidences.

The family? In statistical terms, that was the most probable. He hadn't met them personally, but from what he'd heard nothing had emerged so far that pointed in that direction. And Sjöberg's interest in that homeless thing would soon die out on its own. The contributions of the homeless to the characterization of Erlandsson were not insignificant to them, but they would not find his murderer at the trailer encampment.

In any case, the phone call to acting police commissioner Malmberg on Sunday morning was the most concrete thing they had to go on. Perhaps one of the many vultures who frequently sat listening to what was being discussed on the police radio could have been struck by a sudden need to make himself important. But it could also be the murderer himself who called. Or someone who had reason to direct suspicions in the wrong direction. Under any circumstance, it was of the greatest interest to find out where that matter stood as soon as possible.

During the afternoon Hamad went through the log printouts from the Hammarby police switchboard for the time Malmberg could have received the call, plus or minus fifteen minutes.

The switchboard also kept track of the calls that went directly—that is, not via the receptionist—to the landlines on every desk in the police station. He traced the incoming calls not dialed from unlisted numbers and then linked them up with the respective recipient, whom he then contacted.

None of these calls were addressed to Malmberg, and they also concerned completely different matters than the murder of Sven-Gunnar Erlandsson. Strangely enough, none of the calls that had been made from unlisted numbers had gone to Malmberg's landline, either—directly or via manual forwarding.

As the time approached six and he was still no wiser, he got ready to go home. Then the lists from Telia showed up in his inbox.

A small number of calls from unlisted numbers had come in via the switchboard during that time period. The subscribers behind these numbers were named and their addresses had also been listed. Hamad immediately contacted the police officers who took the calls and none of them had any problems explaining them. They were all of a private nature.

Two calls had been received by Gunnar Malmberg's cell phone during the time period in question. One of these was thirteen minutes wrong in time and came from Malmberg's own home phone besides. The other had arrived at 9:36 a.m. From a phone card.

TUESDAY MORNING

On Tuesday morning Bella Hansson came by the police station and Sjöberg called an informal meeting in his office. It was crowded, but he expected that what Hansson had to say was of interest to everyone.

"The gun we're looking for is a Glock 38," she began. "Unfortunately, I should add, because they aren't too hard to get hold of and are common in criminal circles. As long as you have the right contacts, it's no problem."

"And if you don't?" asked Andersson, who was standing, leaning against a bookshelf. "What do you do then? We haven't encountered any armored car robbers in this investigation yet."

"There are quite a few shady sites on the internet," Hansson answered from her place in one of the visitors' chairs. "So far we haven't been able to connect this weapon to any other crime."

"Do you mean we're not going to find the murderer through the weapon?"

"I think that might be difficult. Not to say hopeless," she added and then changed track. "According to Kaj, the theory that the victim was first shot in the back from about five meters away and then from a close distance in the neck when he fell down adds up. That shot was immediately fatal."

"So we're talking execution," Sandén observed. "The fact that his cell phone was then stolen doesn't make this a robbery. It's primarily a murder."

"At 12:24 a.m. he sent a text message to his wife," said Sjöberg. "It could be that he had the cell phone out when he was shot, and that the murderer took it on a momentary impulse. It's an iPhone, after all. Expensive and attractive."

"It could also be the case that he was murdered because someone wanted that cell phone," Andersson countered. "For some other reason than that it's so expensive. Far-fetched, maybe, but still a possibility to take into consideration."

Sjöberg nodded thoughtfully.

"Speaking of telephones, Jamal—how's it going with Telia? Have you seen any call lists?"

"I haven't got Erlandsson's yet. But it's been confirmed that the call Malmberg received at 9:36 a.m. Sunday morning came from a phone card."

"So it's a dead end there, too?"

"In principle."

"Tower?"

"I'll get back about that."

Wallin changed subject. "Those playing cards, Bella, were there really only four?" she asked. "There weren't five?"

"No, there were four," Hansson attested.

"Where did you get that bit about poker from? You were talking about a poker player at the golf course, when you got the call."

Hansson thought before she answered.

"It was Lundin who was on duty, I seem to recall. He must have been the one who mentioned poker."

"But he couldn't reasonably have had any idea about that," Wallin continued stubbornly. "That Erlandsson was a poker player. They might just as well have been playing bridge. Or Go Fish. What cards were they, by the way?"

Hansson opened the plastic folder she had in front of her on the desk and pulled out a bundle of photographs. Among them she found one that depicted the four cards.

"It was the eight of spades, ace of clubs, ace of spades, and eight of clubs," she answered.

"Two pairs then," Hamad announced. "That explains it."

Wallin did not look completely convinced.

"Were there any fingerprints on the cards?" she asked.

"No, there weren't."

"Should there have been? I mean, considering the rain."

"Absolutely," Hansson replied. "If someone had touched them with bare fingers there would be prints. Which seems to rule out Erlandsson putting them there himself, because he didn't have gloves on."

"A message from the murderer perhaps," Wallin thought out loud. "But what's that scribbling there?" she asked with reference to some bluish stains on one of the aces.

"I was just getting to that," Hansson answered. "Do you remember I mentioned that besides these playing cards we also found a slip of paper in Erlandsson's pocket? The handwritten text became blurry as a result of the rain. It proved to be written with an ordinary ballpoint pen, and that kind of ink doesn't tolerate dampness too well. The stains on the ace come from that piece of paper. But the playing cards have a glossy surface, which doesn't absorb any of the ink. Instead it looks like scribbling, just as you said, Walleye. However, the lining of the breast pocket of the jacket, where we found the cards and note, had soaked up a little of the ink. With the help of the ink on the lining, the ink on the scrap of paper, and some impressions on the paper from the ballpoint pen itself, I've managed to extract part of a message from this mess. It's a mixture of letters and numbers, maybe a code of some kind. It looks like this."

In the middle of Sjöberg's desk she placed a piece of paper with an arrangement of sloppy curlicues. Sandén and Sjöberg, who were already sitting at the desk, leaned forward to study the incomprehensible text. The other police officers crowded around the table to try to decipher the content of the mysterious slip of paper.

"I'll take that!" Wallin called, before anyone had really managed to process what was on the paper. "I love codes, I'll make sure it gets solved. If that's possible," she added with an inquisitive look.

"I'm in," said Sandén without taking time to think. "What the hell, you know we'll work this out, Walleye!"

All the others looked with surprise from one to the other before they started laughing. No one showed the slightest disappointment at being deprived of a task that could not be considered anything other than hopeless.

Odd Andersson found himself in a slumped position in the chair in front of the computer. With every fruitless phone call and every failed search he sank down a little more. The task of tracing a Glock 38, as Hansson had quite rightly pointed out, proved to be completely hopeless. Periodically he caught himself totally unfocused and thinking about different things altogether.

The visit to the trailer folks in the Huddinge forest had made a deep impression on him. There was no problem understanding what Sven-Gunnar Erlandsson saw in these people. Both the woman and the man gave an impression of being reasonably intelligent and insightful. Despite everything. Even though they had both been convicted of minor crimes, even though they had drugged away their lives and that once in the past the woman had lost custody of her two children.

Unfortunate circumstances had caused them to give up any dreams of honor and respectability, but they were thinking individuals and reasonably harmless to their surroundings. At least as far as he knew.

And then he really could not let go of the thought of that young girl who for a time had shared life in the trailer with them. What reasons could there be for a child to leave her regular life, her school and family, to live at the bottom of society?

Many reasons, he unfortunately had cause to believe. His own time growing up had not been the most fun, tinged with mental illness and abuse behind the charming facade of Volvo, dog, and suburban happiness. However, he had never considered fleeing the sinking ship; instead he had endured, counting the years and months until the day he could move away from home.

But he had revolted. He refused to get in line and live that false pseudo-life. And he found freedom in music. As a rock musician you could be wild and crazy, and he bought the whole concept, which infuriated his parents. He let his hair grow, got a tattoo the day he became a legal adult. But above all was the music. During his teens he was in lots of bands, wrote his own songs, and both sang and played guitar. They never achieved any great success, and he didn't get into music school. So when he was forced to choose an alternative path, it had been the police academy instead. His father the contractor despised the tax collectors and the cops in equal measure, but to Andersson the policing life seemed considerably more fun.

Of course there could be many reasons for a young girl to want to get away. But so many that she ended up among the riffraff in the trailer park? And in the middle of winter besides? It must have been bad. Really bad. The only question was whether anything could be worse than dragging yourself around homeless. As a fifteen-year-old. Uneducated.

Insignificant.

He decided to look her up. Rebecka. Hoped that Erlandsson really had managed to talk her into returning home. And that things weren't too terribly bad for her.

Petra Westman decided to get to the bottom of the missing Russian summer child. She had gathered together most of the existing material, and now devoted herself to plowing through files and close-reading witness interviews.

The last time the girl was seen was right before eleven o'clock on a morning in August eight years ago. According to both Marie and Staffan Jenner, she had been out of sorts those last few days because only a week remained of her stay in Sweden. But the evening before the disappearance, Staffan Jenner came home with a bicycle for her. As an assurance that she would get to come back soon and then, hopefully, stay.

The next morning it was pouring rain. Staffan Jenner was a freelance journalist and worked that day. This work partly consisted of running around among various assignments, and there were enough assignments to support his claim that he had been busy working all day, but none that gave him a complete alibi for the entire time span that mattered. Despite the bad weather, Larissa Sotnikova took off on the bicycle at quarter past ten. The other children stayed behind, inside, with their mother.

It was Marie Jenner who first began to worry. When it was almost one o'clock and she still had not heard anything from Lara, she called Ida Erlandsson, who was at home alone. Ida had contracted an ear and throat infection and didn't have the energy to be at the soccer camp with the rest of the family. But she was definite that she had not had a visit from Lara that day. On the other hand, she had slept several hours, so it was conceivable that Lara had been there after all and rang the doorbell, but that Ida had not woken up.

In late afternoon the circus started. People went outside in the area and searched high and low for the girl. Without success. The bike was never found, either. It was known that Lara had visited the soccer camp at Mälarhöjden playfield around 10:40 a.m. Then the rain let up, but despite that she had a conspicuous orange raincoat on and was therefore easy to identify even for those who didn't know her. There she had spoken with several of the children and the coaches at the camp. Among them were Anna, Rasmus, Adrianti, and Sven-Gunnar Erlandsson. Not at the same time, however, because they were in different parts of the sports facility and involved in different things.

But there were several statements from witnesses. A few individuals had seen the child in the orange raincoat cycling around in the morning. Whether these sources were credible or not was hard to know, but if what they said was true, she seemed to have moved in wide circles from her home in Herrängen and was seen as far away as the Älvsjö forest. The last sighting of Larissa Sotnikova was made about eleven, on Murgrönsvägen heading toward Konvaljestigen. This was questioned by the police, however, because she was said to have been seen in the company of a younger girl without rain gear. And no such girl had shown up in the investigation.

In Staffan Jenner's favor it appeared that the adoption plans were far advanced. Considerably farther than they would be if he was against the whole thing. Which according to both Jenner and the rest of the family he was not at all. There was also the bicycle he had bought the girl the day before the catastrophe. On the other hand, that might as easily have been a well-thought-out diversion. His car had also been searched with a fine-tooth comb for leads. And of course traces of the girl were there, but no signs of struggle or that anything unseemly might have taken place during the day before the disappearance.

What primarily spoke against Jenner was the fact that his alibi didn't hold up. That his wife committed suicide a year later did not help the matter. Nor the fact that she did so by means of sleeping pills. There was nothing that proved she had taken them of her own free will. And if she had done so, she probably had rather strong reasons. Perhaps the knowledge of what had gone on in her own home? Jenner gave a brittle and fragile impression besides, both physically and mentally. His medical records might hold a thing or two of interest, but there was no way to get access to them when evidence of his involvement in these cases was so lacking.

If you were to work according to the hypothesis that Larissa Sotnikova's disappearance had something to do with the murder of Sven-Gunnar Erlandsson, then perhaps it was time to expand the outlook a little. Or reduce it, depending on how you framed it. Westman decided to search for common denominators, and Staffan Jenner was perhaps not the only one. How were things with the Wiklund and Siem families? They too were soccer families, and could have been among those who were at the Mälarhöjden athletic field that morning eight years ago.

In one of the boxes on the floor she searched out a bundle of lists of participants from the soccer camp and browsed through them in the hope of running into a familiar name. And sure enough: a Carolina Siem, born in 1989; a Lovisa Siem, born in 1992; and a William Wiklund, born in 1993, were among the names on the lists. In addition there were Jan Siem, Katarina Siem, Ingela Wiklund, and Lennart Wiklund among the organizers. The last was named as a coach, but with his name crossed out with pencil and replaced with another, namely Rasmus Erlandsson.

This was interesting. Why had Lennart Wiklund been replaced as a coach during the camp? And with the Erlandsson boy to boot? Sjöberg had said that Sven-Gunnar Erlandsson had replaced Lennart Wiklund, moving from a girls' team to a boys' team. True, that was only a year or two ago, but the problem could have come up earlier. An inordinate interest in young girls? Or girls who exaggerated his interest out of pure wishful thinking?

Westman decided to contact him and get an answer to the question. Somewhere among all the papers on the desk she knew she had his information, but it seemed simpler to turn on the computer instead. On hitta.se one page was taken up by nineteen Wiklunds residing in Älvsjö, one of whom was Lennart. To be on the safe side, she called his cell phone number. After two rings she had him on the line and explained who she was.

"I really have just one question. You were listed as a coach for the soccer camp held at the Mälarhöjden athletic field during the week that a Russian girl disappeared. Larissa Sotnikova. But I see here that you were crossed off the list and replaced by Rasmus Erlandsson. How did that happen?"

"Jenner's summer child? But wasn't that ten years ago?"

He sounded surprised.

"It was eight years ago," Westman answered. "2001."

"What does that have to do with—" Wiklund started, but stopped himself and answered the question instead. "I was sick. Really sick, in fact. Had a fever of over 40° for more than a week."

"Were you home alone during that day?"

"Yes, the rest of the family was at the Mälarhöjden athletic field."

"Little Alexandra too?"

"She was with Ingela. Taking care of the food."

"Okay," said Westman, meaning to say goodbye, but Lennart Wiklund was not done talking.

"It was probably mono," he continued. "Which didn't keep me from helping to search for the girl. That afternoon I stuffed myself with Alvedon and something else that I don't remember what it's called, and searched for her until midnight."

"Thanks, that's all," said Westman and concluded the call.

Sometimes it's better to keep your mouth shut, she thought. If you could be out running around for hours, then you could have managed quite a few other things besides. In theory.

Of those in the investigation who had been more or less grown-up enough to carry off an eleven-year-old and were at the athletic field the morning Lara disappeared: Rasmus, Anna, Adrianti, and Sven-Gunnar Erlandsson; Dewi Kusamasari; Jan and Katarina Siem; and Ingela Wiklund. Lennart Wiklund, Marie, and the three Jenner children were at home. Staffan Jenner was out in his car, working. Lennart Wiklund and Staffan Jenner obviously lacked an alibi. The rest of the Jenner family confirmed each other's. The soccer folks' alibis would presumably not have been scrutinized too hard during the investigation.

Why should they have been? No suspicions had been directed against them, and the police surely had no reason to ask each and every one of the more than a hundred individuals at the soccer camp for a watertight alibi. The fact that they had all been there during the morning seemed clear. But had all of them been there during the *entire* morning? Presumably it would be near impossible to get clarity this long afterward.

Let's say, Westman thought further, *that the very last pieces of information about Larissa Sotnikova are reliable.*

That the witness who saw the girl from the kitchen window on Murgrönsvägen was not way off base. In that case, Lara would have gone past along with a smaller girl without rain gear on a bicycle. A girl with a blonde ponytail hanging down below her bicycle helmet. What little girls were there to whom Lara could conceivably have loaned her bicycle? And the helmet? Josefin Siem was five years old at the time. Alexandra Wiklund likewise. She had no idea what color hair they had. It could of course have been Ida Erlandsson, blonde but one year older than Lara.

Where were the two girls headed? She grabbed the desktop and pulled the chair up to the computer. The hitta.se website was already up, so she deleted the name Wiklund from the "What are you looking for?" field, entered Murgrönsvägen before Älvsjö in the "Where?" field and clicked on "Find."

It took a fraction of a second for the map image to come up. But in that moment she glimpsed something on the screen that caused her to click back to the previous page. And quite rightly—seven places above Lennart Wiklund was yet another familiar name. Ingela Wiklund. With the address Konvaljestigen 1.

What the . . . Didn't the witness on Murgrönsvägen say that the girls were going in the direction toward Konvaljestigen?

She jumped back to the map page and got an overview of the area. Followed the possible girls' possible route with her gaze: Murgrönsvägen south, then left onto Konvaljestigen, over to No. 1. *And what do we find there?* A bicycle path that led in among the trees. Plus a freestanding house bordered by a school empty for summer vacation and a leafy greenbelt.

Långbrokungens Väg was where Lennart Wiklund was living nowadays, but it was more than likely that at the time of the disappearance he lived at this address in the Herrängen district. Together with his wife and their two children.

But on that particular morning he was alone at home.

Sandén and Wallin took to their assignment with the blurred ink with great enthusiasm. Sandén really didn't know why he had volunteered—this type of problem-solving had never been one of his favorite tasks. But what he did know was that it was a true delight to work with Walleye. While the rest of the group seemed to consider her objectionable in some way, perhaps because she was not refined in any respect, Sandén thought she was a rather amazing mixed bag of surprises. She was damn capable too, at almost everything she undertook. She had a very personal way of attacking the problems they were faced with, but no one listened to her; the others simply thought she was strange. Even Sjöberg, which really bothered Sandén.

How Sjöberg, the warmest and most loving of all people, could think badly of a person like Walleye was a mystery. But it amused Sandén that Sjöberg had a hard time concealing his skepticism about his and Walleye's good relationship. He actually seemed a bit jealous.

Now they were sitting beside each other behind Sandén's desk with the enlargement in front of them, scale 1:5.

"Nietzsche," said Wallin. "The philosopher."

Sandén looked perplexed.

"Uh, I just threw out the first thing I happened to think of. There are way too many characters. But the first one could be an N, and then we have S and I a little farther along."

"Heinz," said Sandén. "The ketchup."

"Yes, that too," Wallin said. "Though I wonder if there aren't more numerals than letters. Shall we go through one at a time and write down all the possibilities?"

"That sounds wise," said Sandén, reaching for a pad and pen. "The first one must be N."

"I agree. We'll go with that for the time being. Then we have an S or a five."

Sandén wrote.

"Nine or seven maybe?" Wallin continued.

"And a ball?"

"Exactly, write 'ball.' Or O slash zero. Then we have an I or a one."

"And a nine or a four. Or what do you think, Walleye, is there any letter that looks like that?"

"Doubtful. Then an I or a one again. S or five. And then a pear."

"A six maybe?" Sandén suggested. "Or a really messy A."

"And then a flying box."

"You have to keep in mind that this is handwritten," Sandén pointed out. "A sloppy D maybe, that landed above the line?"

"Or an O."

"Seems a little too square for that, do you agree?"

"Yes," answered Wallin. "An H then? Where the legs have run together?"

"Then we have a C, G, or E, I'd say."

"I or one."

"And a seven. Or a T?"

"And then the ball again," Wallin said. "Write O or zero. Although maybe it could be a plus sign?"

Sandén wrote down all the alternatives.

"Five or S, nine or four," he said.

"And then a little blip," said Wallin. "What is it?"

"Maybe it doesn't belong there," Sandén speculated. "Maybe it's just a stain that happens to be there."

"In that case it would be blank there, and I don't believe that. An apostrophe, maybe?"

"Good idea, I'll make a note."

"A Z or a two."

"A six or a G?"

"And then another blip that doesn't go down. Although thicker."

"A U maybe?" Sandén guessed. "Or an H. Or a messier apostrophe."

"A quotation mark, possibly."

"How do we continue?"

Wallin thought for a few moments before she answered.

"I think I'll throw together a Perl script that generates all combinations of the characters we've decided there can be."

Sandén did not understand a word of what she said.

"You're speaking in tongues, my dear Walleye. Rewind and start over."

"I'll write a computer program that tests all numerals and letters we've guessed at. Then we'll get a list of all conceivable combinations of those characters. If you stare at the list a little maybe it will be easier to see a pattern, figure out what it's supposed to represent. Are you with me?"

"I think so. But . . . can you simply 'throw together' that kind of computer program?"

"It's no problem," said Wallin casually. "I've played around a little with such things. In a previous life. When I didn't have anything better to do."

Sandén shook his head with a resigned smile.

"You are full of surprises, Walleye. What should I do in the meantime?"

"I guess you can research on your end. Google a little on what we have. Who knows—maybe something inspiring will show up."

Then she left the room with purposeful steps, the caftan-like garment she was dressed in fluttering in the draft behind her. Sandén did not feel one hundred percent convinced that he understood what he was expected to do, but he turned on the computer anyway, as he was asked. And damned if he didn't already feel a bit inspired.

TUESDAY AFTERNOON

Hamad spent the morning going through Sven-Gunnar Erlandsson's computer, a particularly uninteresting task. His email communication was routine, mostly about work and soccer. The tone was often warm and friendly but otherwise neutral. Nothing secretive, nothing beyond the normal. Nothing surprising among the contacts or calendar, either.

Photography did not appear to be a major interest; there were no pictures on the computer, in any event. Among the documents the most exciting was a confidential business plan from SEB. Judging by the rather extensive Google and internet history, Erlandsson neither surfed porn nor indulged in anything startling. A wasted morning, in other words.

The requested information from Telia showed up after lunch. He skimmed through Erlandsson's telephone lists and decided that it would be a lot of work to map the family's telephone habits. The cell phone records interested him more than the family's landline account. First and foremost, he wanted to verify that the SMS received by Adrianti really had been sent from this account right before twelve-thirty on Sunday morning. It had been.

But when he discovered that against all odds there was another entry on the list, his heart took an extra beat. The last registered outgoing call from Erlandsson's cell phone had been made several hours after he was killed. To a prepaid phone card number. And what was more, the call originated in Södertälje.

With fumbling fingers he navigated into Eniro's map image of the area where the cell phone tower was. A stone's throw from the soccer field where Jan and Josefin Siem were at that exact same time.

Maybe she wasn't so dumb after all, Wallin. Could it be that one of them, or both, were involved in the murder of Sven-Gunnar Erlandsson? Another alternative of course was that the girl, when she caught sight of the desirable cell phone next to her coach's lifeless body, put her hands on it. Impulsively or otherwise. Regardless of who and for what reason—why had the person in question used it in that case, without first removing Erlandsson's SIM card?

Hamad needed that cell phone. A plan was slowly taking shape in his mind. A plan that he hoped would turn everything upside down.

Sjöberg had gone over yesterday's gathering at home with the Erlandsson family again and again all day. More or less. Now he was sitting with pen and paper in front of him, trying to dissect the conversation, as he recalled it, into its various component parts. He wished he'd had that digital recorder Åsa had given him, which he had used so diligently at first. But it started to break down after about six months, and he never took the time to do anything to fix it. Partly because he felt maybe he was losing focus, that he was not on his toes during a conversation when he knew he could listen to it afterwards. So now he had to do it the long way. He did have his notes to fall back on, but it wasn't facts he wanted to get at, but something else. The underlying mood. The emotional situation there in the kitchen on Vaktelstigen in Herrängen. The heart of the matter.

Wallin had distinguished herself right from the start with her way of oscillating between ingratiation and sternness. Her shocking opening, holding Adrianti Erlandsson accountable for answering the cell phone in the middle of the night. Which to be sure she had not done this particular time, but—it was the reaction that was being investigated. And right after that, praising Adrianti for her sense of style. And then to start talking golf. Which truly was off topic. "Why don't you play anymore?" "There are lots of nice courses here," and so on. Just as Sjöberg was about to draw out of Adrianti what had happened when she met Erlandsson. Really irritating, if Wallin didn't have something particular in her sights. Which he was quite sure she did. In which case, why couldn't she have informed him of it? But all right, maybe he didn't invite that.

On the other hand, Wallin had squeezed out quite a bit of interesting information about the Siem and Wiklund families in an exemplary way. So she was evidently not completely half-baked. Even if it felt like they were two singles players on the same side of the net rather than a doubles team.

Then to the most startling: when Wallin dropped the bomb about Adrianti's daughter, Dewi Kusamasari. This was doubtless the most revealing thing that happened during the interview, he was the first to admit that. Because he too had a feeling that Adrianti had been trying to conceal the fact that she had a daughter. But there was no reason for Wallin to let that bomb explode without his knowledge. She made him look like an idiot. Perhaps not so it was obvious to the Erlandsson family, but she did it in triumph and it felt more than a little competitive from Wallin's side. True, she was the one who discovered the girl's existence, but she was also the one he'd put on the civil registry job, so how much of a feat was that really? In Wallin's defense, they had come to the Erlandsson family's villa from different locations and in separate cars, and for that reason had not had time to draw up a plan together. But there was this thing called a cell phone, and she could have briefed him if she had wanted to.

In summary, he had two questions that he meant to ask Wallin, if he found it worth the effort. Why had she kept her plans regarding the revelation of Dewi Kusamasari's existence secret? And why all that chatter about golf and home decor?

But now to the essentials. Was it the case that at their first meeting Adrianti had avoided talking about her daughter? Yes, Sjöberg was more or less convinced of that. But why? Was there any particular reason to keep her outside this investigation? Or could Adrianti simply not bear to talk about her daughter? Heavy emotions had settled over the room after Wallin mentioned her. An enormous loss seemed to mark everyone involved. Not so strange perhaps, considering that the girl had been away from home for four years. But was it that simple? If everyone loved Dewi as much as it was hinted, why had she left them in the lurch? With a sorrow so dense it felt like you could take hold of it.

There was something in that that didn't add up. Something must have happened. Something the whole family knew about and that gave them no hope that she would come back. But what? And where was she? Did it add up that after four years she was still out traveling, or had she settled down somewhere? Did they have any contact with her at all? Adrianti said that she got reports from time to time, that the girl was doing fine. But perhaps that wasn't true? And if such were the case—what motives did Adrianti have to lie about it?

Sjöberg cursed himself for not asking those questions. But then he had not had time to think through the matter beforehand, either.

Staffan Jenner had also aroused strong emotions in the Erlandsson family. The children were convinced that he had nothing to do with their dad's death. Or with the Russian summer child's disappearance. Adrianti had been close to a breakdown when Staffan Jenner's name came up, so where she stood on the issue was hard to say.

In other words, there was every reason to make contact with Adrianti Erlandsson again. The one who cheered and washed team jerseys, as Ida Erlandsson put it. A real win-win situation.

———

That the first character on the slip of paper in Erlandsson's breast pocket was an N was the only thing Sandén felt reasonably convinced of. The following curlicues were considerably harder to decipher. But he had to start somewhere, so he decided to take a chance on "59OI9." And so he googled that, as Walleye had ordered him to do. And a list of semiconductor electronic components showed up on the screen. Followed by an extract from an old book by Carl Friedrich Gauss, who upon closer inspection proved to be a nineteenth-century German mathematician. Then yet another scanned German mathematics book from the beginning of time with handwritten calculations of tangential functions. And a whole lot of other things that brought no clarity about anything. But he followed each link that came up on the screen and carefully noted what he could understand of the text. Then he realized that he had forgotten the initial N during the search.

"NS9019" led him into trains, instructional media, and Balinese jewelry. While the search string "N59019" led him to a red Chevrolet Impala in Endicott, New York. Followed by a street address in Columbus, Montana, where a Portuguese restaurant was located. "218 E 1st Ave N, 59019" was, in Sandén's opinion, an overly complicated description of the restaurant's location. But it struck him that the N in this case stood for "North," and it was not at all inconceivable that the N he was working with did too. What appeared next on the screen was an inspection copy of a map image of Campbell County in Virginia for use in surveying.

Just as he was about to study this in detail, Wallin came into the room. She went around the desk and set a list of conceivable numeral and letter combinations in front of him. Many combinations.

"So you're through programming now?" said Sandén. "Well done. I'm sitting here surfing. I now know enough about German geometry to put Jessica in her place." He was referring to his twenty-three-year-old daughter, who would soon be a graduate civil engineer.

"German geometry?" Wallin laughed. "Do you think geometry is different there than anywhere else?"

"Have you seen their grammar?" Sandén countered. "It's a hell of a lot more complicated than everywhere else, I promise."

Wallin took a look at the screen and her gaze remained there.

"Did you come up with anything?" she asked. There was now no trace of the smile. Wallin changed facial expressions at the speed of lightning.

"No, I wouldn't say so," Sandén replied. "Possibly a seed of an idea. That N at the beginning of the text could stand for a direction."

He noticed how her gaze was running across the screen image, how her eyebrows were knit together. Evidently she had not heard him.

"Or something completely different," he added to be on the safe side.

No reaction. What was it she saw? It did not seem to be the image of Campbell County itself that interested her, but the table to the side of it. A table that clarified the connections between various lines on the map, their length and something called "bearing." What could that mean—bearing? In the top field of the column it read "S71°04'25"E." In the next "N48°01'13"W." And so on.

"Yes. You have no idea how right you are," said Wallin, grabbing the paper with the blurred text in enlargement from the desk. Compared the format with the one in the table on the American land survey map.

Sandén took pen and paper, got up from the chair and placed himself beside her.

"N," said Wallin, and Sandén wrote. "Five, nine. Or possibly seven."

Could the next character on Erlandsson's paper be a degree sign? Sure, the ball.

"Degrees," Wallin continued. "One. Nine or four. Minutes."

"Is that what it's called?" Sandén asked.

"It's called prime and expresses minutes. When it concerns angles, navigation. We thought it was an I or a one, but it has blurred considerably, should look approximately like an apostrophe."

"I get it. Then five. And a six maybe? A really messy six."

"And seconds," Wallin established. "Double prime."

"No wonder we didn't get that," said Sandén. "Looks like a square."

"Then I presume we have an E. It can't very well be a W, can it?"

Sandén agreed. "Shall I google a possible continuation on this formula?" he asked.

And now Walleye was laughing again.

"You don't need to. It's only the same thing one more time. Degrees, minutes, seconds. Although different numerals. These are position coordinates. Describes an exact spot on the earth. Damn, we're good!"

Then she raised her hand and Sandén by reflex slapped it with his own. Just like on the tennis court, when you're playing doubles. He agreed completely.

"We're the best," he said. "Damn, how surprised they'll be, the others. That we cracked it!"

"Now we only have to find this place. Find out what's there. And what interest Erlandsson had in it."

"If we're on the right track we still have three uncertain numerals," Sandén pointed out. "How many combinations will that be?"

"Eight. Two to the third power. In other words, these," tearing the pen out of Sandén's hand and starting to circle the relevant alternatives on the list.

When she was finished they had a short list, as she called it, containing the following:

N59°19′56″E17°59′26″
N59°19′56″E17°54′26″
N59°14′56″E17°59′26″
N59°14′56″E17°54′26″
N57°19′56″E17°59′26″
N57°19′56″E17°54′26″
N57°14′56″E17°59′26″
N57°14′56″E17°54′26″

"Now we'll figure out where these combinations lead us. May I borrow your computer?" she asked, as she sat down without awaiting an answer.

"Sure," said Sandén, placing himself behind Wallin's back to follow what was happening on the screen.

"We'll go to hitta.se and start from here."

Wallin keyed "Östgötagatan 100, Stockholm" into the address field and ordered the application to take her there. A map image centered around the police station showed up on the screen, and up in the corner even a photograph of the building facade was visible.

"Let's see what coordinates this address has."

A click on "Show coordinates" conjured the information "Lat N59°18′16″ Long E18°4′49″."

"So we're on the fifty-ninth parallel," she stated. "That sounds promising. I'll zoom out."

Which she did, whereupon a map depicting a large portion of Sweden appeared, with Ockelbo to the north and Västervik in the south.

"How far do we need to go to end up on the fifty-seventh parallel?"

She dragged the marker south on the map, as the numbers on the calculator reset in the coordinate display window. Due north of Nynäshamn, the latitude coordinate changed to 58° and in the sea inside Gotland to 57°. An insignificant move westward caused the longitude coordinate to change to 17°, and then to 16° right outside Västervik.

"I don't know what would interest Erlandsson in the middle of the sea between Småland and Gotland. A treasure?"

"Maybe you could dump something there," Sandén proposed. "Narcotics. Weapons. But the fifty-ninth parallel seems more interesting. To start with, in any case."

Wallin dragged the marker back north. Slowed down at 59°17' and with small movements managed to get to 59°19'. Then she moved slowly eastward until at last she found herself at N59°19' E17°54'. Zoomed in a little and tried to find the coordinate display marker, which had vanished from the image. The same procedure one more time, and the resolution was fine enough that it was clear they found themselves in Nockeby. Only now could the marker be moved so that only the second indications were changed.

Right after that they found the first position: a multifamily building on Tyska Bottens Väg with the position N59°19'56" E17°54'26". Then she maneuvered eastward, stopping at Tranebergs Strand, a street by the water next to the Traneberg Bridge with the coordinates N59°19'56" E17°59'26". Then south again, to the crossing of Gesällvägen-Norrängsvägen in Stuvsta with the position N59°14'56" E17°59'26". Less than two kilometers from Sven-Gunnar Erlandsson's residence.

"But why would you make use of coordinates to indicate the position of a street intersection?" Sandén asked. "Or a building?

I believe more in the Baltic in that case, I must say. Even if that Gesällvägen seems gruesomely close to the murder scene."

"Agree completely," Wallin mumbled, concentrating on moving the coordinate display marker to the position indicated by the coordinates N59°14'56" E17°54'26".

At last the calculator reset so that all numerals were in agreement. They now found themselves in Huddinge, a kilometer farther away from the Erlandsson family's villa. But in the middle of the forest. A stone's throw from the homeless trailer encampment.

WEDNESDAY MORNING

Almost twenty-four hours after Odd Andersson had found a social worker who knew about the girl from the TV4 documentary, she called back. For confidentiality reasons she had been unable to provide Rebecka's surname during their previous conversation, which made it hard for him to continue with his investigations.

"I've made contact with Rebecka's mother," she now reported over the phone. "And she's willing to meet you. But they're out of town and coming back this evening. So if you're still interested, it's fine to call or visit her tomorrow."

"I'm still interested," Andersson confirmed. "In a visit. Assuming, of course, you can say where they live."

"They live at Bronsgjutarvägen 7 in Norsborg. And it's fine after ten o'clock in the morning. Her name is Jeanette Magnusson."

"Does that mean the girl's name is Rebecka Magnusson?" Andersson asked.

"That's right."

"I really have to thank you. It was nice of you to help me with this."

"Not a problem. I'm doing it for Rebecka's sake," the woman from the welfare office answered, and the conversation was over.

Andersson pondered what those last words might mean. Unfortunately, it probably meant the fifteen-year-old had still not been found. Or that she had, but had now run away again. Which explained why both the social worker and the mother were prepared to let the police into the matter.

He entered the address on Eniro's map search page and chose the hybrid variation, which showed an aerial photo, but with the street names indicated like on a regular map. To his surprise he discovered that the Magnusson family lived in a pleasant townhouse area bordering the forest and very close to Mälaren. What had he expected? Probably something from the Million Program, a large public housing program implemented in Sweden decades earlier. A high-rise in the concrete jungle.

His thoughts were interrupted by a quiet knock at his door. It was father and daughter Siem, who had unwillingly come to the police station to answer a few questions. Sandén had declined to be part of the meeting, occupied as he was by the deciphering work.

Andersson rolled his own chair to the other side of the desk so that it was next to the visitor's chair. Then he invited them to sit down, crossed his arms over his chest, and leaned against the desk. One more visitor's chair wouldn't have hurt, but in this particular case there was nothing wrong with the slight power advantage the perspective from above gave him.

The girl did not look all that distressed, more likely excited to meet the *Idol* star again. On the other hand, her father had already made clear to Andersson over the phone that he would have pre-ferred to avoid the trip into the city. So Andersson opened with a question directed at him.

"Have you ever gone with Sven-Gunnar Erlandsson to the trailer encampment at Huddinge?"

"Trailer encampment? Why would I have done that?" Siem answered with surprise that seemed genuine.

"Where the homeless hang out. He used to help them."

"You mean where that TV story was filmed? Now I see. No, I've never been there."

Josefin Siem sat smiling in cheerful ignorance of what was approaching. She really was unusually cute. She was dressed in a short skirt and a sporty chemise that revealed a well-conditioned body. This time she had let out her thick hair and it fell beautifully over her bare shoulders. It was dark, however, in a way that made it hard for Andersson to believe it had once been light.

"You didn't happen to be blonde as a child?" he asked anyway.

Both Josefin and her father attested that such was not the case.

"You see, we need information about a blonde girl who was between five and ten years old in 2001. Namely, the girl that is said to have been seen with Larissa Sotnikova right before she disappeared."

"Oh Lord," said Jan Siem. "Are you rooting around in that again? Is this supposed to have something to do with Svempa's death?"

"To be honest, we really don't know anything about that," Andersson answered politely. "But we're trying to look at things from all angles. What do you think happened?"

Siem shrugged his shoulders.

"No idea. But there was talk that the girl ran away because she didn't want to go home. Which you can understand."

"Yes, sure. It might very well have been that way. But in any case, we would like to know whether you remember any little blonde girl that age."

Josefin looked at her father. He shrugged his shoulders again.

"Both of our bigger girls were at the soccer camp. They're dark-haired as well."

"Alexandra?" Josefin suggested. "She's blonde."

"Are you referring to Alexandra Wiklund?" Andersson asked.

Josefin nodded. She looked childishly innocent.

"We'll be asking questions there too. But according to reports from the time she, just like you, was at Mälarhöjden athletic field that morning, even though she hadn't started playing soccer yet.

"Speaking of Wiklund, Josefin—from what I've understood, you reported Lennart Wiklund to the club management because he was looking at you. Is that right? Or bothering you? What was that all about, really?"

Josefin Siem's expression shifted. Her eyes opened a little wider and a flash of something reminiscent of excitement lit up in them.

"I know," she said politely. "He was super-icky. He looked at us all the time with that sick look. You know, like he wanted to have us, like. And then he would like hug and carry on. It was super-annoying."

"Us?"

"Me and my friend. It was super-annoying."

"Yes, you said that. Are you completely certain that it was that way? That you didn't misunderstand something?"

She nodded big-eyed several times, and with exaggerated movements. Like a little child. Revealing a less attractive feature around her mouth and suddenly no longer looking nice at all. Not even cute.

"Hundred percent certain," she said officiously.

Andersson noticed how her father was studying her while she made her statement. Possibly with a trace of doubt in his eyes.

"But you took hold of the situation?" Andersson asked, directing himself now to him.

"Took hold of . . . I mentioned it to Svempa. Josefin and her friend also talked with him."

"But you didn't talk with Wiklund himself about it?"

"No, we didn't actually," Siem answered with a sigh. "I didn't want to harm our relationship. As perhaps you can understand."

Andersson did not at all. If it was the case that the guy was hitting on twelve-year-olds, then wasn't it time to call him to account? Now they succeeded in shoving him one step to the side, certainly upsetting his self-confidence, without him even having been informed of where the rumors came from. Much less having the opportunity to defend himself. Yes, Erlandsson of course. But the credibility was significantly reduced when you had no chance to look the accuser in the eyes.

"But you swallow this story hook, line, and sinker?" Andersson wanted to know. "Without the slightest suspicion that the girls maybe exaggerated a little? Or outright made it all up?"

Josefin looked embarrassed now. Her gaze wandered.

"Why would they have done that?" Siem asked angrily. "It's obvious I'll protect my daughter when this kind of thing happens. Speak on her behalf. And Svempa resolved it in the best way.

Without anyone having to suffer. What the hell does this have to do with anything, anyway?"

"I'm the one asking the questions here," Andersson informed him. "If this isn't true, there may be reason to suspect that other things you're saying are not in accordance with the truth, either. I have it from another source that this is simply nonsense. That Wiklund isn't interested in twelve-year-old girls at all, but instead perhaps it was little Josefin Siem who was upset that Lennart Wiklund *didn't* pay her enough attention."

Now Josefin was blushing. Despite the suntan, he could see she was blushing. Jan Siem looked as though he wanted to sink through the ground. It was time to change the subject.

"I would like you to each send me an SMS, so that I have your cell phone numbers in my phone if I need to reach you."

Jan stretched his right leg and pulled the cell phone out of his jeans pocket. Josefin looked perplexed, but she too did as she was told. Neither of the cell phones was an iPhone.

Andersson gave them his number and while they were involved with their phones, he took the opportunity to question them about what he was really interested in.

"Do you have any other cell phones, Josefin?"

"No, just this one," she answered, sending off the message.

"And you?" he asked Siem, who answered with a shake of his head.

"So neither of you has an iPhone?"

"No, apparently not," Siem answered obstinately.

There were two notifications in Andersson's cell phone and he noted that neither of the messages had been sent from Erlandsson's number. Which he would not have expected, but which he had to confirm. Not even a thirteen-year-old would go around calling from a murdered man's phone account. More than once, anyway.

"You see," said Andersson, "what happened is that Sven-Gunnar Erlandsson's cell phone disappeared the night he lost his life."

"And now you think that Josefin or I would have stolen it," said Siem with a sneer. "Now this has, God help me—"

"Did you, Josefin?" Andersson interrupted.

If anything, she looked surprised.

"I realize that one of those nice iPhones must surely be high on your wish list. And if you're thirteen and don't have any money, then . . . Anyone at all might have done the same thing in your situation."

"I didn't take it," she said indignantly.

But he already suspected the girl was good at lying.

"The main thing is that I get the cell phone," he said calmly. "I promise to turn a blind eye to this little theft, if you just give me the phone. It is very important for the murder investigation. Just give it to me, then we'll forget the whole thing."

"But she's saying she doesn't have it," Siem hissed. "Leave her alone now, damn it."

"Do you happen to have it, then?" Andersson continued stubbornly.

Jan shook his head with a look of contempt on his face.

"No, I said. Anyone at all could have gone past the corpse and picked up that phone. The murderer himself must be a likely candidate."

"Yes, that was just it. Because it happens to be that someone called from Erlandsson's cell phone on Sunday morning. When he was already dead."

"I see now. But it wasn't either of us."

"And the call was made at eight thirty via a tower in Södertälje. A tower which in principle is at the soccer facility where we met you. Strange, isn't it?"

All the color disappeared from Siem's face. Only now did he seem to understand the seriousness of the situation. Josefin stared at her father with her mouth half-open, looking pitiful there in her seat.

—⁓—

In radiant sunlight under an almost cloud-free sky, Wallin and Sandén left the path to continue straight into the forest. They had parked the car at the end of a small road in sparsely populated Glömsta, and then navigated into the woods with the help of a printout from hitta.se and Wallin's late husband's handheld GPS. It was wet in places, but they were prepared for the worst and brought their high boots along.

They looked a bit funny on Wallin, who had dressed for the day in a white knee-length ruffled dress and a short black leather jacket with rivets on it. A pair of aviator sunglasses were pushed up on her forehead now that they had stepped in among the shadows of the trees.

It was hilly, the terrain rolling in this part of the forest around the small Lake Gömmaren. But it was lovely. Blessedly quiet, moss-covered and magical.

Sandén walked right behind Wallin, who was leading the excursion. There was no question of walking side by side, the vegetation did not allow it. He avoided the slaps the tree branches doled out at regular intervals, but from what he could see Wallin got one or two.

"Not far to go now," she said, stepping over a fallen limb with her hands in front of her face to protect it from yet another blow. "I need to rest a little. We'll go up to that glade there, then we can sit in the sun."

"Are you such a lightweight, Walleye?" Sandén teased, not feeling the slightest bit tired. "I thought you were the athletic type."

She took the last steps up to a flat rock and sat down in the bog moss on a spot where the rays of the sun reached through the crowns of the trees. They reached Sandén too, who was sitting beside her. She was clearly out of breath.

"No, not exactly," she answered. "Yes, a little maybe. Or . . . Uh, I'm actually too lazy. I play some golf. But that doesn't really count. And then I like to play tennis and soccer and bandy and everything, but I never do. So no, I'm not the athletic type. I would never set foot in a gym."

"Tennis?" Sandén repeated with surprise. "Why haven't you told us that? Conny and I play an hour every Friday at seven o'clock. You should join us sometime."

"I think my interest in tennis is modest at that time of day," Wallin said. "At seven o'clock I'm sitting with my Friday highball."

"Ha, me too. But I'm talking morning here."

"Then that's another matter, of course. But I imagine maybe Conny wouldn't be so enthused at having to put up with me then either."

She was right, of course. Sjöberg had his misgivings as far as she was concerned—Sandén knew it and apparently Walleye did too.

"What kind of bullshit is that?" he started, but then it struck him that it was silly to be hypocritical. It was not his style and just as little Walleye's. It was better to get straight to the point.

"Uh, I take that back," he said instead. "What I really want to say, I guess, is that we'll have to try to change that. Conny's a good person. You're a good person. I don't like it when good people can't see each other's greatness."

A streak of genuine delight passed over Wallin's face. It was heartwarming. She really was something else and deserved to hear it, too.

"I see his," she said, getting up. "Now let's go." She staggered a little, but recovered her balance and started walking.

They made their way around the outcropping and another fifty meters into the almost impenetrable forest. A hare appeared from nowhere and crossed their path with long hops only a few meters ahead of them.

"Now we're really close," said Wallin. "Only a second, then we're there. Keep your eyes open now. We're within the margin of error."

"A second? So we're already there?"

"Think double prime, Bucko."

He looked around, smiling. Bushes. Moss and mushrooms. The outcropping at a distance and a few large boulders. But mostly trees. And more trees.

"Here," said Wallin, stopping. "Now we're in the zone. The accuracy is fifty to sixty meters, so we'll have to search that far in all directions."

"What's up?" Sandén asked. "You look pale."

"No problem, just a little tired," Wallin answered. "Imagine a circle around this point." With her hand she made a sweeping motion around her to visualize the circumference of the circle and then its diameter.

"You take that half, I'll take this one," she instructed.

Sandén walked what he estimated as sixty meters back in the direction of the outcropping where they had rested, moved fifteen or twenty degrees and then made his way back to the middle again, without seeing anything conspicuous. Wallin's approach was similar. Sandén repeated the procedure several times until he had searched approximately three fourths of the area he was assigned. He could no longer see Wallin.

"How's it going, Walleye?" he called.

"Nothing so far," he heard at a distance. "But I'm not done yet, have a little left to search through."

He moved out again and then into the middle of the circle. The whole time he let his gaze wander over the ground and among the tree trunks, even searching up in the treetops. But nothing of interest came in his way, nothing other than what you would expect in a forest like this. A few more turns without any surprises and then the whole semicircle was done.

"I'm done!" he called. "I haven't found so much as a popsicle stick!"

"Me neither," Wallin answered from a point considerably closer than he'd thought. "Maybe we're in the wrong place after all."

There was movement among the branches, she was on her way toward him, only about ten meters away. Her voice was fragile, toneless, and she was very pale now. Something was not right. Did she look a little unsteady too? Maybe he ought to do something? Then she turned and drew away from him again. Oh well, she knew herself best.

His phone rang. He had a sense of being in the middle of the wilderness, but when he thought about it, he was not very far from civilization. Half a kilometer as the crow flies at most.

He pulled out the cell phone and saw that it was his wife who was looking for him. Which seldom—not to say never—happened during work time. His stomach was tied in knots.

"Sonja?"

To start with he heard only sobbing on the phone. *Cool and calm*, he thought. Whatever happened he must remain calm, not get agitated so that it turned out like last time.

"Sonja, what happened?"

He took a deep breath, tried to steel himself against what was on its way. Looked for Wallin, but he no longer saw her.

"It's Jenny. She . . . Forgive me for calling while you're at work, but I couldn't—" Then the weeping took over.

Sandén felt completely powerless. Far from Sonja when she needed him the most, in the middle of the forest with Wallin who now suddenly was no longer visible. Where the hell was she? Waiting for his wife to regain control over herself, he held the phone away from him.

"Wallin!" he shouted at the top of his lungs, but got no answer back.

His shout echoed between the tree trunks and boulders, but not a sound was heard from Wallin. He put the cell phone to his ear again and started walking in the direction where she ought to be.

"Forgive me, darling," he resumed the conversation. "I'm in the middle of the woods and Wallin has disappeared. Try to tell me now."

He looked to right and left, but no Wallin. She had a white dress on, damn it, shouldn't be so hard to find in all the green. Sandén was in a cold sweat.

Sonja was breathing uncontrollably, let out an extended whimper before she started sobbing again.

"Jens . . . Jenny is pregnant," she got out at last between sobs. "I can't bear . . . We can't . . ."

That couldn't be. Jenny couldn't be pregnant, Sonja had helped her with contraceptives. To prevent what mustn't happen. He started moving now in the direction he had seen Wallin disappear, as well as he could in the thicket. Plowing his way ahead between protruding branches, covered with needles, sharp.

Jenny could not take care of a child, they were not prepared to become parents again with all that entailed of sleepless nights and other sacrifices. Finances, time—didn't they have the same right as everyone else to leave all that behind them, to be able to grow old in peace and quiet? He stumbled over a protruding root hidden among the moss. He could not let his emotions run away.

"We'll work it out, Sonja," he said gently. "You and I and Jenny together."

"It's far advanced. Much too late for an abortion."

He was starting to get out of breath. A spruce branch gave him a rap on the cheek.

"We'll solve this," he said. "We're strong, positive people . . ."

Then he caught sight of something white a little to his right, a large bundle lying on the ground. A white, bloody bundle. He sped up, squeezing in sideways among the brambles, completely unconcerned about the needle-covered branches that whipped him in the face. Stumbling, he made his way the last few meters to his colleague, who had now lost all color in her face.

"I have to go, Sonja. Have to call an ambulance."

He ended the call, entered the number for SOS, and sank on his knees with his cell phone between cheek and shoulder. Searched for a pulse without immediately finding one. Gave up and instead placed his hand on Wallin's forehead.

To his astonishment, her face felt completely cold. The fine summer dress was completely bloody below. He lifted up a corner of it and determined that the underwear was also drenched in blood and that a good deal had run down along the legs.

Now it was urgent. Every second could make a difference. When he heard the voice at the other end he conveyed what he wanted to say, factual and well articulated, but without leaving room for any questions.

"My name is Jens Sandén, I'm a police inspector with the Hammarby police and I'm in Huddinge, in the forest around Lake Gömmaren. I have a fifty-five-year-old female colleague with me, Hedvig Wallin, and she is unconscious, bleeding profusely from her abdomen, and has lost a lot of blood. Her body temperature is low and she has no color in her face. I am now going to try to take her to Barrskogsstigen in Glömsta. My position is—listen carefully now—fifty-nine degrees, fourteen minutes, and fifty-six seconds north, seventeen degrees, fifty-four minutes, and fifty-six seconds east. Meet me at the road."

Then he lifted Wallin in his arms and began the most demanding undertaking he had ever embarked on, by far. Without allowing himself to feel ahead at all, he forced his way through the dense thicket with the over-120-pound woman in his arms almost the entire way to town. Not for a moment did he stop to catch his breath or shake out his arms.

With only a bit of the almost impassible trail remaining, he was met by ambulance personnel who at last released him of the burden. Not even then did he throw himself on the ground to breathe out. Instead he followed the instructions he got and did his best to be helpful.

Only in the ambulance could he rest a moment while his face and arms were bandaged. The next three hours were spent in a hospital corridor outside an operating room, hovering in uncertainty about whether Wallin's life could be saved. Hovering in uncertainty about how his own and his family's lives would look. In short, he had a lot to think about.

—◦—

"Alexandra Wiklund has no memories at all from the day when Larissa Sotnikova disappeared," said Westman. "She alleges. She doesn't even remember the soccer camp at Mälarhöjden athletic field."

"She was five years old," Hamad pointed out. "That may very well be correct."

The two police assistants were sitting on either side of Hamad's desk, waiting for Staffan Jenner to come in for yet another interview. A third chair was borrowed from Westman's office so that all three could sit, and on this one Hamad had now set his feet. He did not seem bothered in the slightest by the heat, though he had long pants and a long-sleeved shirt on. True, a thin sports shirt—checked and with rolled-up sleeves as per this summer's trend—but Westman herself was sweating like in a sauna, though she had on only a sleeveless blouse and short skirt.

"Fair," she answered as she fanned herself with something she found on the desk, which happened to be Hamad's calendar. "According to the mother, there was no possibility whatsoever that she could have left the sports facility even for a short while. They were together the whole time. True, she was—and still is—blonde, but she doesn't seem to be the girl that was seen with Lara on Murgrönsvägen right before eleven. She doesn't even seem to have known Lara."

"Was she part of the search party?"

"No, they left her with some good friends and kept her outside of it all. Didn't think something so horrid was suitable for such a small child."

Hamad nodded thoughtfully.

"So we still don't have the slightest idea who the little blonde girl might have been," Westman continued. "If we choose to believe that last witness. But I really want to. I think the place where she was seen is much too interesting to simply dismiss. A stone's throw from Wiklund's villa, where the ladies' man Lennart was at home alone."

"I'm inclined to agree," said Hamad. "Above all because Lara had such a conspicuous raincoat on. If the lady on Murgröns-vägen says she saw one like that on the street outside, and a bike besides, then of course it's worth taking seriously. Good research, Petra."

Westman soaked up the praise. Especially because it came from Hamad. Not that he was stingier with that sort of thing than anyone else, but his blinding-white smile was something special. Made her feel good. She didn't allow herself to enjoy it too long, however, as they still found themselves in something that resembled a dead end.

"But of course Lennart Wiklund denies even having noticed any little girls," she said with a resigned gesture. "He was down with mono and could hardly get out of bed. Until it was time for a search party, when he turns into Sergeant York. Even his ex-wife subscribes to that, and they aren't even on speaking terms. And no little blonde girl who knew Lara has shown up in eight years, so why should we be able to locate her now?"

"She doesn't need to have been all that little," Hamad noted. "She was able to ride an eleven-year-old's bike, and there are very few five-year-olds who can ride a bike at all. So Alexandra Wiklund and Josefin Siem are completely out. However, it may have been Ida Erlandsson. Blonde and the same age."

"One year older."

"She may have looked younger than Lara, in any case."

"By Swedish standards, Lara was not especially tall for her age," Westman reported. "Rather delicate besides. She probably didn't have it too rich at home in Russia."

"And Ida was also sick in bed that day," Hamad said dejectedly. "Why should she lie about that? No, we'll have to attack the problem from another direction. Until we think of something. The Wiklund lead is good, but we don't even know if Lara went past his house."

"Bring up the map of the area on hitta.se," Westman ordered.

Hamad did as he was asked. Westman went around the desk and placed herself behind him.

"Lara was seen here on Murgrönsvägen for the last time," Westman continued. "She comes straight from the soccer camp, where she spoke with several members of the Erlandsson family. From them she found out that Ida was sick and at home in bed. I'm assuming she's on her way there. Which do you think is most likely: that she turns right on Konvaljestigen and then takes the long detour over to Vaktelstigen, or that she takes the easy way through the woods and past the school?" Westman followed the alternative routes with her index finger along the screen.

"Exactly," said Westman before Hamad had time to answer. "Lara took the route past Wiklund's house. Which is also a prime location for a kidnapping. And Ida says no one came to the door during the day. Which is true. Because Lara never got there."

Hamad nodded. Westman went back to her chair and sat down.

"The reasoning is brilliant," said Hamad.

"Really?"

"More than that, I think Wiklund seems to be a pretty harmless guy."

"Who hits on little girls?" Westman spit out. "Drunk on his butt the night of the murder, with memory lapses and everything."

"We've experienced that, both you and me, Petra. So I think that's a poor argument."

Westman felt herself blushing, which she hoped was not visible under her vacation tan. But he was right. Who was she to moralize about other people's alcohol habits?

"Besides, a number of things indicate that he actually doesn't look at little girls," Hamad continued. "And that possibly they're the ones looking at him. And if you think about that young woman he dragged home . . ."

"His 'female acquaintance,'" Westman sniffed. "She's not even half his age."

"Then there's a pretty big difference between a twenty-year-old and an eleven-year-old, isn't there?"

Westman unwillingly had to consider herself defeated in this particular exchange of opinions, but knew she was right in principle. Regardless of whether or not the guy hit on girls who were *too* young, he had a view of women that she didn't appreciate.

"Yeah, sure," she agreed, without feeling completely convinced.

There was something about that type of man and their sexual proclivities. You didn't know how much power it had over them, how far they were prepared to go. If the circumstances were right.

"The question is whether Wiklund isn't the least suspicious in that poker club," said Hamad, as if he were reading her mind. Although thinking the opposite.

"If it weren't that the circumstances in this case were the right ones. That Lennart Wiklund would be able to kidnap an eleven-year-old without being noticed." Westman stopped short.

The phone on the desk rang.

"The prime suspect is approaching," Hamad rounded off the conversation and picked up the receiver. Westman got up to open the door to the corridor.

Staffan Jenner looked tense in the visitor's chair in front of Hamad's desk. Westman noticed that he had dressed up a little, in comparison with how he had looked when they saw him at home in Herrängen. But it was possible that this was an ordinary workday for him, and that was why he had on a rather nice-looking corduroy jacket and well-ironed white shirt with a discreet blue-checked pattern.

"Did you happen to go along with Sven-Gunnar Erlandsson to that trailer encampment at any time?" Westman began.

Jenner looked perplexed, but answered straight out.

"I was there on one occasion."

"Why?"

"He wanted to show me what it was he did there. Who he was helping."

"Why is that?" Westman asked again.

"Because we were friends. I was curious, he was proud. Rightfully."

"But you never went back there?"

Jenner shook his head. He was so thin and sunken he could almost be mistaken for a homeless person himself.

"It wasn't my thing."

"No?"

"Svempa listened to them, talked with them. I have no problems listening, but talking is not something I'm very good at. As you've probably noticed."

"But maybe you've spent time in the area around there anyway?" Westman coaxed, with a far-fetched hope that he would mention the place at Wallin's and Sandén's coordinates.

"I've been to the Gömmar beach with the kids a few times. It's very beautiful there. Both a sand beach and rocks. And grass."

"No other place? Recently?"

Jenner shook his head.

"I don't think I've been in the woods there for ten years. Apart from that time with Svempa."

"And Erlandsson—did he have any business there? Anyone else to visit besides the homeless, I mean?"

"Not as far as I know," Jenner replied.

"Did you happen to think of anything concerning the murder?" Westman tried. "Anything new we ought to know about?"

It could clearly be seen how Jenner's jaws tensed. He was on his guard now, prepared for the worst.

"No, I really can't see any motive for a single human being to want Svempa dead. As I said, he was loved by everyone."

"We're not so sure of that," said Westman. "According to what we've understood, Jan Siem was not a hundred percent satisfied with the outcome of the poker club you were involved in. We have a feeling he feels tricked out of money. And certain items found at the crime scene also indicate that the murder was poker-related. That maybe Erlandsson outright cheated."

"Also, Erlandsson's cell phone was gone when the police came to the crime scene," Hamad continued. "We have certain indications that Jan or Josefin Siem took it. A call was made from it the morning after the murder. From a cell phone tower in Södertälje extremely close to the place where they both were at exactly that time."

Jenner relaxed in the chair. Hoped, perhaps, that the danger to him had blown over. In any event, he was no longer the lone suspect.

"What do you think about that?" Hamad asked.

Jenner thought for a few moments before he answered.

"Maybe Siem does look out for number one. That I can agree with. And he wasn't really happy that in principle he had to pay everything this time, that was noticeable. But to go from that to shooting a person with premeditation . . . ? I can't explain that cell phone call. But it doesn't seem very clever. Couldn't it have been the daughter who . . . couldn't keep her fingers under control when she . . . ?" He shrugged his shoulders, looked uncomprehending.

"It has also come to our attention," said Westman, "that Lennart Wiklund has been previously accused of having an unhealthy interest in young girls. Erlandsson is said to have removed him as coach of one of the girls' teams. It was hushed up, so Erlandsson was one of the very few who knew the circumstances. But in any event that may have aroused a number of emotions in Wiklund. What's more, we've gone through Larissa Sotnikova's files."

Jenner had had only a short breather. He blinked nervously and drew up his shoulders, preapring to absorb any new blows.

"If the testimony from the woman in the window on Murgröns-vägen is right," Westman continued, "Lara ought to have passed Wiklund's house only a minute or two after she was last seen. And Lennart Wiklund was at home alone."

Westman paused, letting the information sink in.

Jenner's intensely blue eyes looked attentively into hers. But he said nothing. What should he say? No connection between Wiklund and the missing summer child had ever come out.

Staffan Jenner was taken by surprise. And relieved? Quite certainly, if he was guilty and the suspicions were aimed in a different direction for the first time. But then it was also crucial that he play his cards well.

"It could be like this," said Westman, "that Erlandsson—with his specific knowledge of Wiklund's interest in young girls—found out about this. And maybe held Wiklund accountable. Which would be as good a motive for murder as any. Or what do you say, Staffan?"

He looked confused, almost on the verge of tears.

"I . . . I . . ." he stammered. "I don't know what I should say. I've socialized with this man for several years after Lara disappeared. It can't be the case that . . . It seems much too cold-blooded. Lennart . . . I like Lennart. He's happy. Livens things up. Would he . . . ? I have a very hard time believing that, I must say. We didn't know each other at that time. He and Lara had never met."

"Perhaps just for that reason?" Westman suggested. "She was only a girl, any girl at all."

"But . . . No, I refuse to believe that. Not Lennart."

Jenner was more definite now, starting to get used to the idea. But did not accept it. Or pretended that he didn't.

"Have you confronted him with this?" he wanted to know.

"We have," Westman answered. "He denied it, of course."

Jenner caught sight of the water glass they had set in front of him on the desk and emptied it. He looked thoughtful, kept shaking his head. Put the glass back with an almost exaggerated slow movement.

"Adrianti," said Hamad.

Jenner appeared not to hear at first, but suddenly looked up at him with a look that was almost pleading.

"Have you spoken with her since the murder?"

Westman was smiling inside. Jenner vacillated between hope and desperation, but now it was time to apply the thumbscrews in earnest.

"I mean only that because Erlandsson was such a great support to you after Lara's disappearance, then I guess you'll pay that back in a situation like this?"

Jenner seemed to be gasping for air.

"No," he admitted, "I haven't had any contact with Adrianti."

Hamad studied him awhile, with a hint of a smile on his lips. Jenner was now holding onto the arm support so hard that his knuckles were white.

"Do you know what I think?" Hamad continued. "Do you know what I thought the last time we spoke, at home in your house on Blåklintsvägen? Yes, that a man who has lost a child—for I think you can say that you have, Staffan?—you were going to adopt the girl? A man who has lost a child and a wife and his good reputation in that house, and with the children moved out besides, should have sold the house a long time ago and moved away from there."

Jenner, breathing heavily, looked at Hamad with terror in his eyes. Westman feared that he might collapse at any moment.

"I think you *can't* sell the house. Because the new owners would find something very embarrassing if they started digging. Namely the body of an eleven-year-old girl. Sven-Gunnar Erlandsson, the hub of the social machinery, knew everything about everyone. And when it occurred to him what had happened to Lara and he confronted you, then you were forced to do something about it.

"For that reason it's a little hard for you to see Adrianti. Because you're not very good at talking, as you said. Not very good at acting. And maybe it's even the case that you actually don't have the nerve to lie to the grieving widow right to her face."

But Staffan Jenner collected himself. Westman saw how he was able to gather up the remnants of himself during Hamad's monologue. How he took hold of his collar, straightened up in the chair, and made a decision.

Kamikaze, she thought. *He's thinking about confessing.*

"I haven't spoken with Adrianti, that's right," he said with a deep sigh.

Not a trace of the anxiety that had tormented him was now visible. He looked distressed instead.

"And you're completely right, I don't have the nerve to. But it's not because I murdered her husband. It's out of respect for Svempa."

Hamad raised one eyebrow. Westman didn't know what she should think. The air in the room was quiet.

"I'm in love with Adrianti," said Jenner. "We've had an affair. Or whatever you want to call it. We have . . . slept with each other on a couple of occasions, and I felt deep remorse both times. Due to the betrayal of Svempa."

Hamad frowned. Westman sat speechless and waited for what came next. Jenner threw out his arms and sighed again.

"Svempa was my best friend. What I did was unforgivable. It was Adrianti who took the initiative both times, and I couldn't stop myself. I have loved her since I first saw her. Without doing anything about it. Besides, I had no idea she felt something similar towards me."

"When did this so-called affair take place?" Westman asked dryly, in an attempt to conceal how disappointed she was.

"About four years ago. For a month. Then we decided to break it off. It was best that way. And if I were to come running as soon as this had happened to Svempa . . . It wouldn't look good. Even if the intent was only to console and support.

"I simply can't bring myself to do it. And Adri understands. I know that. But in time, perhaps . . . For that reason, I think I'll stay in the house a while longer."

Sjöberg was brooding. He sat leaning over the desk with eyes closed and his face in his hands, brooding. The noose was starting to tighten. But around not one, instead no less than three, potential murderers.

Siem, a stingy, ungenerous type who found himself at the exact place from which the mysterious call to the acting police commissioner had been made, and at the right time besides. Rather unsympathetic, according to Andersson and Sandén, who had met him. But with a weak motive. Money, with all due respect, but a few thousand kronor? Hardly likely. The motive must be something else in that case.

Jenner? Absolutely. He had been in the line of fire during the investigation of Larissa Sotnikova's disappearance. A year later, his wife had taken her own life in a manner that raised the suspicion of a camouflaged murder. He was shy, with few friends and nerves exposed. A criminal profiler's dream.

Motive? With perhaps one or two violent crimes behind him, it was conceivable that he had committed a third. To conceal the earlier ones. Besides, now suddenly another motive had come to light. An affair with the victim's wife.

Combined, this was clear as a bell—if it weren't for the fact that the joker Wiklund suddenly showed up. Which comprised a previously unknown connection between Larissa Sotnikova's disappearance and the murder of Erlandsson. Wiklund lived a minute from the place where the girl had been seen for the very last time, was alone in a house without public view, and besides had indecent inclinations. According to doubtful sources to be sure, but in any event Sven-Gunnar Erlandsson had taken the rumors seriously. The motive here too would be to conceal a previously committed crime, and that was a strong motive.

But suppose, thought Sjöberg, *that we leave out the missing Russian girl for a moment.* What did they have to work with then?

Well, the playing cards in the victim's pocket. The more Sjöberg thought about them, the more convinced he was that they had significance in the case. The four men were part of a poker club. The cards lacked fingerprints and therefore were in all likelihood placed in Erlandsson's pocket by the murderer. Who else would have cared about fingerprints? Definitely not Erlandsson himself, who did not have gloves on a mild August evening. A message then, or a greeting. It obviously had to do with poker, even if one card seemed to be missing. But he could not understand what the four cards meant. And poker as a motive for murder among a gathering of reasonably well-off middle-aged Swedes was so ridiculous, he could hardly bear to accept it.

Then there was that scrap of paper in the same pocket.

The wet piece of paper with the blurred coordinates, which Wallin and Sandén had managed to decipher. The fact that the coordinates indicated a point in the Huddinge forest, not very far from the homeless trailer encampment, looked like more than a coincidence. Possibly, of course a point in the middle of the Baltic could be an alternative.

Was it Erlandsson's paper, or was it also placed there by the murderer? But what could it be about? Drugs? Weapons? A hiding place for stolen property? As it was in the vicinity of the trailer encampment, none of these alternatives seemed too unreasonable.

Odd Andersson was extremely engaged with the trailer folks, and that was good. Talked with all of them, everyone who had had anything to do with Erlandsson. For the time being it was the fifteen-year-old runaway who was under discussion, and she was evidently not the easiest to get in contact with. It would be interesting to hear whether she had anything new to add concerning

Sven-Gunnar Erlandsson. Something seen from a perspective that was different than the other friends' and the family's.

The family. A grieving widow and three grown children. Or four, to be more accurate. The fourth one had not been in the country for four years. Perhaps she too was on the run. Or . . . ?

It struck him like a cudgel on the head. Could it be that she had disappeared? That Dewi Kusamasari had *also* disappeared?

Like the Russian summer child?

Sjöberg sprang out of the chair. Drummed on the desktop with his fingertips. In that case, why hadn't anyone said anything? Everyone loved Dewi: the stepsiblings, the mother, the deceased stepfather. What reason in the world could there be for an entire family to keep silent about something like that? The mother said she had sporadic contact with the girl. How often was it, and when did it last happen? Two missing girls in the same investigation were two too many. He had to get in contact with Adrianti Erlandsson again as soon as possible.

He was interrupted in his musings when his cell phone rang. It was Sandén.

"Conny. Something has happened."

There was something about his tone of voice. Not the usual happy-go-lucky. Sandén sounded tired and . . . depressed?

"What? Where are you?"

"At Huddinge. Sitting and waiting in a corridor."

"At what? How are you?"

"It's not me. It's Walleye. She collapsed in the forest."

"I'll be damned. What's the matter?"

"She was completely cold when I found her. Lost a lot of blood, apparently. Too much."

"Found her? Weren't you together?"

"We were searching a pretty big area. Dense thicket. We got separated from each other. I already thought earlier that she was pale, but she said she was feeling fine. She's a real fighter, that woman. She'll manage it."

"Manage it? Do you mean that maybe she—?"

"They're operating on her now. Several liters of blood had run out of her belly. Her face was white as chalk. And me, the stupid jerk, didn't react."

"She herself could have—" Sjöberg attempted, but Sandén interrupted him angrily.

"None of that shit now, Conny."

"I only meant that you didn't—"

"Walleye is golden, get that sometime. She doesn't back out in the middle of an assignment just because she has a stomachache."

Sjöberg felt accused. Certainly with good reason. But what he had tried to say was not meant as criticism. He only wanted to free Sandén from the burden of guilt.

"Did she regain consciousness?" he asked instead.

"No. And I have no idea whether we should contact her family. The children. What do you think?"

"So she's hovering between life and death?"

"Yes. The operation may take three or four hours, and the outcome is uncertain," Sandén replied resolutely.

Sjöberg thought a few moments.

"What good does it do for the children to sit there outside? If everything goes well, they can always visit her afterwards. If it goes badly, they won't get there in time to see her anyway."

"You're right about that. I think they live abroad. I'll wait here until they're through with the operation."

"Do you want company?" Sjöberg asked.

"No, damn it. I have a few other things to think about, too."

"Yes—how did it go, by the way? Did you find anything?"

"Not a thing. But that's not what I meant. Jenny's pregnant."

"You're joking," said Sjöberg.

Sandén was not one to worry unnecessarily, but if there was something that worried him it was just this: that his disabled daughter would get herself in so-called trouble. She was not capable of taking care of a child herself. Which meant that Jens and Sonja would be booked up for about the next twenty years. *What darkness.*

Sandén did not answer.

"Who's the father?" Sjöberg ventured to ask.

"No idea. I haven't had a chance to talk with her. Not with Sonja either, actually."

Catastrophes came one after the other. Sjöberg did not know what he should say. What cliché he should choose.

"I'm sorry, Jens. Truly. Speak up if we can help out in any way."

"I guess you can tell Simon there'll be money to earn in a few years when we need a babysitter."

Sandén let out a sound that vaguely resembled a laugh. A hollow one. But he tried.

WEDNESDAY AFTERNOON

Hamad, Westman, Andersson, and Sjöberg had a late lunch at Lisa's Café, a place on Skånegatan frequented by the Hammarby police. Despite Lisa's customary cheer and the lovingly prepared sandwiches with sausage and fried egg, the mood was anything but good. Sjöberg kept looking at the clock. Sandén still had not phoned; the operation must have been going on for almost three hours now.

"No news is good news," Sjöberg tried to convince himself and his colleagues.

"Good health keeps quiet," said Andersson, which appeared to be somewhat of an overstatement.

"And they didn't find anything out there in the woods," Hamad sighed.

"There must be something out there," Andersson said. "I don't think the coordinates were jotted down on that scrap of paper for no reason."

"So what do you guess this is about?" Sjöberg asked.

"Guns, maybe."

"The murder weapon?" Westman sneered. "Do you seriously think the murderer would have left information on the body about where he intended to bury the gun?"

Andersson absentmindedly fingered the silver ring in his ear.

"No, that's not what I mean of course. But there could be a cache of weapons there. The gun might have come from there."

"Could they be that cunning, those homeless people?" Sjöberg asked. "Isn't it more likely this concerns drugs or stolen property?"

"It's not that close," Andersson replied. "The trailer folks don't necessarily have anything to do with it."

"Look who's talking," Westman teased. "You're the one who's chasing the homeless high and low."

Andersson looked embarrassed. Everyone's eyes were now directed at him, and that did not seem to amuse him in the slightest. A little funny, considering how he stood out with his shoulder-length hair, the earring, and the numerous tattoos on both arms. He was well-known from TV besides, and no one had forced him into that, thought Sjöberg.

"I think we ought to excavate there in any event," Andersson answered.

"It's a big area," said Sjöberg. "A big project. Expensive, too."

"It's a national park besides," Westman pointed out. "Which means we would never get a permit."

"There are other places where we ought to excavate first," said Hamad. "Staffan Jenner's yard, for example."

"Ingela Wiklund's, is another," said Westman.

"Or Siem's," said Hamad. "If you follow the cell phone lead."

"We would never get permission to dig in their yards either,"
Westman noted. "We need more meat on the bones. But this is
about the Russian summer child."

"It's about rape," said Hamad.

"You sound very convinced," said Sjöberg.

"It must be about the missing girl," said Westman.

"I know it's about rape," said Hamad.

There was no reason to question that. Murder of a young girl
was usually preceded by rape. And Sjöberg's own musings concerning Dewi Kusamasari were gnawing at the back of his mind.

There was silence around the table, each one submerged in
their own thoughts. Sjöberg brushed a few crumbs into his hand
and set them on the plate. Glanced at the clock and made sure
his cell phone was not turned off. A couple of older gentlemen
sitting a half-stair up at the table closest to the kitchen laughed
loudly. Lisa looked out from the doorway and got involved in
their conversation. But at the police officers' table, no one felt
any great joy.

Sjöberg's cell phone rang. Andersson, Hamad, and Westman
watched with rapt attention, which turned to horror as the tears
welled up in Sjöberg's eyes.

"Walleye is wondering if one of you can stop by with her
laptop," Sandén reported. "She's afraid we'll lose momentum in
the investigation otherwise."

Sjöberg felt jubilant. He cried and laughed at the same time and
could not get out a sensible word. Then the moment of paralysis
released the other three, and to the surprise of the other customers
there was suddenly such tumult at the police table that it drowned
out even the two gentlemen up in the corner.

—᷄᷄᷄—

Five hours after the supervising physician delivered the report that Wallin managed the operation well, she was ready to receive visitors.

"Damn it, Walleye, you scared me," said Sandén as he pulled the chair up to the hospital bed.

"Sorry," she answered with a tired smile. "You look like shit."

She received him semi-reclined in the bed with a couple of pillows behind her head. Her face was full of scratch marks and bandages, but thank heavens she had regained her color. Sandén had not thought about his own appearance during the hours in the corridor, but he guessed there were certain similarities between them.

"Thanks, the same to you," he said, placing his hand on her cheek. It was warm now.

"You were completely cold out there in the woods. It was a shock." She placed her hand over his. Squeezed it.

"Thanks," she said. "They say it was a matter of minutes. Did you carry me?"

"No, I let you lie there on the ground and went to the nearest town and looked for a pay phone."

"Come on now," she said seriously. "I want to know what happened. Then I won't embarrass you any more by thanking you for saving my life."

"Thank the doctors. And the ambulance personnel. I don't know how to revive old hags."

"Jens, I have stitches in my belly, I can't laugh. Did you carry me?"

Sandén sighed self-consciously.

"Of course I carried you. I ran like a scalded troll with you in my arms. Right before the parking area, the ambulance personnel showed up and took over. I have to apologize that I didn't take any particular notice of the spruce branches that were whipping you in the face."

"Come here and let me give you a hug."

He got up and carefully placed his cheek against hers. She placed her arms around him, giving him a kiss on the cheek.

"Thanks," she said again. "You're the best."

"With no competition. But you'll have to be a little careful with me, my face stings."

"I know."

Sandén sat down.

"What really happened?" he asked. "Why didn't you say anything?"

Wallin shrugged her shoulders.

"I felt tired and a little shaky. Had a stomachache. But I didn't think it was anything to worry about, thought it would pass. They say I lost almost two liters of blood, mostly internal."

"There was quite a bit on the outside, too, you should know. Was it abdominal bleeding?"

"Until a few weeks ago, I actually thought I was pregnant."

"Get out of here. At your age."

Wallin nodded.

"It wasn't really according to plan, but I thought life often turns out really cool when unexpected things happen."

A typical Wallinian analysis, and one that greatly deserved to be committed to memory.

"I didn't know you had a boyfriend," said Sandén.

"I didn't either," she answered with a wink. "Maybe I'd been out and was a little careless. But it turned out to be a tumor in the uterus. Big as a tennis ball. So they removed it."

"The hell you say. Benign, I hope?"

Wallin nodded.

"A myoma."

"But what were you doing at work?"

"They sent me home after three days and gave me sick leave for two weeks. I felt strong and bored, had no desire to try to get a longer sick leave. But I guess they'd done a poor job. Evidently something burst."

There was a knock at the door and Hamad appeared in the doorway.

"Are you having a party, or . . . ?" he said with an uncertain smile.

Wallin looked surprised, happy, and a little self-conscious all at once.

"Come in," she said with a movement that vaguely resembled a wave. "What do you have there? Is it my laptop?"

Hamad went up to the bed and placed the computer next to her.

"By agreement. Nice that everything went well. We were a little worried there for a while."

"Thanks, that's nice. What kind of agreement?"

"It was Jens who—"

"Uh," Sandén interrupted, "I thought you needed a little stimulation. I think I'll leave you now, Walleye, since you have company. I have a few things to take care of on the home front. Is that okay?"

"Absolutely. And listen—thanks for everything."

"No problem. Get better now. You're needed."

Hamad listened attentively as Wallin recounted the day's events. She left out the exact reason for the bleeding—not because she was worried about the consequences, but because she didn't want to embarrass him. What had happened was extremely personal and Hamad was a pup—a very pleasant, talented pup, but much too immature and with far too many preconceived notions about her to want to share that with him.

With Sandén it was different. He was a grown man who despite his moments of boorishness had his heart in the right place. And, contrary to what everyone believed, he was completely free of prejudice. For what were prejudices, really? Wasn't it about not judging? Sandén might generalize his impressions, faster and more openly than the politically correct establishment, but he was not quick to judge. And generalization was the very framework of all kinds of philosophy, the only way to structure existence into theories. Sandén's theories were often simple, but well grounded. And he was happy to let himself be persuaded. He was not frightened, either, in that way that was so common among men, of the less agreeable aspects of the female body. He was not disgusted, didn't cover his eyes and ears. And there was something extremely beautiful about men who respected women. For real.

Hamad, on the other hand, had a ways to go. She felt reasonably convinced of that. For that reason she spoke in sweeping terms about abdominal bleeding, a generally familiar, not particularly terrifying part of the body.

When the subject was exhausted, it struck Wallin that the situation was optimal to take Hamad's pulse a little concerning Sven-Gunnar Erlandsson. During Monday's meeting in the police station he had given certain signals that perhaps he shared one of her viewpoints, in any event. Hamad had expressed some doubt as far as Erlandsson's character was concerned. Which had not been questioned by a single other person during this investigation, except herself. And here was Wallin now, right after an operation and miserable, and there was no one else in the room that Hamad could be influenced by or ingratiate himself to. It was crucial to take advantage of the occasions that came up.

"You said the other day that Erlandsson wanted to be top of the roost," she attempted hesitantly. "What did you mean by that?"

"We shouldn't be talking work, should we?" Hamad replied. "Forget that for a while now and rest up instead."

"I want to talk work," she answered. "Rather than just lying here thinking about it."

Hamad hesitated a few moments.

"I was just saying that cheating doesn't necessarily have to do with greed," he answered. "That instead it might be about . . . a sense of power. But I don't think this case is about poker. Despite the cards we found in the pocket."

"So what do you think it's about?"

"I think it's about rape."

A strange way to put it, thought Wallin. *Strange choice of words.* Sure, she understood what he meant; it was obvious that Hamad and Westman were convinced that the Russian girl had been kidnapped and murdered. And that an eleven-year-old girl most likely was raped before she was murdered. But still—why did he call the crime rape and not murder?

"And rape clearly is mostly about power," she said. "Who do you think raped and murdered Larissa Sotnikova?"

Hamad sighed.

"There are several different alternatives," he answered. "All equally probable."

He then recounted his and Westman's investigations concerning Siem.

"Where was that call to Commissioner Malmberg made from?" Wallin asked. "Have you managed to figure that out?"

"From Södertälje," Hamad answered after a second of hesitation, which did not escape her.

"I see, goodness. The same tower as the call that was made from Erlandsson's cell phone?"

Hamad nodded.

"And at what time was the call made from Erlandsson's cell?"

"Both calls took place at about the same time. At 9:35."

"So there," Wallin said meditatively. "But excuse me for interrupting. What's your thinking about Jenner and Wiklund?"

Hamad continued his account. Wallin listened attentively and determined that there was good reason for any one of them to end up under the magnifying glass in this case.

"But Erlandsson himself is free from suspicion?" she coaxed. "Despite what you said about power?"

"That was purely hypothetical. As I said, I don't think the murder of Erlandsson has anything to do with card playing."

"Or that he was a dictatorial type?"

"No. In my assessment—and everyone else's too, it seems—he was an upstanding and well-liked citizen."

"In my assessment he was a poser," Wallin interjected, with complete certainty that this would hardly be well recieved.

"Erlandsson was committed to the weak in society, besides," Hamad continued, "I think he stumbled across who was behind

Lara's disappearance. And he decided to get to the bottom of it. I see that as the most apparent motive for this murder."

As expected.

"But you may be right," he continued. "It may also be that someone found out he had something to hide. I see that as the only alternative motive."

Will wonders never cease? A convergence.

———

Adrianti Erlandsson went over the house with the vacuum cleaner. Wednesday already, Svempa had been dead for four days. It was unreal. That the earth was still spinning around its axis, that she was still moving about in her fine house, in her new country.

Rasmus and Anna had gone back to Uppsala on Tuesday. What else was there to do? Life must go on. Her own life seemed to be doing that, even if it was on idle. For in just a few weeks, right after the funeral, Ida would also be leaving. Little Ida as she still called her, although she wasn't so little anymore, a university student for more than a year. She would be out traveling. Like so many other young people nowadays. Work in Australia, rest and amuse herself on sandy southeast Asian beaches.

She took off the nozzle and passed the hose under the kitchen benches to vacuum up crumbs that weren't there. Stopped occasionally to adjust some object that perhaps ended up a little crooked on the kitchen shelf. *Because it should be as it should be.* Trying to convince herself that she fulfilled a function. To fill life with something. What was left of it. For what was the point of keeping it nice here when no one cared any longer? Yet here she was, doing it, out of pure routine. She, who had neither a job nor education, would hardly have the means to remain living in the villa anyway.

She set the hose down on the floor and turned off the vacuum. Then she went over to Svempa's office and turned on the computer. Went into MSN and checked whether she had any email. She didn't. On Sunday she had sent a message about what happened to the address from which Dewi had last written. For some reason she changed email addresses from time to time, and she actually never commented on anything that Adrianti had written. Which made her think that what she sent did not get there.

During the four years Dewi had been away, Adrianti had received eight emails. Two per year. Briefly worded messages about where in the world she was, that everything was fine and that she hoped they were doing fine too. Nothing more. No heartfelt emotions, no wish to come home again, to see them. Now it had been three months since the last one. "Happy birthday, I'm in Bolivia."

Her eyes were filled with tears. Only now did it occur to Adrianti that her only fixed point in existence, her only tie to her own history, to her blood, was Dewi. Beloved little child. How could she have let her simply disappear like that? How could she let herself be convinced that it was normal for young people to want to get away, go off on adventures? Maybe it was to start with, but four years? And without a parting word?

That was when she had sought consolation with Staffan. When Dewi disappeared and it occurred to her that her daughter did not intend to come back for a long time. Svempa didn't want to hear that, he was not one to get unnecessarily concerned. Those who worry in advance often have to grieve twice, he would say. But Staffan was a good listener. He had taken her seriously, seen her with completely different eyes than Svempa. And one thing led to another. She had been weak. Risked everything she had built up in Sweden for a few moments of pleasure. To feel loved for a few hours.

She drew her finger under her nose. It didn't help. There were more tears, more snot. The world was crumbling around her. Everyone who meant anything to her disappeared. Suddenly she felt like the loneliest person on earth.

Dewi, she thought. *I want you to come home. Wonderful, beloved little person. I miss your laugh. Your warmth. Your flashing intelligent eyes. I want you back. We'll stay together. Like we always did. I can't bear to live without you any longer. Where are you?*

Adrianti tried to collect herself. Got up and went out in the kitchen to blow her nose. Remained standing by the kitchen counter with the damp tissue in her hands. Was it really her considerate, loving little Dewi who simply left her that way? Who maintained only sporadic contact? No, you could hardly believe it was even she who had written those empty, basically meaningless messages. Dewi was poetically inclined, she liked words, loved to tell stories. And why did she change email addresses all the time, so they couldn't have a dialogue? What if . . .

What if it wasn't really Dewi who sent those messages? What if she wasn't out traveling at all? What if Adrianti was being kept in the dark? What if something terrible had happened to her?

She had to talk with someone. Someone who listened, who took her seriously. Despite the agreement she had with herself, even though it wasn't appropriate, even though he certainly thought the same. She had to talk with Staffan.

Sandén expected a family in dissolution when he came home. It wasn't really that bad, but the mood was subdued to say the least.

Jenny was the one who seemed least affected by the situation. She did not understand the seriousness, looked forward to the change in her life, but was a little dejected for the moment because her mom was. Sonja restrained herself and concentrated on dinner preparations, but her posture as well as tone of voice revealed how she really felt.

Thank heavens Jessica was there, strong as usual. She helped her mother with whatever she could think of, while making small talk about things both unessential and more essential. Primarily to dampen the worry. She looked slightly relieved, however, when help showed up in the kitchen door. Even if perhaps he didn't look his best purely in terms of appearance.

"Dad, you look really terrible!" she exclaimed.

Jenny rushed up and threw herself around his neck.

"Is it true you saved the life of another police officer?" she asked while he tried to defend himself.

"No, it really wasn't like that," he answered, pushing her gently away from him. "But I can tell you what happened. If you're interested?" he added, kissing his wife on the lips.

She looked tired and sad, and shook her head when she saw his mangled exterior. He caressed her on the cheek and then went over to the kitchen table and sat down.

"I want to hear," said Jenny.

"Maybe Mom doesn't have the energy to talk right now?" he answered with a glance over to Sonja.

She stood with her back turned and seemed barely interested.

"Tell us now, Dad," said Jessica, fixing her eyes on him.

He guessed she had her reasons. It had probably not been very cheerful for Jessica here at home the last few hours, and there was no big rush, after all, to discuss a future that would not present itself for a few months. All the tough parts could probably wait a while. Both daughters were so eager that, despite Sonja's threatening back, he found it best to do as he was asked.

So he told the whole story there in the kitchen. The girls listened solemnly, and even Sonja let go of the potato peeler after a little while and came and sat down at the table.

"And you know what she said, Walleye I mean, when I talked with her afterward?" Sandén concluded the story. "'Life often turns out really cool when unexpected things happen.' I thought that was a memorable comment. Something we all ought to have in the back of our minds when things happen in life that maybe we haven't counted on. That it can turn out really cool in the end."

Jessica looked curiously from her father to her mother, then got up and—in a perhaps slightly ungentle way—gave Sandén a big kiss on the cheek.

"Oh, shit!" he cried, his hand flying up to his face.

Jenny started to laugh, and Sonja smiled for the first time since he got home.

"You're quite right, darling," she said, drawing her hand through his hair.

"*Walleye* is quite right," said Sandén. "Walleye is always right. So when is our little cutie-pie coming?"

"In November," Sonja answered.

"In November? But you're not showing?"

"That's because I'm so fat to start with!" Jenny said.

"No, no, listen, you're just right," Sandén said. "But what worries me is with such a mom, the kid is going to be insufferably cute. Ugh, how we're going to spoil her. Or him."

"Jenny says she doesn't know who the father of the child is," said Jessica, a bit more seriously now.

This rubbed off on Sonja, who gave Jenny a worried look.

Sandén was forced to think for a few seconds before he decided what he thought on the issue. When he opened his mouth, however, he was completely clear.

"Great. Then we won't investigate the matter any closer, and we'll have our little darling all to ourselves."

No one had any objections.

Then they moved out into the garden and spent the rest of the afternoon and evening with their bare feet in the lush grass that had grown a few days too long. Jessica grilled T-bone steaks and let herself be beaten by Jenny in croquet.

Everything was almost as usual.

———

When Sjöberg showed up Adrianti was on her way out, but she turned around at the door and let him in anyway. She seemed worried, stressed. The foreign accent was more apparent now; she stumbled over words and was careless about grammar.

They sat down at the kitchen table. Grief had not left any visible traces in the house, it was just as tidy and well-kept as before and smelled newly-cleaned besides.

"Well, there was a matter that came up in our previous conversation that I have a hard time letting go of," Sjöberg started.

Adrianti looked at him fearfully and pulled nervously on her fingers so that they cracked. Something must have happened that had frightened her.

"Your daughter. Dewi. I didn't really follow that. Surely you must know where she is?"

Adrianti shook her head.

"How could that be? I mean, all of you seem to be extremely fond of her. Doesn't she feel the same toward you?"

"Yes. Dewi loved people. She loved us. All of us."

"You say 'loved.' That sounds a little ominous, I must say."

"Loves. Excuse my bad Swedish."

Sjöberg chewed on that a while, but decided to go on.

I want you to tell me what happened when Dewi left. The exact circumstances."

She looked at him with an inscrutable expression, but took a deep breath and began.

"It was in the middle of the summer. She had taken her entrance exams a few weeks earlier. With fantastic scores. Then she packed her backpack and went to the Roskilde music festival. Together with Lina Jenner. Lina is a few years older, but they've always gotten along extremely well together."

"Roskilde festival?" said Sjöberg. "Did you approve of that?"

"No. But they were adults, both of them, and Lina's a good girl. What could we do?"

"And then?"

"After two days Lina came home. Without Dewi."

"Without Dewi? Did she contact you?"

"Two times. First, she called and said they would be staying until the festival was over. Then Svempa and Staffan went down to Denmark to talk sense with her. They divided up and looked in different places, talked with a lot of people, but came back empty-handed."

"And the second time you heard from her?"

"She called and said that she intended to go on a round-the-world trip. That she hadn't said anything before because she didn't want to make me sad."

"How did she sound?"

"Dejected. I got sad, she knew that."

"And then?" Sjöberg saw how tears were forming in Adrianti's eyes.

"That was the last time I talked with her."

"When was this?"

"It was the same day that Svempa and Staffan went down. It's a large area. It was like searching for a needle in a haystack."

"You must have been extremely worried."

"I was mostly sad. A little worried too. With her foot and everything. But Dewi usually knows what she's doing."

"Her foot?" said Sjöberg. "What do you mean by that?"

Adrianti looked at him with pleading eyes. Was he pressing her too hard? Maybe, but he had to have answers to these questions. Now she was no longer able to hold back the tears.

He placed his hand on her arm and waited until the weeping calmed down. Had she been this desperate for four years? But held it back for the family's sake? Had the murder of her husband perhaps contributed to the dam breaking? Or had she suddenly been struck by the same suspicion as Sjöberg?

"Adrianti, had Dewi hurt herself?" he asked gently.

"She was handicapped," Adrianti answered mournfully. "Dewi was disabled."

Sjöberg was completely taken by surprise, could not get all the pieces of the puzzle to fall into place.

"Disabled? But as I understood it, she was . . . a great soccer talent?"

"She was," Adrianti confirmed. "Until she had her accident."

"How old was she?"

"Fifteen. Just got a moped. She loved that moped. But she could never ride it again."

"I'm terribly sorry. What kind of accident was it? Can you bear to tell me?"

"No, I really can't," said Adrianti, managing to force a dejected smile in her misery. "But I'll do it anyway."

"Thanks," Sjöberg said sincerely. "Forgive me for pressing you in this way."

She shook her head deprecatingly and made a fresh start.

"Dewi was home alone one afternoon during summer vacation. She was looking for something and was out in the garage rooting around. We had an old washing machine out there, stacked on a pile of duckboards. She was a little careless, and the washing machine fell on her. She was lucky, however, strange as that may sound. Only her foot was crushed, but that was serious enough. She had severe crush injuries."

"How awful," said Sjöberg. "It must have hit her hard. All of you. The whole family must have been affected."

Adrianti nodded.

"She was never really the same after that. Stopped soccer, stopped laughing. She withdrew and mostly kept to herself in her room. Devoted herself to schoolwork, listened to music, wrote poetry and other things I never got to read."

Suddenly it occurred to Sjöberg that this was what all the strange verb forms were about. Not that they believed Dewi no longer existed, but the fact that Dewi had become a different person. When they spoke in the past tense, they were talking about Dewi as she was at one time, the way she really was. That also explained the oppressive sorrow that seemed to permeate everything when she was discussed. Their beloved Dewi had left them, gone into herself, and it was tough for all of them. The fact that later she physically left them only added to the burden.

"That was partly why we let her go to Roskilde," Adrianti continued. "That Dewi wanted to do something like that, together with other people, was unusual. I was happy and worried at the same time."

"You seem worried now, too," said Sjöberg. "What is it that's worrying you?"

"That she . . . that maybe she's gone for real."

"Is that a new thought? You've never wondered along those lines before during these four years?"

Adrianti shook her head.

"Why now, suddenly?"

"Svempa is gone. The children have all moved away. I didn't have so much time left over before. To think about Dewi. And Svempa always used to calm me and say that Dewi is certainly doing fine. That she had made her own choice. Then I started thinking about those short messages she sends. It's not like . . . her."

Sjöberg feared the worst. If Adrianti Erlandsson had started suspecting that Dewi had disappeared, there was probably reason to be worried. He asked her to describe the communication that had gone on since she disappeared, and none of what he could see now changed that. Eight meaningless check-ins, sent from just as many email addresses. Dewi could be anywhere. Or nowhere at all.

"Does she use a wheelchair?" Sjöberg asked.

"No, not anymore. She did for a short period in the beginning, but then she changed to crutches. Sometimes she walked without crutches too, tried to pretend that everything was like usual again. But that could never be. I think the pain was awful in what remained of her foot, but Dewi endured it. Never complained."

"I'll look into this," said Sjöberg. "I promise. But there is another thing, too. The affair with Staffan Jenner."

Adrianti considered whether she should simply deny it, but thought better of it. Exhaled all the air she had in her lungs and collapsed in the chair. She looked embarrassed.

"I know," she said. "I'm an idiot, should have told you of my own accord. But not in front of the children, and . . . I thought it was awkward. It *is* awkward. Is it Staffan who talked about it?"

Sjöberg nodded.

"It wasn't particularly nice," she continued. "The children, who were such good friends. And Svempa and Staffan, who . . . Yes, they were best friends of course. It was a betrayal."

"Do you think Svempa knew about it?" Sjöberg asked.

"He shouldn't have known anything. I mean *no one* knew about it. But in any case . . . I think he knew anyway. He had a sixth sense. A special ability to know everything about everyone. But he never said anything. And it lasted only a month. We met two times before we got sensible. Svempa never said a word about it."

"Why did you do it? Why did you initiate the relationship?"

"It was when Dewi had left. I missed her so incredibly. Needed warmth. Consideration."

"You didn't get that at home?"

Adrianti got an uncertain look in her eyes.

"Yes, of course, but . . . I can't explain. I was weak. It was a stupid thing to do. I regretted it just as quickly. And Staffan too. So we broke it off."

Well. Not much to say about that. The flesh is weak. The reasons many and complicated. Adrianti Erlandsson and Staffan Jenner had not done anything stupid for four years. After a relationship that lasted for a month.

Conny Sjöberg had not done anything stupid for a year and a half. After a relationship that lasted for six months. No doubt prevailed as to who had committed the more serious transgression. Neither of them had gone home and begged for forgiveness, talked things out, given their life partner a chance to have an opinion. Who was he to judge? He was a cowardly wretch. A manipulator with an instinct for self-preservation. Or—if you looked at it a different way—a man who carefully weighed advantages and disadvantages against each other and came to a decision that hopefully favored all parties. Perhaps there was something good about that.

"We're going to be discreet about this information," said Sjöberg. "I'll see to it that this doesn't come out if it's not necessary."

Adrianti looked grateful, and that was heartwarming. He was not one to run around gossiping, in any case.

WEDNESDAY EVENING

Wallin felt beat up. She did not recognize her body, swollen as she was, and it hurt all over. Although they were pumping her full of pain meds, it hurt in the operation scar, in her face, in the crooks of her arms. She was tired besides.

She slept off and on, exhausted by all that her battered body had gone through during the day. Of course she ought to make some calls. Her children, friends, relatives. But right now she did not have the energy to talk with anyone, much less have more visitors.

During her waking time she tried to read, but even though the book was good she could not concentrate on the contents. Her senses, her thoughts led her off in other directions and she had no way to resist, had to allow herself to float out.

Enchanted forest. Light and dark. The play of the shadows among the trees. Sweat, cold, birdsong. The play of the wind in the leaves.

Odors. Pine needles and leaves, mushroom and moss. Blood.

Death.

Erlandsson.

Poker.

The poker lead had amounted to nothing. Rightly perhaps, but now she decided once and for all to get to the bottom of that talk about poker. Other things had intervened, but now there was all the time in the world. Why had there been talk about poker long before anyone knew that Sven-Gunnar Erlandsson and his friends spent the poker treasury the night before the murder? Already, out there in the pouring rain on the golf course, poker was mentioned. Her colleagues dismissed her musings about this, and very possibly they were right to, but until it was proven the question was still relevant. Four cards was not a poker hand. That's just the way it was.

She stretched toward the handle hanging above her head and carefully pulled herself up to a sitting position. Turning toward the nightstand, she took out her cell phone. Then she entered the number for Lundin, the young policeman who had been on duty the morning when Wallin and Hansson called in from Nacka Golf Club at Värmdö. And despite the rather late hour and the fact that she had a blocked number, he actually answered.

"Excuse me for disturbing you," said Wallin, who with a vague hope that her health condition was not general knowledge tried to sound as if she had not just been brought back from the dead. "You had duty on Sunday morning and called Bella Hansson and me to a crime scene in Älvsjö. Do you remember that?"

Of course Lundin recalled that very well.

"Is it correct that you talked about poker then? That poker in some way had something to do with the murder?"

"That came from the county communication center," Lundin answered. "I didn't come up with that on my own."

"Can you find out who the uniformed officer was who reported to them?"

Lundin promised to do that, then called back after less than ten minutes.

"It was Camilla Ericksson from the response unit in Farsta. I've got a phone number if you're interested."

Wallin was, whereupon she ended the call and started another one.

"Hedvig Wallin, Hammarby police. Excuse me for disturbing you so late, perhaps you're not at work?"

"I remember you," said Eriksson. "We met at the crime scene in Herrängen on Sunday."

"That would be correct," said Wallin, wondering how it was that Eriksson remembered her in particular.

"There's nothing wrong with my memory," Eriksson continued, an explanation that Wallin was content with.

"Are you the one that poker rumor came from?" she asked.

"What poker rumor?"

"When I was called in by the on-duty officer, poker was mentioned in connection with this murder. The thing is, it was not until several hours later that it came out that the victim belonged to some kind of poker club that had been out having dinner together. So I'm simply asking: Where did you get that?"

Eriksson laughed, sounded like a nice woman.

"Haven't you heard about Wild Bill Hickok?" she asked.

It took a few seconds, then the lightbulb came on.

"Naturally. What a nobody I am. Thanks so very much for the help. And excuse me for disturbing you."

"Not a problem," Camilla Eriksson said. "Good luck."

Now Wallin was buzzing, took out the computer, and placed it in her lap. Verified that she had contact with cyberspace, went onto Google, and entered "Wild Bill Hickok" in the search field. The first hits led her to Wikipedia, which had quite a bit of text about the old Wild West hero.

Wild Bill was shot from behind, in the head, by Jack "Crooked Nose" McCall, on the second of August 1876 at a saloon in Deadwood. At the moment of death he had five cards in his hand, but only four of them were known to posterity. Namely the black eights and the black aces.

Dead man's hand.

How could she have missed that? How could everyone besides Camilla Eriksson in the uniformed police have missed that? It was sloppy, but that's the way it was. Now it was a matter of managing this newly won knowledge in the best way.

Erlandsson, like Wild Bill Hickok, had been shot from behind. A coincidence? Perhaps, because Erlandsson was shot in the neck and Wild Bill in the head. But what was more, both shots were fired on the second of August. True, with 133 years in between, but the date was apparently not randomly chosen in the Erlandsson case. And the four cards in the breast pocket certainly had their significance. Probably it did have something to do with poker in some way.

Still, none of the poker players involved acknowledged any disharmony at the gaming table. Siem was possibly bitter, perhaps he was a stingy bastard who complained about rules and other things, and even thought that Erlandsson was not playing fair. But to go from that, to destroying his own life and many others' . . . ? Wallin wanted to believe that well-situated middle-aged men would have more interesting reasons to murder each other. Poker as a motive for murder felt both out-of-date and childish. Out-of-date because it belonged to the nineteenth century, childish because . . .

Well, because it was childish to be a sore loser.

But Josefin Siem was a child. Perhaps a downright manipulative child. *Daddy's little girl.* And the last call from Erlandsson's cell phone had actually been made from somewhere in the vicinity of the athletic field in Södertälje where both of them happened to be. No, the Siem family was of interest in this investigation to the highest degree, no question about that.

Then, naturally, this whole poker angle could simply be a wrong track. "Dead man's hand" could mean something else. It could refer to the dead man, rather to than a poker hand. It could also be a greeting from the murderer, a signature that perhaps had more to do with the murderer himself than with the victim.

One thing she was quite sure of: Erlandsson had been a bastard. The others could say what they wanted. That he was then murdered because he was a bastard Wallin was not equally sure of.

Mais il avait une vite dans la tête, she thought. Could not think of an adequate way to express that in Swedish. He held up a perfect facade of minutely proper suburban idyll with the latest in-home decoration. Fine, well-behaved children, well incorporated in a social activity that gave him the authority and influence he so avidly coveted. Had they chosen that life themselves? Hardly. Even if perhaps they hadn't given it a thought. And then a little charity on top of it all. To put the halo in place.

And in order to succeed in all this, he had imported a loyal and grateful slave from a place where you didn't even dare to dream about such a life. Where you worked as hard and as long as survival itself required. A servant who shopped, cleaned, did the dishes, prepared food, and laundered soccer jerseys without uttering a word. Who gave up everything that was her; devoted herself to soccer instead of golf, because that suited the family better. Who was nice to look at besides and loving both to the children and to the man of the house. So well trained that she had her cell phone on while she slept. In case he sent an SMS in the middle of the night that said he was on his way home.

So she could prepare herself.

THURSDAY MORNING

As Andersson had already figured out, Bronsgjutarvägen was in a pleasant area of townhouses, close to a forest and lake. The area was ideal for families with children, with a soccer field, nearby beaches, and large areas for adventurous little tykes to climb trees and play hide-and-seek. Plenty of other children to play with, small quiet streets to bicycle on, and well-maintained gardens ideal for barbecues with the neighbors.

The Magnusson family's home was one of many similar single-story houses, and in the driveway was a shiny, clean, fairly new Audi with a roof rack. Andersson was let into the house by a boy about ten, dressed in swimming trunks, who slipped past him as soon as his mother showed up in the hall. She suggested they should sit in the yard, where she offered sponge cake and home-made elderberry juice.

"Isn't Rebecka home?" Andersson asked when they had sat down on plastic chairs with yellow-and-white-striped cushions.

"No, she's not. It's been a long time now since she came to see us."

That was a statement, nothing else. Jeanette Magnusson was in her forties, ordinary looking and a few pounds overweight with medium-blonde hair that she gathered in a carelessly thrown-together knot at her neck.

"You see her time here as a visit?" Andersson asked. "Not that she lives here?"

"She still has her room. And she knows she's always welcome. But she doesn't want to live here. She's quite definite about that."

"She's fifteen years old. Aren't you the ones who decide?"

"Yes, you might think so," the woman answered, reaching for her glass. "But it's not that simple. It has never been simple with Rebecka."

She paused while she drank. Andersson took the opportunity to sample the sponge cake. It was crumbly, but good.

"Rebecka has ADHD. She has extremely definite opinions about things and a rather aggressive disposition. When she was little, she often ended up in fistfights. She makes it easy to be on bad terms with people."

"She's very pretty," said Andersson. A statement that was meant to be disarming and based solely on the few-seconds-long clip from the TV documentary.

"She is pretty, that's right. And certainly she's had some joy from that. People tend to have a little more patience with a cute child. But despite everyone who has tried to help her, she has only kicked back. She's an anarchist to the tips of her fingers." The last she said with a resigned smile. "Maybe you think she doesn't feel loved here at home, and that's true enough. But believe me, all of us love her and we've done all we could so that she would feel that, to get it to work. But it doesn't work. She doesn't want it to."

I see, thought Andersson. *So she just runs off then? And the rest of the family sits at home twiddling their thumbs and hoping she'll come back? Is that how it works in Welfare Sweden?*

Jeanette Magnusson seemed to be reading his thoughts. "We've had child psychologists and family therapists involved for years. The social services are also involved, as you know. Rebecka doesn't want to live here at home. She wants her own apartment, but she can't. She's fifteen years old and has a well-functioning home. The social services agency won't pay. Which I have great understanding for. We can't pay. So she runs away instead. What should we do? Chain her up?"

Andersson was speechless. This was not what he had imagined, and he had no answers. He swallowed the last piece of sponge cake he had in his hand and wiped his fingers on his pants.

"And the other children?" he asked stupidly, mostly just to say something. He really had no idea what he wanted to know about them.

"It feels horrible to say this," the woman answered, "but the boys actually do better when Rebecka is gone. There's always trouble around her. She's destructive, makes everyone around her feel bad. Even worse, she's self-destructive too."

"How does that express itself?"

"She doesn't take care of herself. Runs away in the middle of winter without having proper clothing. Sleeps any old place, according to the few reports we've gotten. In a stairwell. In a public restroom. She associates with the most horrible characters."

"Do you know whether she uses drugs?" Andersson asked.

Jeanette Magnusson shook her head. "We don't think so. They've brought her home several times, dirty and miserable. Hungry. But she hasn't seemed intoxicated. Then she stays a while, and then it's time again."

"Nice that it's summer anyway," said Andersson in a lame attempt to look at the matter a little more lightly. "When was she last home?"

"In March."

"In March? That's almost six months ago!"

"We keep our eyes and ears open. But no one has seen her since then. She has apparently changed city. Or country. There's nothing we can do, more than hope."

Could it be that terrible? If the girl had committed crimes she could have been sentenced to juvenile detention, but as the situation was now, there was evidently nothing they could do to keep her there.

"You're aware that she was living over in Huddinge for a bit?" Andersson asked. "In the woods there? With a bunch of homeless people in a trailer?"

"I found that out yesterday, yes. From the social worker. But that's five months ago. And that's the last report we've received about Rebecka."

"She ever been gone for so long before?"

"No. But it has kept escalating the whole time. The first time she ran away she was eleven. She was gone for four days."

"I think it may be time to send out a missing persons report," said Andersson.

"Thanks. We've suggested that before, but with her record, you know . . . The police haven't taken it seriously. Which is pretty understandable. So why are you getting interested now?"

Andersson was not sure how what he had to say would be received. That one of the last individuals her fifteen-year-old daughter had met before vanishing had been murdered. True, Jeanette Magnusson seemed rather hardened at this point, but still.

He answered evasively. "Rebecka figures on the fringes of another investigation. I was curious to hear what she had to say, so that's why I'm trying to get in contact with her. Nothing serious on Rebecka's part, so there's no reason to worry."

The last he added so that Jeanette Magnusson's interest in the case would cool, but it seemed rather to have the opposite effect.

"What kind of investigation is it?" she wanted to know.

"It's a murder investigation, but—"

"What murder investigation?" she interrupted. Evidently, Jeanette Magnusson was not receptive to diversionary maneuvers.

"It concerns the murder of a fifty-two-year-old bank official from Älvsjö, Sven-Gunnar Erlandsson. He used to visit the homeless in the trailer park she stayed at and hand out food. But as I said, Rebecka is peripheral in that connection."

"She's not peripheral to us. She's been gone for five months now, without the police having been interested."

"I'm sorry," said Andersson sincerely. "I'll see to it that changes."

He thought about underscoring yet again that it was scarcely probable that the girl's disappearance had anything to do with the murder. But on second thought, it was perhaps best not to make any promises.

Wallin was on her back in the hospital bed, staring up at the ceiling. At her dentist there was a poster on the ceiling for you to look at. A really boring poster to be sure, depicting Swedish provincial coats-of-arms, but something to look at anyway. Here there was just a white ceiling. She could sit up, that was no problem, but if she wanted to lie down it had to be on her back.

Her stomach was a color palette. She looked like she had been literally beaten yellow and blue, and it felt that way, too.

Now she was lying there thinking about grammar. "Him who shot him you're never going to find." That was what the telephone voice had said in Gunnar Malmberg's ear on Sunday morning. Who said that? A man, according to Malmberg. But he left it open that the voice could be distorted. Which meant that it was impossible to deduce the voice by how it sounded. That the call came from a well-defined area in Södertälje was established, and this directed suspicions at members of the Siem family.

Malmberg thought he'd heard traffic in the background. What did that say? Possibly that a car passed nearby. Nothing to go further with. But the grammar was interesting. "Him who shot him." It sounded uneducated. Not to say crazy. Or perhaps just youthful? "Fucking losers," the call had concluded, which caused her to lean more in the youthful direction. Intuitively she would say a young, uneducated man somewhere between fifteen and thirty.

Rasmus Erlandsson? No, he was made of different stuff. No member of the Erlandsson family would express themselves that way, she was sure of that. Any of the Jenner children? She had never met them, but no. The diction oozed suburban ghetto, hillbilly, WT or "white trash" as it was called, although it was seldom written out these days.

So why not entertain yourself by trying to look at the case from that perspective?

—⁓—

He woke up in a cold sweat. He reached for the pack of cigarettes on the nightstand and lit one with shaking hands.

Pulled himself up to a sitting position in bed and tried to shake off the nastiness. But the dream was much too real, it wouldn't leave him. He had never experienced anything like it before; he even lifted the covers to make sure the girl from the dream was not really there.

Childish.

With his hand against his neck he felt his pulse pounding as he pulled on the cigarette, and then lit a new one from the butt. He was still out of breath, panting as if he'd been running a marathon. Shit, how they would laugh at him now, his brothers, if they saw him.

There were four brothers, brothers and half-brothers to be exact. He was the youngest. But he was growing, had filled out a lot during the past year, both physically and mentally. He had become cunning. His brothers still didn't take him seriously, still didn't want him along when they did their "deals." So it wasn't to them that he turned when he needed tips and advice, when he needed someone to talk with. Which usually wasn't about dream interpretation, but more down-to-earth things.

Simon got out of bed and went over to the computer.

Jiggled the mouse so the screen lit up and then logged onto Flashback. Started a new topic in the forum for "Dreams and sleep-related phenomena," a forum he had never visited before. He usually moved amongst harder stuff, like drugs and criminality. He wanted to learn, and he learned fast. A lot faster than his brothers could suspect. He was the smartest one of them, which deep down they surely knew and which they would soon benefit from. But here he was now at a fairy forum for psychology. On the other hand, no one would find out about it IRL.

I had a super-fucked up dream last night. I usually wouldn't care, but I'm totally shaky and can't get the fucking nightmare out of my head.

As I remember it I'm in bed having wild sex with a well-endowed blonde when I hear angry voices outside the house. Then there's loud knocking on the front door. I don't get too worked up because I think it's her boyfriend who's there to take her home, 'cause it's a girl I know and her boyfriend is an idiot but also a fag. I go up to the window anyway and outside is the worst biker gang. I'm completely paralyzed but then I throw myself into the closet. Through the crack in the closet door I see how they break down the door and attack my brother and two buddies with iron pipes. The whole time they're yelling something about me squealing on somebody who sells dope, which I would never do.

Then I realize they're after me too and after searching awhile they find me there squeezed in with the winter coats. They drag me out on the floor and one of them shoots me right through my body so my guts are hanging out. I try to stuff them back in with my hands, but then everything turns black and I die.

Then I wake up and now I'm feeling really lousy. Maybe it sounds stupid, but this is the worst thing I've experienced in my whole life.

It already felt better, just being able to write it off a little. He got up and pulled on a T-shirt before he left the room. Carefully opened the door to his mom's room. She was still sleeping. Lying in the bed, with only half of her naked, formless body covered under the blanket. Snoring.

Nice. Then maybe he could avoid seeing her for a while.

—–—

Wallin decided to poke around what she frequently referred to as the numbskulls' favorite internet forum, Flashback. However, this forum, with free and open communication in both a positive and negative sense, was not populated solely by numbskulls. People from all professions congregated here, all social classes and all ages. And certainly all conceivable intelligence quotients were represented too. Certain categories, in fact, were somewhat over-represented in her opinion. Not least the moronic WT category.

And so it was for that reason Wallin on pure impulse went here to search for the man who had called and taunted the acting police commissioner and possibly had also taken Erlandsson's phone.

Wallin decided to start searching for "Dead man's hand," the name for the pairs of aces and eights found on Erlandsson. But except for one entry concerning one of the military's classic rations—pieces of sausage with white beans in tomato sauce—which evidently went by that name, it was only about poker in general and Wild Bill Hickok in particular. Nothing new, that is.

When she continued searching for "Sven-Gunnar Erlandsson," it proved that the murder now had its own heading on Flashback. She went carefully through the whole thread, without finding anything other than curious questions and mindless speculation. No interesting gossip about Erlandsson or observations previously unknown to the police were discussed. Nor did those who were posting on the subject do so for any reason other than simple curiosity.

She knew about Odd Andersson's fruitless attempt to locate the murder weapon. Despite that, she wanted to give it one more try. While he had searched all over the internet, she intended to limit her searching to Flashback. Because if you supposed that Gunnar Malmberg had made a proper analysis, that the voice belonged to a young man, and that her own linguistic theories were not completely off the wall, that was to say that the caller was not the sharpest knife in the drawer—and that he had not only made that call, but was also the one who had shot Sven-Gunnar Erlandsson—then there was actually a small chance this is where he first tried to buy a gun. That he had asked for advice concerning handling and care of the weapon. That he wanted to dispose of the gun after the murder. Or—considering the triumphant tone he used during the call—that perhaps he needed to talk about what he had done. To boast.

Simon went downstairs to find something edible, in the belief that he would have a moment to himself at the kitchen table. But the youngest of his elder brothers, Jakob, was sitting there, vacantly staring in front of him while he had his coffee. He did not even look when Simon entered the kitchen.

The two older brothers were easy to deal with. They were crude, loud, rough, but it was to the point and no funny business. It was different with Jakob. He was only a couple of years older than Simon, but even though they had grown up together they never got along. Perhaps it was for just that reason. Because the competition between them had always been tough, because they were so close in age.

Jakob was a smarmy type and you never knew where he was coming from. He could be nice one minute, almost like a buddy. Only to want something in return the next minute. Something that was so much tougher, often downright dangerous. Sure, Simon had run the other brothers' errands many times, but that was as it should be. If they were dissatisfied with him he got a good smack, and then everything was okay. But Jakob, he could torment you for hours, for days. Just for the fun of it.

But that would soon be over. It *was* over, he felt it now. Simon had caught up and passed his brother and he never intended to let anyone bully him again. Even Andreas and Matteus, the older brothers, would soon fall into line. They would respect him, do as they were told. Like Michael Corleone. Even though he was the youngest, Simon would soon be the head of the family. Since he unquestionably had what it took.

"Get up," he said brusquely to his brother, who answered without looking up.

"What the hell for? Fuck you."

"Because I say so," Simon answered calmly. "Get up."

Jakob looked at him, with his broad, disgusting sneer. He got slowly up from the table and placed himself with his face threateningly close to Simon's.

Without warning, Simon headbutted him right between the eyes. With a howl Jakob fell to the floor with his hands over his face.

"What the hell are you up to?" he screamed. "You're out of your fucking mind! You broke my nose!"

Simon stood completely still and watched the blood pulsing out between Jakob's fingers where he was lying on the kitchen rug. He felt completely relaxed. Not the least bit worried about what aftereffects there might conceivably be this time. He intended to see to it that there weren't any.

To the sound of his brother's howling, he went up to the kitchen counter and sliced two pieces of bread. Took the soft cheese out of the refrigerator, made his sandwich, and poured a large glass of milk. Then, his brother still on the floor, he calmly left, up the stairs and back into his room. There he set his breakfast on the desk before he locked the door behind him and sat down in front of the computer.

He already had a reply to his thread about the horrible nightmare. A user with the handle Mentalbreak wrote: *A few days ago I dreamed I strangled my mom with my bare hands, I could really feel how the life was running out of her. Oh shit.*

Simon thought about it. How it would feel to squeeze his hands around his mom's throat. Or twist a knife in her back.

Evidently he was not alone in having strange, realistic dreams. It felt nice.

For several hours she kept at it, reading page up and page down about this, in Wallin's opinion, completely uninteresting topic. Throngs of weapons enthusiasts flocked to Flashback. Mostly to discuss choice of weapon, advantages and disadvantages of various brands, various calibers. And the great majority were involved in sport shooting and nothing else, but police weapons were also frequently discussed.

From time to time, however, a contribution showed up that seemed to be about something else. That is, about weapons for less than up-and-up purposes. Nothing that caused Wallin to go into a tailspin, but she made notes in any event. To be on the safe side.

Until she stopped short.

It started with a single entry. It was written by someone calling themselves The Saint and was very brief:

I have a Glock 38.

Only when she read the entry did she catch sight of the name of the thread. Which was "I want to kill someone. I'm going to kill someone." It was created by this same account, The Saint.

She went back to the begining of the thread, started there, and then read all entries with great interest.

> *The Saint: For a long time I've thought about becoming a hired gunman, but don't know how to get started. I have access to weapons, so that's no problem. I also have some experience. I've used a pistol once before but that time I chose to be merciful for economic reasons. As it is I could go into town and murder the first available person, but I prefer to do it for payment. So now I'm wondering how to get in touch with employers. Is there anyone who can share their experiences with me? Maybe you*

think this is a sick question, but it's really just a way to make a living and I can think of many jobs that are worse.

This was followed by lots of scornful comments, with a few traces of seriousness.

Brother Fuck: You don't say. Like passing out mail at the office maybe, or cutting grass? No, damn it, you wouldn't want that kind of drudgery. Better to slaughter innocent people and spend 25 years in isolation at Kumla. I see a bright future in the crystal ball for you, Saint.

The Saint: What are you doing here if the subject doesn't even interest you?

strm999: Because he wants to point out to you that you are completely sick in the head.

The Saint: Don't think so. I'm just goal-oriented. Just you wait.

strm999: Where is the world headed anyway? But empty barrels rattle loudest, as luck would have it.

The Saint: Please, can't you all be a little serious? The question is meant seriously.

strm999: We are serious. Don't you get that we're trying to help both you and the poor souls you're thinking about killing? So I'll give you a good piece of advice: Play a little less computer games, eat healthy and start exercising. I would even advise you against my principles to get saved. The Christian message could be the way out in this case.

The Saint: I've thought about that too. But at the same time there has to be balance and I think my qualities are better suited for the other side.

strm999: Qualities, permit me to smile . . . But it feels comforting that you've thought this through properly . . . not! Now I have to rush off to my honorable, completely risk-free job. The worst that can happen is that I happen to get a paper cut on my finger. Bye now and bad wishes.

Brother Fuck: I have a job for you, Saint. Go into the bathroom and stand by the sink. Do you see that ugly bastard who's gaping at you? Put a shot in his head, then I'll see to it that you get paid in kind.

The Saint: You can keep making fun of me, I'll grant you that. I know what I'm about and that I'll make it happen.

Spitfire: How much do you have to pay to have someone "eliminated"?

The Saint: I would do it for 100K.

Yo Gurt: I wouldn't even crush someone's foot for so little money.

Goyz: Do you even have a gun?

The Saint: I have a Glock 38.

Goyz: I think it's time for a diaper change now, Saint.

*The Saint: I'm going to do it even if no one will pay me. That's
just how it is. You can think what you want. I'm strong in
my conviction.*

And so on, and so on. The Saint's last entry in the discussion
was dated the twenty-fifth of June 2009. Other interested parties
still kept going, but The Saint himself had withdrawn more than
a month ago.

Could it be that he had decided to take action?

———

Through the keyhole he saw Jakob, that idiot, standing there
waving the bread knife. He looked like a clown more than anything, all bloody both on his face and on his shirt. And he was still
screaming, like a little pig.

Simon put the key in the lock again, lifted the screen from the
air vent above the bed, and took down the Glock.

"Listen up, little lady!" he shouted. "Just so you know what to
expect if you rush here in with the knife."

The noise outside the door actually stopped. He racked the pistol
with that classic sound that no one could mistake.

"What the hell . . ." he heard from outside.

Then he went up to the door and turned the key in the lock, took three steps back, and raised the weapon. Saw the handle lowered and the door carefully being opened.

Jakob looked like a scarecrow standing there, with his arms at his sides, still with the bread knife in his hand. He stared into the muzzle of the pistol and seemed to hardly believe his eyes. Then he dropped the knife on the floor and put his hands in the air.

"Okay, we'll forget it," he forced out.

Simon said nothing for a few seconds, enjoying the situation, the advantage. The terrified look on his older brother's loathsome face.

"Good," he said calmly. "But you have to watch your-fucking-self. From here on, you do as you're told."

Jakob nodded. Convincingly.

"Go and wash up now. Your face looks like a pussy."

Jakob nodded again. Ashamed. Then he slinked away.

Simon went up to the doorway and followed him, satisfied, with his eyes. His brother was cowed. Not to say annihilated. When the bathroom door slammed behind Jakob, Simon bent down and picked the knife up off the floor.

Still no sign of life from his mom's bedroom. The damned Muppet didn't even notice when her sons were almost killing each other.

What made Wallin interested in The Saint, besides the guy's explicit desire to murder, was the fact that he claimed to be in possession of a Glock 38 plus that he disappeared from the thread more than a month before the murder. There was nothing more of interest on The Saint's thread about his murder fantasies. But there were other routes to take if you wanted to find out more about him.

She started by carefully reading all the threads he created. Almost all of them were about narcotics. Even if only half of what he wrote was true, he clearly had problems. The Saint had tried most things and despite his apparent tender age was a hardened drug user. In the thread "Around 80% pure amphetamine—report," he revealed a great deal about himself, which perhaps was not very well thought-out if he was considering a career as a hit man:

Sex: male
Age: 20
Weight: about 85 kg
Height: 182 cm
Substance: amphetamine (80-90% pure)
Dose: 2 bennies
Previous experience: cannabis, morphine, cocaine, amphet-
amines, benzodiazepines, oxycontin, dolcontin, tramadol,
mephedrone, methedrone, methadone, fentanyl etc.

Then followed a well-informed account of how he made a solution of a benny that he shot into himself, how after a magic rush he fixed another shot that was a good boost to the benny. And so on.

Common to all threads where The Saint was involved was that he was often scorned for his naive attitude. The more Wallin read, the more sorry she felt for him. He seemed completely lost in life and vacillated between hope and desperation, love and violence, amazing ecstasy and deep depression. And again and again he was put down by ill-intentioned, scornful Flashback users, but always answered nicely, excused himself, and thanked the few well-meaning answers he got.

Wallin became depressed as the image of the lost boy started to become clear. How had he ended up there?

Once again she took a look at the distressing thread about the nightmare. Only now did she realize that it was only a few hours old. And that since the last time she looked, a number of new entries had shown up. Most, as usual, condescending, cluttered by smiley faces hitting themselves on the head and LOLs. What was difficult and frightening for The Saint was a laugh for most others who hung out on the forum. Wallin sighed mournfully.

An entry popped up before her eyes. It was the thread-creator's own reply to the only other serious entry on the thread:

Mentalbreak: A few days ago I dreamed I strangled my mom with my bare hands, I could really feel how the life was running out of her. Oh shit.

The Saint: Thinking about doing the same. I dare to, I can, I have fresh blood on my hands. She's disgusting lying there spread out in the bed. Naked and fat. Naked and fat.

Wallin felt the hair raise on her neck. The message itself was awful enough. But the repetition . . . The repetition of the last sentence. There was something almost poetic about the whole thing. In a way that made her stomach turn.

What should he do now? To be on the safe side, he locked the door behind him again; what Jakob might do was impossible to predict. Jakob was completely out of his mind. A psychopath. But now he was shaken. That his life would be threatened by his little brother, whom he had dragged in the dirt for twenty years. It was a matter of respect and now it was Simon who demanded respect, not the other way around. A solid headbutt, and the roles were reversed.

But Simon did not feel satisfied. Now that he'd lost his innocence, he wanted more. Even if he actually didn't feel any happier. Strong in a way, but also restless. And then these super-terrible nightmares. But that could have to do with him putting a fucking lot of shit into himself since . . . that happened, mostly to ease up. Which he apparently had not succeeded very well with. No matter what he took.

A joint was what he needed now. So that he could think. He took the things out of the air vent, sat down at the desk, and started rolling. While he worked, his thoughts ran off in various directions. His heart was pounding in his chest. Cold sweat formed on his forehead. His hands were shaking so that he had to start over several times. What the hell was happening? An anxiety attack? A mental breakdown?

Only after a few puffs did his bodily functions calm down. And his thoughts started to clarify. When you thought about it more closely, it was not really so strange that the body reacted. There had been a lot recently. During the past week he found himself far outside his old comfort zone. Took a big step into life and was well on his way to taking yet another, bigger one. But this was about realizing his dreams. Living in the present and the future. Not about what had been. Adapting yourself to your new reality. With all that entailed of good and bad. And out into real life. *La dolce vita.*

Simon took a deep puff on the joint, with his gaze fixed on the bread knife still lying where he'd placed it alongside the keyboard. Then he closed his eyes. Tried to retain as much of the salutary vapors inside him as possible until at last he exhaled.

"Mental breakdown," he mumbled to himself, opening his eyes.

And noted that Mentalbreak had still not answered his latest entry. Then he heard Jakob sneak out of the bathroom and into his room. Good, he was still afraid, trying not to make himself noticed.

———

It was enormously frustrating not to be able to do anything about the fact that a young man somewhere in the country was considering sticking a knife in his mom. A boy who for a long time had harbored a dream of murdering, and who claimed to be in possession of a Glock 38 besides. And who now, according to his own statement, had fresh blood on his hands. Blood that purely theoretically could be Sven-Gunnar Erlandsson's. For how many people in Sweden could have been shot with a Glock 38 during the past week? In statistical terms—no one. But in practice this concerned at least one.

So instead of just sitting with her arms crossed, Wallin fought on. Now she had plowed through all the threads that The Saint himself had created and then proceeded to go through the entries he posted in threads other than his own. And there were a lot of entries. The Saint spent a good deal of time at the computer, that was obvious.

After some skimming, she stumbled across something. Namely a thread a couple of years old where curious Flashbackers followed the development of a serious fire at a farm outside Katrineholm. The rumor was that a person was missing who might have been in the house, and when The Saint posted his entry the fire department was still struggling to get the fire under control.

> *The Saint: An old schoolmate from grade school lives there. Really hope that she or someone in her family isn't still in there. I'll run over and check out the situation. Maybe I'll be able to take some pictures with my cell phone that I can post.*

This was exactly what she needed. With rising pulse, she browsed through the rest of the thread until it was clear that a then-eighteen-year-old girl by the name of Veronica Bengtsson had tragically perished in the blaze. The name of the farm was already indicated in the thread, and by means of this information she had enough meat on the bones to go further.

Eagerly she logged in on Stay-Friends and soon had a whole class list in front of her. One of the girls in grade six at Forssjö School during the academic year 2001/2002 was named Veronica Bengtsson. With a little luck, The Saint should be one of the boys on the list. The question was only—which one of them?

Wallin examined the class photo. He was 182 centimeters tall now, weighed 85 kilos. That told her nothing about how tall or heavy he might have been in sixth grade. Did he look sad maybe? Or dangerous? Mistreated, poorly dressed, unkempt? All the boys obviously looked cute and nice, like kids mostly do. And torn knees on pants was part of childhood.

What did the signature itself—The Saint—say about who he was? Nothing, of course. He was anything but a saint.

Possibly that he had self-awareness and an ounce of humor.

Once again, she took a look at the names on the list. And there it was. Clear as a bell.

In the back row second to the left he stood, and Wallin had not been mistaken: he really did have an ounce of humor.

His name was Simon Tampler.

The Saint.

Sjöberg was not receptive. To what was being said in his ear; to the facts set forth; and the ideas, essentially different from his own, now being presented to him. He was convinced that among the theories they were working on so far, one was right. That they had not all as a group rushed off in completely wrong directions. And that it was not Wallin who would serve the murderer's head to them on a silver platter.

Wallin, whom no one really took seriously—well, apart from Sandén of course, but he didn't always deserve to be taken seriously either. Should she be the only one who hadn't followed the usual trails, the only one who didn't let herself be guided by other people's convictions? To put it mildly, it was not what he had imagined.

The only reason he actually listened was that he had a bit of a guilty conscience about Wallin. Plus, Sandén had talked back in her defense on several occasions, which was not like him. So for that reason Sjöberg decided to give Wallin a chance. In no way was this about intuition, simply about common sense. He had simply *decided* to meet her halfway. Before she came up with this astounding maneuver. But during the course of the conversation, it occurred to him that she had actually approached him, the contrary one, on her own initiative, and not Sandén who she could be certain would take her seriously. And that was brave, he had to admit that.

"Listen now, Conny," said Wallin. "His name is Simon Tampler, he's twenty years old and lives in Forssjö outside Katrineholm. Look him and the other members of his family up in the crime registry. I guarantee you're going to find something. He has a broken childhood. He can be a nice, friendly guy, but mentally unstable."

"How sure are you he's the one we're looking for?"

"Ninety percent sure."

"Only ninety?"

"He could be a troll."

"A troll?"

"Someone who isn't what he makes himself out to be. On the internet, that is. But I don't think so. Everything adds up. He has a Glock 38, he says explicitly that he has a need to kill, and he claims he killed someone quite recently. Besides, his behavior reveals that he really has."

"How so?"

"I don't have time to explain it right now, but believe me. I'm good at reading people."

Really? thought Sjöberg. *Can you be and at the same time have such a hard time behaving in a way that appeals to your colleagues? But sure, maybe you can.* He shouldn't be so damn narrow-minded.

"I recommend in the strongest terms that you send a national response team there. At once."

Sjöberg sighed. Deeply.

"I can't do that, Wallin. It just won't work."

"Because the evidence is too weak? Because deep down you don't believe it? Sure, I understand. But go yourself then. Armed to the teeth."

"To bring in a nice, friendly twenty-year-old?"

"Yes. Because he has a Glock. Which he won't hesitate to use. Because he's not responsible for his actions, maybe psychotic. You have a good way with people, Conny. You have to talk sense with him. In a nice, friendly way. And don't forget that respect is an important word for this kind of guy. But it's urgent."

"How can you be so sure of that?" Sjöberg asked.

"I'm not. Not at all. But I do know he's thinking about murdering his own mother. So it's urgent. And we don't want it on our conscience. Even if no one could blame us for not figuring it out before it happened."

Sjöberg thought awhile. Thought maybe it was just this occasion he had been waiting for. He could show Wallin the respect she really deserved. Like all other people. And even if she was out on a limb, no great damage was done. As long as they didn't involve the national response team, but instead took action at their own risk so to speak, then there was no major loss of prestige. And when he thought about her remarkable effort where that coordinate code was concerned, he had to admit she really had put her best foot forward. Even if it hadn't given them anything. And if it were the case that Wallin really was right . . . that this Simon Tampler really had murdered Sven-Gunnar Erlandsson, that they found the weapon and Erlandsson's iPhone in a house search . . .

Well, then it would just be hats off to her. Even though new facts, new leads, new secrets in this mess were showing up all the time, nothing had come of it. So, for the time being, the investigation was more or less at a standstill. He was prepared to take the risk.

"I just have to ask one thing," said Sjöberg. "What was he doing at that athletic field, this Tampler? Or do you still think it was Josefin Siem who grabbed Erlandsson's cell phone when she found the body?"

"Simon Tampler wasn't at the athletic field," Wallin replied. "He was on the train between Stockholm and Katrineholm. It should have left the Central station at 8:29 that morning, but it left forty-six minutes late, that is, at 9:15 a.m. The trip to Södertälje South takes twenty-two minutes. So he was in Södertälje at 9:36 when the call was made. And the track runs next to the athletic field. The traffic sounds that Malmberg thought he heard were train sounds."

"Stop and verify. Are you confusing two different calls? Or do you mean that both calls were made from the same tower at the same time?"

"More or less, yes. That's what I managed to drag out of Hamad."

What the hell. Why hadn't Hamad told this to Sjöberg? He hadn't asked directly, while Wallin apparently had, but still.

Thoughts were swirling and for a few seconds he just sat shaking his head. Sjöberg was speechless. What if she really had cracked the case? The only thing to do was gather the group and be off for Katrineholm.

"Impressive work, Wallin. That I must say. I'll take over now. And maybe you should take the opportunity to rest up a little, so we get you back soon?"

"Absolutely, I'll do that!" Wallin laughed on the other end. A little too loud. But maybe that wasn't so important.

"I'll keep you updated," said Sjöberg. "If it's okay to call and disturb you?"

"No problem. But listen," she said, suddenly serious again in that typical Wallinesque way. "There was one more thing. Not because this has any great significance any longer, but still. Those cards Erlandsson had in his pocket were not just any old cards. It was a dead man's hand. The cards Wild Bill Hickok had in his hand when he was shot in 1876. On the second of August, which is worth noting. Just wanted you to know."

"Uh . . . thanks."

"Take it easy now, and good luck," Wallin concluded the call.

Sjöberg again just shook his head.

THURSDAY AFTERNOON

The weed had left his body and the sweats came over him again. Racing heartbeat and hands that wouldn't obey. Dives. Surges. Like an old woman in fucking menopause. He heard motorcycle sounds outside, Matteus and Andreas were home. He had to get rid of these strange feelings, wanted to be in form when he saw his brothers. So he made himself a fix with half-and-half jack, banked with dextrose and creatine, but that was what he had at home.

While he was busy with that, he listened to the sounds in the house. He heard his mother make her way out of bed, out of the bedroom, and down the stairs. His brothers were on their way in, the outside door slammed, and then he heard them exchange a few words with their mom in the kitchen. From Jakob's room not a sound had been heard for several hours. He was probably lying low—licking his wounds.

Now he got a shot of amphetamine, felt good again, and got up. Raised his hand in front of him and noted that it almost wasn't shaking at all anymore. The sweating had stopped. He cleaned up after himself, pulled on a pair of jeans, and opened a window. The room needed to be aired out. Then he went out in the hall and started going down the creaky stairs. Heard how the voices fell silent in the kitchen—it sounded ominous somehow, as if it had something to do with him. Not because his mom usually said very much, but Matteus and Andreas made a lot more commotion when they were together. Which they almost always were.

When he came into the kitchen his mom was standing with her back to him, measuring coffee into the coffeemaker. The brothers were sitting on either side of the table on chairs angled out toward the room, toward him. Straddle-legged, leaning forward with their burly forearms placed across their thighs and their hands hanging loosely between their knees. They looked serious. In logical terms he realized this wasn't good. But his body and brain were disposed to something else, the jack was rushing around in his veins and wanted him to disconnect logic, laugh, and be strong. Logic said that Jakob, that little rat, had not submitted to the treatment, that like the snot-nosed brat he was he had tattled to the older brothers instead of just swallowing the humiliation. And that was not good. Not good at all.

"How's it going?" he simply said, sauntering completely relaxed over to the refrigerator.

"Are you high again, you little bastard?" said Matteus.

"So what?"

"Stop. Look me in the eyes."

Simon stopped. Looked Matteus in the eyes. With a foolish smile that he couldn't get rid of.

"You're so high on that shit you don't know what the hell you're doing anymore."

Simon did not agree. But didn't answer.

"Do you get what you've done?" Andreas asked. "Do you understand what a mess you've made? The whole operation can go to hell."

Mom was busy at the kitchen sink. She still had not turned around.

"Too bad about business," Simon answered. "But I don't give a damn about life and death."

The brothers exchanged glances. Two shaved heads, two big beards.

"Then maybe it doesn't matter so much if we kill you? Because that's what we do with types like you. Types who steal our stuff," said Andreas, getting up, taking a step toward him.

Powerful, angry, threatening. But Simon felt nothing. He couldn't care less about any of it.

"Jakob is a little cunt," he said.

"Jakob is loyal. He understands what you can and can't do," said Matteus, who also stood up.

"It was just a loan. You'll get the pistol back. I don't need it anymore."

"You don't borrow things from us without asking for permission," Andreas hissed, taking yet another step in Simon's direction. "Remember that. If you wake up again."

Matteus raised his hand just as Andreas was about to attack Simon.

"What do you mean you don't need it any longer?" he asked suspiciously. "You haven't fucking used it, have you?"

"Maybe I have," Simon answered with a shrug of his shoulders.

Still with that smile that he himself didn't know the origin of. He ought to be scared, but he just felt . . . deadened. It was like it didn't matter what happened, it was all the same.

"What have you done, you fucking idiot?" Matteus roared, aiming a kick right at his belly.

Bent double he fell to the floor, but Andreas quickly got him up on his feet again and held him under his arms while Matteus went at him with his fists.

The last thing he saw before everything turned black was his mom, who had now turned around and witnessed the scene with a stupid smile on her face.

Sjöberg decided that the five police officers working on the investigation would have to be enough. Not counting Wallin of course. She was very convincing in her arguments, but this concerned a lone twenty-year-old who had not previously been convicted of any crimes.

All of them crowded together in one van and Westman drove. During the course of the journey, they made contact with Chief Inspector Torstensson with the Katrineholm police. A few of them had dealt with him before, during the intense work on several murders at various places in central Sweden a few years back. True, he was on vacation, but despite that had nothing against answering the questions they had.

"The Tamplers, yes," his voice echoed from the speakerphone. "I know them. Very well, unfortunately. They live in the Forssjö area, on a farm that's pretty isolated. There are four brothers, each one worse than the other."

"Simon," said Sjöberg, "what do you know about him?"

"That must be the youngest. I haven't had anything to do with him. He's probably been the least trouble of them. So far, in any event. I think he does a lot of drugs, but to my knowledge he's never been in jail for anything. The two oldest ones are not exactly little angels. Motorcycle guys involved in really heavy things. Burglary, robbery, threats, assault, weapons violations. There are suspicions that they were involved in a break-in at a military armory, but as stated, those are only suspicions. Andreas and Matteus are their names. Go to jail at regular intervals.

"Then there's one more, Jakob. They all have Biblical names, ironically. He runs the big brothers' errands and is well on his way to becoming a heavyweight too. But so far he's only been convicted of minor crimes."

"And the parents?"

"The mother was married once upon a time and had the two oldest ones. The old man was a brutal bastard who drank and abused her. He died young, in a traffic accident I seem to recall. Then there's been a new guy or two, but none who stayed very long. The thing is she's mentally disabled, that woman. Mildly."

Sjöberg could not keep from glancing at Sandén, who was sitting in front of him in the car. He looked neutral, but Sjöberg could well imagine what was going on in his mind.

"But not incapacitated," Torstensson continued. "So it wasn't possible to take the children from her right at the hospital. And the situation for those kids hasn't been the best, but not so serious that social services thought there was reason to take them from her. They had food and clothes. Went to school. That's enough to call yourself a parent these days. Difficult balancing act, that. Personally I think—"

"That's probably all we needed to know," Sjöberg interrupted. "Thanks for taking the time in the middle of vacation. Go lie down in the hammock now."

"Haha, no problem. And if anything, happens call me again. I'll send a car. Or two."

The trip continued in silence. There was not far to go, and there was a good deal to think about what Torstensson had told them.

The Tampler family's farm was located in a beautiful area with both forest and open landscape. Along the last stretch, which was not even paved, cows were out on picture-postcard pastures among oak groves, juniper slopes, and outcroppings of rocks. On the other side of the road was a glistening lake.

They parked the van out of sight and walked the last stretch up to the farm, which consisted of one large residential house and one somewhat smaller, a few small outbuildings, and a good-sized barn. No traces of livestock tending were visible, nor did there seem to be any agricultural activity on the property.

With his Sig Sauer in the holster and a bulletproof vest under his shirt, Sjöberg should have felt somewhat secure, but there was something ominous about the whole enterprise, about the poorly tended farm and the people who lived there. And before they slipped up to the grass-covered farmyard, he considered Torstensson's invitation one last time, but dismissed those thoughts.

Suddenly he heard something. He stopped and the others did the same. Pricked his ears and listened. Voices. Loud men's voices coming from the main house. Sjöberg looked around the farmyard and noticed two motorcycles parked over by the barn; only two. The two oldest brothers were at home, but hopefully there were no other motor-borne young people on a visit.

"Petra," he whispered. "You sneak up to the house and try to see what's happening. Andersson will find out if there's any other door into the house."

Andersson did as he was asked and disappeared, crouching over toward the yard and behind the corner of the house. Westman followed the sound of the voices and stopped under the window just to the right of the porch. Stuck her head up to get a picture of what was going on inside, and then quickly down again. Then she jogged back to the waiting policemen.

"There are five people in the kitchen," she explained. "One is standing passively in the door watching, and two burly biker types are assaulting a man lying on the floor. You're not going to believe me, but the mother is standing by the sink, laughing."

"Are they armed?" Sjöberg asked.

"Not as far as I could see."

Andersson showed up again.

"There's a door on the back side too. But it's locked."

"We'll call in the Katrineholm police," said Sjöberg, making yet another call to Chief Inspector Torstensson.

"They're killing him," said Westman. "We have to go in."

"Sjöberg here again," said Sjöberg into the cell phone. "Send two cars to Tamplers' farm, quick. And a couple of ambulances. There's a serious assault in progress. We're going to intervene, but you'll have to take care of the perpetrators, the older brothers. It's like something out of *Deliverance* out here."

Torstensson confirmed and Sjöberg ended the call. Gave signs to his colleagues, whereupon the five police officers ran up to the outside stair with guns drawn.

"One, two, three," said Sjöberg, and they stormed into the hall.

Sandén, who was first, took hold of the kid in the doorway, a tall rascal with bad posture who was reminiscent of the dueling banjos. He was taken by surprise and lay flat down on the hallway floor at Sandén's order.

At the same time Hamad rushed into the kitchen, followed closely by Sjöberg, Westman, and Andersson, all with pistols drawn.

"Police! Down on the floor!"

The two brothers, who looked like the prototype for motorcycle gang members, slightly overweight with shaved heads and blond beards, were still standing over the boy on the floor. He was curled up in a fetal position with eyes closed. And strangely enough, something that looked like a smile on his face. Leaning against the kitchen sink was a fat woman in her fifties, in a bathrobe and slippers with fur trim, giggling nervously.

It was Westman, standing on the far right-hand side closest to the kitchen table, who noticed what was going on. Her angle was different and for that reason she was the only one who could possibly see how Andreas Tampler's right hand was reaching in under his pants leg and down into his sock.

"We won't hesitate to shoot!" she shouted. "Up with your hands in the air! Now!"

When he then pulled out the little pistol, it was natural that she was the one he shot at. Hamad reacted, taking a step to the right to improve his angle, and put a shot in Andreas' thigh, only a second after the bullet hit Westman right in the trunk. She fell headlong backwards and struck her head on the kitchen table before landing on her back. The big man howled, crashed into the refrigerator, and collapsed to the floor, still with the pistol in his hand.

Andersson and Sjöberg had released focus for a moment on the other brother, Matteus, who now suddenly rushed forward with a knife in his hand and aimed a blow at Andersson's upper arm. While Hamad rushed up and tore the weapon out of the hands of the still howling Andreas, Andersson raised his hand to defend himself and took the blow in the palm of his hand. Andersson did a 180-degree pirouette, which for a brief moment made a clear shot for Sjöberg, who fired a shot that grazed Matteus Tampler's calf. Which was enough for him to let go of the knife and collapse on the floor.

Andersson glided down to the kitchen floor with blood pumping from his injured hand, while Hamad put handcuffs on Andreas. Sjöberg ran up to Matteus, cuffed him, and let him lie there so he could devote himself to Andersson instead. Sandén came rushing in from the hall to Westman, who was now lying stretched out on the floor.

"Breathe, Petra, damn it! You've got to breathe!" he called, while he tried to shake life into her.

When the sirens were heard at a distance, Sjöberg grabbed a towel to wrap around Andersson's hand. As he did that, Andersson lost consciousness and he had to help him down into a prone position on the floor.

"Come on now, Cod," he tried with a light pat on the cheek.

But Andersson did not want to be present any longer, and they were unable to get signs of life from Petra, either. Sandén straddled her and pressed several times with the palm of his hand against her rib cage. Then he leaned over and breathed air into her mouth.

The cars were in the farmyard now and Hamad cut the pants leg off Andreas, who was breathing jerkily and apparently was in shock. Then he tied the piece of cloth around Andreas's thigh as hard as he could and turned toward the unconscious boy on the floor.

Then the police made their entrance.

"We need medical personnel, in with them!" Sjöberg called.

"One, two, three, four, five, six, seven . . ." Sandén counted, while he pressed his hands against Westman's rib cage.

"I don't know if she's breathing!"

He blew air into her lungs one last time before the ambulance personnel took over and he stumbled away exhausted, sitting down on one of the kitchen chairs. At the kitchen sink, Mama Tampler was giggling hysterically.

The whole drama was over in a few minutes. Now the ambulances and one of the police cars had left the farmyard. Still in the kitchen were Hamad and Sjöberg, with the mother and four Katrineholm police officers. Sandén had gone with Westman and Andersson in the ambulance, and the Tampler brothers were under heavy surveillance by uniformed police at the Kullberg hospital awaiting recovery. Andersson's hand injury seemed to be relatively unproblematic, according to the EMTs, and Sjöberg's towel had already put a stop to the bleeding. Westman had suffered a slight concussion, and she was breathing again when the emergency medical technician took over. He could tell immediately that she had a pulse, and he could promise a substantial bruise under the vest.

While the local police took care of their business, the two Hammarby police officers did what they had come here for.

Besides questioning Simon Tampler of course, which would have to wait until he recovered from the beating.

It took Sjöberg and Hamad twenty minutes to find Simon Tampler's air vent hiding place. There they found—besides marijuana, a few bags of white powder, a number of tablets of various colors, shapes, and sizes, plus miscellaneous equipment associated with narcotics abuse—a Glock 38 with ammunition to go with it. They had already found an iPhone with sixteen gigabyte built-in memory, on the desk. It had a red case.

FRIDAY MORNING

After a much-needed morning to sleep in, all of them—except Wallin of course, who was still in the hospital—were back at the office. Something which only sixteen hours earlier would have seemed completely unreal. But here they sat now, gathered around the conference table in the blue oval room.

And as the cherry on top, Brandt the dirty old man and Malmberg the rapist graced them with their presence. Presumably to take credit for Sven-Gunnar Erlandsson's murderer having been arrested. And possibly to grill them concerning the exchange of gunfire. But there was nothing there, everything had been done according to the rulebook.

But wait now, Malmberg, thought Hamad. *Your time is coming. And where have you been hiding yourself the whole week? You who were so interested in this case in the beginning, and blew yourself up like a balloon about to burst because you happened to be the one who got that call? What was it that made you back out, lose interest?*

The answer came quicker than he could have suspected. *An* answer.

"Friends," Malmberg began. "I apologize that I haven't been keeping myself updated with the investigation during the last few days, but I've been at the police and equality conference in Saint Petersburg, and those are urgent matters too of course."

Hm, exactly.

"In any event I'm more or less updated now, and Roland and I would like to thank you for outstanding efforts. And I really mean that. That's the reason for the cake. Help yourselves."

"Agree," said Brandt. "First I'd like to hear how you're all feeling. Odd?"

"No danger, it's just a flesh wound. It hurt like hell, but now I'm on pain relievers. I can still play guitar," he concluded with a wink.

Which produced a hearty laugh from the police commissioner.

"And you, Petra?" he continued.

Westman looked slightly self-conscious. As far as Hamad knew, she had not exchanged a word with the police commissioner since he pulled her onto his lap and tried to arrange a tête-à-tête at the Grand Hotel.

"I guess you could say pretty good," Petra answered with some hesitation. "What happened was very intense. And when you think that the bullet might just as well have hit my head . . . but Sandén showed initiative there. You might have saved my life," she added with her most charming smile.

"Ah, just wanted to take the opportunity for a little kiss," Sandén said jokingly. Embarrassed, actually, at all the positive attention he'd been getting lately.

"But give credit where it belongs," said Sandén. "It was Jamal who saved Petra's life. If he hadn't reacted so quickly, Andreas Tampler would have kept shooting."

"Marvelous," Brandt answered mechanically. "So how does it feel, Jamal? Have you ever shot anyone before?" He asked in a tone as if he wanted to know what the weather would be like over the weekend.

What a hypocrite, Hamad thought. Brandt was not the least bit interested and could not possibly relate to how it felt. That empathy-challenged clown would never be able to understand that in a situation like the one yesterday, where it's a matter of life and death, you act on instinct, hope what you're doing is right. And even afterward, when everything has turned out fine, even then the feeling comes over you again and again that it could have gone differently, you might have been killed, someone else might have been killed, and worst of all: you might have killed someone. The shot might have gone a centimeter to the side and hit an artery. You might have hit the unconscious man on the floor, the laughing woman, or someone else. A ricochet might have . . .

Hell, what fury came over him when he was thinking like that, what anxiety. Sandwiched with happiness that everything worked out, and gratitude. He felt the sweat beading on his forehead, wanted to get up and overturn the table so the fucking cake would go flying.

"No, but it's cool," he answered. Which Brandt was completely satisfied with.

"Conny?"

"Not much to talk about. Just a scratch."

"Did you fire a warning shot?"

"Now will you just leave it alone!" flew out of Hamad. "I'm going to write a detailed report for you to read, but can't we just leave this subject now?"

"Agree," Sjöberg said quickly. "We'll have to let this sink in and at the same time be grateful that—"

"I've drawn a cartoon," said Andersson, whereupon all eyes were directed at him.

Hamad was completely beside himself. Was there a breakdown in progress there too? Andersson blushed.

"In black-and-white. A frame for every second. As I recall it. To put all the pieces in place. But maybe this was the wrong occasion . . ."

Then he pinched his lips together, looked around uncertainly, and sank down in the chair. It was completely quiet. Until Sandén started laughing.

"What an artist you are, Cod!" he roared. "That's just fucking ingenious!"

And as usual, he had everyone with him. The mood in the room was suddenly completely different. Brandt and Malmberg returned to what they were doing and the others sat and chatted a while. The fury ran out of Hamad, who even took a piece of cake.

"Okay," Sjöberg said after a while. "Shall we try to be a bit serious? Simon Tampler is going to be discharged from the hospital at about lunchtime. Then he's going to be transported up here in a police car. Estimated arrival 2:00 p.m. I'm going to lead the interrogation with him."

"I'll sit in," Hamad hurried to say, before anyone else had time to think.

"Good. The rest of you will work on your reports and call it a day. But first we can talk a little about what kinds of questions we want answers to."

"Are we quite sure he's guilty?" Andersson asked.

"We are. Bella has confirmed that Tampler's Glock is the murder weapon. That's enough for me at least to feel certain."

"And the cell phone," Hamad added. "I've taken a look at the contact list and it's definitely Erlandsson's."

"Well, of course we want to find out why he did it," said Sandén. "The motive. Where he got hold of the gun. The playing cards—what was he trying to say with them? The coordinates. If they even are coordinates."

Sjöberg took notes.

"Ask Walleye too," Sandén suggested. "I'm sure she'll have something sensible to contribute."

"Sure, I thought about doing that," said Sjöberg.

"The phone call from Erlandsson's cell," said Westman. "Where did he call from, and why? And was it Tampler who called Malmberg and bragged about the murder?"

Hamad felt his stomach fluttering.

"Was the murder planned?" he said quickly. "Or just an impulse? Why in Stockholm, what was he doing in Stockholm?"

"Did he act alone?" said Sjöberg as he wrote. "Or did he have accomplices? One of the brothers maybe? Or all of them?"

Then no one could think of anything else offhand to ask.

"Get in touch with me if you happen to think of anything," said Sjöberg. "Now, I'm going to sit down in the sun on the Thai boat with an order of *gaeng kiew wan goong*."

He was referring to the Viking ship at the pier right outside the entry to the police building. Thai food was served there in a rather unusual environment, and sun chairs had been set out on the deck where customers could recline, sipping an umbrella drink if they so desired.

"And the crayfish party?" Sandén asked. "That will happen now, since Tampler is arrested?"

"Absolutely," said Sjöberg. "Everyone is welcome starting at 3:00 tomorrow. Bring along bedding and good humor," he added with a wink.

FRIDAY AFTERNOON

After a good, relaxed lunch, Hamad and Sjöberg were now sitting in one of the interview rooms in the basement, along with a bruised, unhappy boy. Outside stood two uniformed police officers, and the whole thing seemed somewhat overwrought. But of course it wasn't, considering that the kid was a heavy narcotics abuser and suspected of having maliciously murdered a seemingly random person with a shot through the neck.

"How are you feeling?" Sjöberg asked.

"Uh. Not so good."

"Because of the assault?"

"No, that's cool. It's just that I've been so f-ing shaky lately. Hand tremor. I sweat like hell and my pulse is racing."

Sjöberg noticed that Simon Tampler looked him in the eyes when he talked. He would not have expected that.

"Did they check that at the hospital?"

"Yes, but they just blamed it on the drugs. Said I was detoxing."

"And you don't believe that?"

"No, not really. I think more some kind of mental breakdown. My moods feel a little wobbly and that." The kid was openhearted, carrying on a dialogue.

Sjöberg didn't know what to think. It was simpler to tussle with unsympathetic criminals. This one felt more like a victim.

"But sure," Tampler continued, "the dope may have something to do with it too. It may be a combination."

"Hm," said Sjöberg. "You are aware that you are sitting here because you have committed an extremely serious crime?"

"Yeah, I really don't get how you caught me," the boy answered with an amused expression that was not particularly becoming under the circumstances. *Didn't he understand what he'd done?* "I thought I did everything right."

"Right?" Hamad interjected. "Can it ever be right to kill another human being?"

"It depends on who it is and how you look at it. But I didn't mean it that way. I didn't think I made any mistakes, that you'd ever be able to trace me. How did you?"

"That's our little secret," Sjöberg answered. "But you can at least tell us how you view this business of killing. And who one has the right to kill."

"I would never kill a child, for example. There's a limit there. Otherwise I guess I'm not too particular."

He looked nice, answered questions politely, seemed interested. Looked at both of them when talking, even though it had mostly been Sjöberg asking the questions so far, and that was more than what most normally functioning people could manage. He was socially competent, as it was so beautifully called. It was undeniably an odd experience to sit and philosophize with such a peculiar mixture of characteristics.

"Would you say that you lack empathy?" Sjöberg asked.

Tampler thought about this before he answered.

"No, I don't think so. I'm nice to people, a good friend. Helpful. But that thing about killing, maybe I have a little different attitude towards. Unsympathetic."

"You see it maybe as a job?" Sjöberg suggested.

The boy shook his head.

"No. Like something I need to do."

"You said your moods feel a little wobbly," said Hamad. "Let me tell you something. Yesterday I shot a person in the leg. Your brother. *In the leg*. I was forced to, to save lives. It turned out okay for him, it was only a flesh wound."

Sjöberg listened attentively, thought he had a sense of where he was heading.

"Despite that, I'm not feeling very well today," Hamad continued. "My mood feels a little wobbly. Do you think it may be a question of something similar for you? That maybe it wasn't so f-ing cool to kill someone after all?"

Simon Tampler looked thoughtfully at Hamad.

The boy was actually . . . cute, thought Sjöberg. Expressive brown eyes and a light-brown mop of hair. In a youthful, charming way. *How the hell could it go so wrong?*

"I've thought a little along those lines," he answered. "But it was something I got in my head that I should try. So I did. I'm pretty goal-oriented."

"Do you intend to continue?"

"Doubtful. But now I guess I'll be in prison for a while. I'll have to think it over. Properly."

Sjöberg and Hamad exchanged glances.

"So this was a fantasy that you lived out?" Sjöberg asked.

Tampler confirmed with a nod.

"Why Sven-Gunnar Erlandsson?"

"I thought he looked like a flipping snob."

"He was a father. Did good work helping the homeless and was extremely committed to children and youth. As a soccer coach, among other things."

"I didn't know that."

"No, I realize that," said Sjöberg. "Because you seem to be a decent kid, actually. But that's just what the concept of unempathetic means. That it's a little hard for you to see a human being as just a human being. Instead of as an object. Do you understand what I mean?"

Simon Tampler thought he did.

"Did you plan the crime?" Hamad asked.

"No. I was just out walking. Thinking a lot about killing someone. And then he showed up in front of me in the dark. So I took the opportunity. Screwed up my courage, because I was freaking nervous. And then I fired. A bad shot that hit him in the back. Then I went up and gave him a shot in the neck. So he would die."

"Did you have gloves on?"

"No," Tampler said. "Why would I? It was warm out."

"So as not to leave any fingerprints."

"But I didn't touch him. I was only holding onto the pistol, then I left."

"The cell phone, then?" Sjöberg asked.

"It was lying next to him. He was texting or something when I shot. So I took it."

"Nothing else?"

"No, I promise. What the hell, he was dead. He looked a little creepy."

"We found some things in his pocket that we don't think he placed there himself."

"I see. What?"

"Some playing cards and a scrap of paper. Are you quite sure you didn't put your hand in his pocket?"

"I swear."

And Simon Tampler did look completely sincere. It seemed improbable that he would lie about this when without hesitation he took the blame for the murder itself. And these details were no longer terribly important, either.

"How did you get hold of the gun?" Hamad asked.

"I can't answer that. I want to, but I can't. You'll have to forgive me for that."

He looked really crestfallen, and Sjöberg thought he might know why he did not want to reveal where the pistol came from.

"It's your brothers', isn't it?"

Shoulder shrug.

"And you don't want to finger them?"

Another shoulder shrug.

"Were they involved in any way? Or one of them?"

"No, damn it. Just me."

"What were you doing in Stockholm?" Hamad asked.

"I was at the DN Gala."

"Cool. What day was that?"

"Last Friday."

"Were you there alone?"

"Yes."

"So you're interested in sports?"

"Kind of. Sometimes."

"Do you still have the ticket?"

"No."

"So how did it go?"

"For the Swedes? To hell."

"Tell us something memorable."

"Tyson Gay beat Asafa Powell in the 100 meter. He ran a 9.78, new Stadium record. But it was disqualified because of tailwind."

"Oh damn. Are you sure you were there? That you didn't just read that in the paper?"

Simon Tampler laughed. "Try me."

"How did the women's 200 meter turn out?"

"She won, the American. Allyson Felix. At 21.88, I seem to recall."

"You're good."

"Yes, that sort of thing is easy for me. Remembering things."

"But so you stayed there all the way to Sunday?" Hamad continued. "How did that happen?"

"I thought it was nice to be in Stockholm awhile. Get away."

"And so you had the pistol with you."

Tamper smiled. Without answering. He was not that dumb, this kid. Firmly resolved not to fall into any traps.

"Yeah, maybe it sounds a little weird," Tampler said. "But that's really how it was. I'd been walking around in town all day and didn't know what I would find. So I just got on the subway, any old one, and rode to the end station. That happened to be Fruängen. So I walked around there a little. First among the houses and then in some forest. Then I caught sight of that old man ahead of me. There was no one else around, and then I decided it was time."

Sjöberg sat silent a while, tried to understand. A really awful story. The thought that when you least suspected it you might run into a total lunatic had occurred to him many times before. But this wasn't how he had pictured the lunatic. A sweet, nice boy, no police record, and reasonably intelligent as it appeared, who murdered for the fun of it. A sport killer. An assassin. Who did not even find any enjoyment in seeing his victim suffer, that's not what it was about. He simply wanted to kill. *Inconceivable.*

Hamad had fallen silent and Sjöberg could not think of any more questions to ask right now, so he decided to round off for now and continue the following week, when the boy would be assigned a public defender.

"You'll be taken to the Kronoberg jail now," he said.

Tampler looked unperturbed. Almost a little curious.

"You're going to be there a while. I want you to know this is not a game. And I'm not saying this to frighten you. But I will inform you that you will be spending the next few years with some very hardened criminals. You're a young, first-time offender, open. It's going to be tough."

"Thanks very much for the warning," said Simon Tampler. With a gentle, friendly expression on his face.

Good Lord. How old would he look when he got out? You really had to hope the boy ended up in the psych ward instead, but

Sjöberg was doubtful. He was much too adaptable, too normal. And too nice. Despite what he had done.

Hamad pushed back his chair and started to get up. Sjöberg was about to do the same when he suddenly realized he had forgotten to ask about the phone call. The telephone call.

"By the way," he said. "One more question. Or two, to be exact. Those telephone calls."

"Yes," said Tampler promptly. "What do you want to know?"

Hamad sat down again. With his face in his hands.

"Was it you who called the acting police commissioner, Gunnar Malmberg?"

Hamad did not move.

"Yeah, that was stupid. I know," Tampler answered. "I felt a little cocky there. Pumped up. But that wasn't how you caught me, was it?"

"No, it wasn't," Sjöberg ventured to say. Well aware that he should not answer such questions at all. But if the boy now felt better because of it, then okay. The case was closed.

Hamad scratched his head, but still did not look up. Was he not feeling well?

"And that other call, where did you make that from?"

"What other call?"

"The one you made from the victim's cell phone."

Tampler looked perplexed, really wanted to please.

"Now I don't really follow you."

"Uh, we'll break here," said Hamad, who suddenly stood up with a sweeping, irritated motion.

Sjöberg didn't know what to think. He wanted an answer to this question. But Hamad went purposefully over to the door and called in the guards, and Sjöberg had no time to react before the boy was on his way out of the room.

"Thanks, Simon," he said. "Good luck in the future."

"Thanks," Simon Tampler answered. "You've been very kind to me."

Then he disappeared through the door with the two constables holding his arms. A deplorable sight.

Hamad shut the door after them with a slam and sat down at the table again. Sjöberg looked at him with surprise, could not for the life of him understand what this was about.

"It's like this," Hamad sighed. "I know who raped Petra. Who the Other Man is."

"You're joking," said Sjöberg, without believing that for a moment. "So who is it?"

"It's Gunnar Malmberg."

"Gunnar Malmberg? It's not possible . . . Why haven't you said anything?"

"For Petra's sake. This simply can't come out. No one but me knows about it. And now you."

"How long have you known about this?" Sjöberg asked, who still could not see the full extent of what Hamad was now telling him.

"For a year and a half."

"And you haven't told Petra? I thought you were close—"

"We are. So close that in confidence she told me she had a short-term relationship with Malmberg. After the rape."

"After the rape?" Sjöberg exclaimed. "That's the worst!"

"You know how they work, those types. It's not about sex, only about power. And when Petra sent Peder Fryhk to prison for raping her, the Other Man, Fryhk's accomplice, wanted revenge. You remember that, don't you?"

Sjöberg nodded. Of course he remembered it; he had been involved to a large extent.

"He called her at night," Hamad continued. "Sent those disgusting pictures to Brandt so she would get fired, and even posted a video sequence from the rape on a porno site. I'm the only one who knows about that, I stopped the mess before Petra found out. Or anyone we know, I hope. What's more, I made certain to direct all suspicions at me. For six months, Petra believed I was the one who had raped her, I was the one who sent the pictures, and so on."

"I did think it was a bit chilly there for a while," Sjöberg murmured.

"You don't know the half of it. She thought of killing me. And I didn't understand a thing. Until it occurred to me how things were and what made it a personal matter between me and him. And because we were constantly putting a wrench in the works for him, he finally staged the most disgusting part of his plan. He started a relationship with her. But because he isn't interested in sex with women who are really there, that relationship was over immediately. Petra saw it as an exciting and somewhat foolhardy adventure, but Malmberg saw it as an opportunity to exercise his power, to get revenge.

"Petra would be completely devastated if she found out about this. Raise hell. And much too soon. Because we don't have any evidence, we would never succeed in putting that bastard away. The only loser would be Petra. My plan is to lie low, lie in wait for him. Sooner or later an occasion will come up—"

"But if we don't have any evidence," Sjöberg interrupted, "how can you be so certain it really is Malmberg?"

"As I'm sure you recall, Petra went to Linköping and had the condoms from the rape DNA tested. That's how Fryhk was convicted. The content of the second condom did not match the DNA from any previously committed crime. But when I had my eyes opened about Malmberg, I sent a sample from him to the lab. Which verified that it matched the Other Man's."

"But Petra made no report and the samples are unofficial," Sjöberg filled in.

"Exactly."

They sat silent awhile staring at the bare walls, as Sjöberg let the whole thing sink in.

"I went and listened to him on Saturday evening," Hamad said gloomily. "At the Pride festival. Do you know what he said? 'All experience indicates that equality is an unbelievably effective force against violence,' he said. I think he got the words turned around."

Sjöberg smiled sadly. He didn't even feel angry. Only frightfully disappointed. Gunnar Malmberg had never been a favorite, exactly. A little too polished, a little too urban cowboy for Sjöberg's taste. But he was a capable fellow: energetic, progressive, with great talent, both socially and intellectually. And now he might also be a rapist, judging by all the videos confiscated at Peder Fryhk's home. And Malmberg had just come home from an equality conference in Saint Petersburg. Had he raped anyone there, too?

"But what in the world does this have to do with Simon Tampler?" said Sjöberg. "Why did you break it off? He was just about to—"

"Because I already knew the answer," Hamad replied. "I realized that I needed to reveal this story to you so you would understand, so I could just as well send him away." Thoughts were spinning in Sjöberg's head. He had thought during the whole investigation that Hamad had been more than necessarily taciturn, not to say secretive, about everything that had to do with that cell phone call. That he threw himself over all telephone-related information. Even though everyone knew that Telia telecommunications was completely hopeless to deal with. And that he had taken the lead yesterday too when they were searching for an iPhone in Forssjö.

Sjöberg was very close now, but he still couldn't quite put the pieces in place.

"Only one call was made," said Hamad. "Simon Tampler called Gunnar Malmberg from Erlandsson's cell phone. *This information must be kept secret at all costs.*"

SATURDAY EVENING

For Sjöberg the cabin was a dream come true. Over two summers and many weekends, he and Åsa had toiled to get it to where it now was. A local construction company was hired to construct the house itself, but they managed the project themselves and were intimately involved in the planning process. Lots of decisions had to be made: colors, materials, faucets, appliances, carpets, and so on. And above all, putting the garden in order.

But here they were now, the whole family in their own summer paradise. A 1,300-square-foot modern Swedish summer house, with large windows and an open floor plan.

Simple, good-looking, functional. Completely marvelous.

The house was on a hillside, and they had to remove a number of trees to get access to the formidable view. And the setting sun. It had cost a few kronor, but it had been worth every cent.

Two tables were set. One for the children and the other for the grown-ups. The kids had decorated for the party by piling on everything they thought of as fancy. There were crayfish bibs, paper plates with crayfish patterns, crayfish napkins, crayfish lanterns, and to the children's great delight even a strand of colorful lights that Sjöberg found in Stockholm before they left.

In honor of the day the Sjöberg children had the company of "Minnow" Andersson, and now they were all on the trampoline. Sitting at the grown-up table were Conny and Åsa Sjöberg, Andersson, Hamad, Westman, and Jens and Sonja Sandén. Jenny was there too, but for the moment she was over by the trampoline supervising that everything was going fine.

It was seven thirty and the mood was exalted. The guests had already arrived in the afternoon and because the weather was beautiful, they went down to the shore. There it was noted that Andersson swam very well with only one hand plus that Westman had one heck of a bruise on her stomach. Then they sat in the garden with their glasses of juice and were forced to sample seven kinds of cookies of varying quality and flavor, all baked by Simon, Sara, and Maja Sjöberg. Then they switched to beer and rosé, all while Hamad mopped the floor with the rest of the guests in croquet, bocce ball, and darts.

Now there was a break between the appetizer, which was a Västerbotten trout roe pie made by Sjöberg, and the crayfish.

"To our absent friends," said Sjöberg, raising his beer glass.

"To Walleye," said Sandén, and did the same. "Or was there someone else you were thinking of?"

"Brandt, maybe?" Westman said, giving Hamad an elbow in his side. "The favorite of the week."

"To Walleye," said Hamad, and the others joined in.

"She sends greetings to everyone," said Sandén. "I went to visit her this morning, she'll be discharged tomorrow. She's feeling much better now, was even up and walking. But you should see her stomach. She looks like . . . Petra, more or less. Although worse."

"That's not possible," Sonja laughed.

"It's possible, I promise. She was extremely disappointed that she couldn't come. She was on the verge of calling transit service to be able to join us."

"What kind of operation was it, actually?" Åsa asked. "Was it ulcers, or what?"

"I think it was something like that. But she'll be at work on Monday."

"You're joking!" said Sjöberg. "She has to take it easy, so it heals. Rest up. I told her that on the phone."

"She probably thinks you can't manage without her," said Åsa with a smile.

"And we can't, either," said Sandén. "That woman has an intellectual capacity like the rest of us combined. Do you realize that?"

He directed himself to all the colleagues around the table and meant the question seriously. Sandén wanted an answer.

Sjöberg took a gulp of his beer. Hamad and Westman exchanged glances.

"I'm starting to think it really is that way," said Hamad.

"Me too," said Petra. "It took a little time for me to realize, but yes, Walleye is something special."

"I've been unjust to her," said Sjöberg. "We've been unjust, all of us. Except you, Jens. The question is simply why. I can't really put it in words."

"She's different somehow," said Westman. "She dresses strange, talks strange, and she's a little silly."

"That sounds like a middle school rationale," Åsa said seriously.

"She talks strange because she hasn't lived in Sweden for thirty years," said Sandén. "She has no dialect and mixes a kind of slightly old-fashioned Swedish with modern, youthful expressions. Whether she dresses strange I'm not the right person to judge. I think Cod dresses strange. But we like him anyway."

And there sat Cod with his hair in a ponytail, an earring, tattoos on his upper arms, T-shirt with Rolling Stones tongue, and a denim vest with something printed on the back. Everyone laughed at him, but he took it with equanimity.

"It's my style," he answered with a wry smile. "Walleye's style is not to have any style."

"So help her with that," Sonja suggested. "Petra, can't you do a little clothes shopping with her and help her with her hairstyle?"

"Why?" said Sandén, casting an irritated glance at his wife. "Isn't Walleye good enough as she is? Do we have to 'restyle' her so she'll have a place in the group? Talk about middle school."

Åsa applauded.

"Well roared, Jens."

"Walleye patrolled for a few years before she moved to Switzerland," Sandén continued. "So she moves back after being a housewife for thirty years, completely updated on everything theoretical in police work and with a PhD in law besides. And you doubt that she has anything to offer because she has an 'ugly' hairstyle? Criminy! You all deserve a spanking. Cheers!"

"I agree completely," said Sjöberg. "We'll shape up. Cheers to Jens, who has given us a much needed lecture. And who saved the lives of two police officers in three days besides!"

After a unanimous "cheers" they all drank, and when they set their glasses down on the table there was spontaneous applause.

—〜〜—

It had been a tough week, with more than usual physical and mental challenges. When the sun had long disappeared in the pink veils of clouds beyond the spruce tops down into the valley, the kids had collapsed, and fleece blankets put on, the tension finally relaxed.

Hamad's jaw muscles were sore from all the laughing. When he summarized the evening, he observed that there had been something slightly desperate about the whole arrangement. They had eaten a little too fast, drank a little too much, settled a few too many topics of conversation in too short a time, laughed a little too loudly and a little too often. If that was possible.

With the alcohol and twilight, relief had slipped up on them, relief that they were all alive, that everything had gone well. Relief that the case appeared to be solved. But above all, he believed, it was relief that they had each other.

Sonja, Åsa, and Jenny had almost completely been left out of the conversation. It wasn't usually like that, not at all. But this time it was different. They had been a hairbreadth from catastrophe and only had eyes and ears for each other. And even Wallin was included in this common embrace. To the highest degree. Without her they wouldn't have been here today. It had been a lovely evening in all respects, he loved these people, loved his job, loved life.

But that still wasn't enough for Hamad. He wanted more. Of what, he didn't know. More of everything. More of life, more of the present.

So he did what he always did when he felt this way, when he hungered for something but didn't know what it was. He did the opposite instead. Toned down what was wonderful, closed off the supply taps.

When no one was looking, he sneaked off down to the lake shore to cool off. Walked on the worn-down paths through the pine forest, filled his nostrils with dew damp August air. Let the beam of the flashlight play among the tree trunks and stumbled on a root that crept across the path. Listened to the silence and felt very small, very insignificant. Which was exactly what he needed. Dampen the interest in himself, in his own well-being. Establish a feeling in his body that everything was fine; he had everything, lacked nothing. Acknowledge himself as a small part of everything here, of nature, humanity, the universe. Accept that everything did not revolve around him.

He threw off his clothes and the blanket on the beach, and waded out into the lake until the water reached his navel.

Then he lowered his body and took in the cold with a deep inhalation. The moon was now completely gone. It was pitch-black, except for the lights from some windows on the other side of the lake and the stars in the sky. It was just him, the water, and the darkness. In a wonderful union with no demands.

He lay on his back in the water and let out his arms. Let his ears be stopped up by the water, and the forces from below hold him up. Without moving he floated around under the stars with a smile on his lips and was satisfied with himself and his smallness. When suddenly he felt a movement in the water.

He was not scared, but curiosity caused him to let his lower body sink down under the surface until his feet reached bottom.

He stood up, the water reached to his chin now. Listened, peered, heard the sound of a body moving in the water, someone swimming in his direction. Thought he could see a silhouette, head, shoulders, movement. Closer and closer, no words, only the sound of rippling water, hands that pushed aside counteracting forces.

He did not move, just stood there and without a word met the life as it swam into his embrace. When its arms coiled around his naked body, its hands clasped behind his neck and its legs locked themselves around him. This was all and much more than he had ever dared dream of.

Then he carried her onto the shore and put her down at the edge of the water. Together they spread the blanket on the sand and made love under the stars again. And again.

At five-thirty they crept into their beds up in the guesthouse. Just so Andersson would not get the idea that no one had slept in them.

MONDAY AFTERNOON

O dd Andersson literally sat twiddling his thumbs at the desk. On Sunday evening he had left Mercury with his mother, Molly, a shift that always left a large vacuum behind. But the weekend had been fantastic, his son loved playing with the Sjöberg children, and both of them had been tired but happy when they came back to Stockholm.

Today, however, it felt different. The weekend's euphoria had settled down, replaced by something more like a hangover. Thursday's drama, the seriousness of the situation, had crept closer in, become more real here in the aftermath than in the heat of battle.

He devoted the morning to paperwork. It was his weakest area, but his drawings helped both him and the others sort out the events in Forssjö and put them into words. Then he caught up on other reporting, but when that was done he still did not feel satisfied. In normal cases it was a great relief to be done with the burdensome process of writing, but not today.

He woke up that morning with a song in his head; he often did. Then he might sit on the edge of the bed with his guitar plucking out chords, and then tear into the song in his own way. Like morning exercise. This usually put him in a good mood. But this morning he hadn't touched the guitar; the song only made him depressed. Why, he didn't know, he hadn't heard it in ages and didn't even remember the words. But it wouldn't leave him.

Jeff Lynne spoke to him from his subconscious, and Andersson was not sure he wanted to know what he had to say to the notes of the melancholy melody. At last he put on his earphones anyway and searched for Electric Light Orchestra's "Latitude 88 North" on his iPod.

He felt the hairs rising on his arms as he listened.

———

Sandén was bored. It was just an ordinary Monday back in reality again, with paperwork and other less essential tasks. He felt emptied of energy, gutted of constructive thoughts. Though Andersson had as usual made existence easier. This time with his drawings of the gunfire in Forssjö, like something right out of *Agent X9*.

Sandén was aware that besides music Cod also amused himself by drawing, but had no idea he was so damn good. Without Andersson's template, the work on the report would have been considerably more demanding, so when he was done with the paper exercise Sandén went over to Andersson's office to express his gratitude and exchange gossip.

Andersson did not notice him when he came in, he was sitting with his back against the desk staring out the window. From his ears two white cords were hanging, so Sandén went up and tapped him lightly on the shoulder.

Andersson started and turned toward him with a serious frown between his eyes.

"You have to listen to this song," he said, pulling out the earphones and handing them over to Sandén. "It's been ringing in my ears since I woke up this morning."

Sandén, who in no way shared Andersson's great interest in music, didn't know what to think, but he did as he was told. And the sound quality was good, so he managed to take in the words besides. Words that spoke of cold days and lost girls. Girls who called out to be found. Words that told him they needed to keep on digging.

"Well, what do you think?" Andersson wanted to know when the music had fallen silent in Sandén's ears.

"I think we ought to have a chat with Sjöberg," Sandén answered with a wry smile. "That there are at least two of us who think that—"

"There is more of this story to be told," Andersson filled in.

—⁓—

Westman had managed to scrape together only a few hours of sleep at most during the night, yet she felt full of energy. Energy that unfortunately she now was forced to channel in a completely undesirable direction. But hopefully it would be that way for a while. If her instincts did not deceive her, if the emotions were as irrepressible from both quarters.

They had spent the night together at her place. And various glances had been exchanged during the day, innocent touching had occurred. In the pantry, when they met in the corridor, on the walk up to Lisa's Café where they had lunch with the others.

It was going to be a challenge. Working professionally side by side and trying to overlook what had happened outside work, what was happening inside their bodies and in their thoughts. They had to remain objective on factual issues, questioning, working as two individuals in the group, not as a couple. And not over-compensating. Such as avoiding talking to each other during a whole workday even though they had a good deal to discuss. Work-related.

Now she tried to see through the pleasing shimmer that had settled over her existence and think constructively about that work. And determined as she compiled her report that all she had devoted herself to during the previous week had been in vain. Completely wasted. Because neither Siem, Wiklund, nor Jenner were the slightest bit involved in the murder of Sven-Gunnar Erlandsson. Because a missing Russian summer child had nothing to do with Simon Tampler and his murder fantasies, nothing to do with her and her colleagues. And consequently, not the nervous Staffan Jenner or the ladies' man Lennart Wiklund.

So frightfully meaningless it would have been if Wallin had perished out there in the Huddinge forests, in search of something that was nothing other than a couple of blurred jottings in the pocket of an unlucky man.

He could barely keep his eyes open. Ever since last Thursday the world had been turned upside down, and his mood had vacillated between high peaks and abysmal depths. And he hardly shut his eyes the whole night. For agreeable reasons.

Hamad hardly knew where to look as he sat blinking over a report that for the most part discussed efforts of zero and no interest. If it really was that simple. Which he had a slightly hard time swallowing. But he was too tired to really be able to think that through.

In any event he managed to complete his reports, partly thanks to Andersson's ingenious comic book perspective on the whole Forssjö drama. Then he remained seated with his gaze directed down toward the Hammarby canal's glistening water, submerged in thoughts that were as far from exchanges of gunfire and internet investigations as one could get.

Hamad was happy. He was completely warm inside and felt how his cheeks were glowing. After all these years, and after all the misunderstandings and other problems, they had finally ended up where they were. In a rush of dammed-up emotions that had been held back for such a long time. The only thing to do was to be grateful and accept it. *Seize the day and enjoy it to the fullest.* And at the same time try to maintain some degree of professionalism. Which required sleep, among other things. Something which he would make sure to get enough of tonight, anyway. Before then he would pluck up his courage and exchange a few words with Petra, just as usual.

He gathered up his things and left the room, walked with pretended goal-oriented steps over to her office in the corridor and knocked somewhat formally on the doorpost before he went in.

She welcomed him with a curious smile. Apparently read him like an open book. He smiled back.

"I think I'll forget about this for today," he said, sinking down in a half-slack position in the visitor's chair. "I have to go home and sleep."

"Oh my, is it that bad," Petra answered. "So how does it feel otherwise?"

He didn't know how he should answer. Should they be formal now, or what did she really mean?

"Are you done with the reporting, are you through reflecting over your wasted week?" Petra continued.

Formal, then. Maybe she was done with this now? Or else she was as uncertain as he was.

"I'm done with the reporting. I'm not through reflecting over our meaningless workweek. I intend to devote myself to that tomorrow, when I hope to be well-rested. I'm not through reflecting over the more meaningful things we were occupied with at the end of the week, either. But you're welcome to help me with that. In Årsta. Under the assumption that lights are out before ten."

This fell on good soil. She gave him an insinuating smile and stretched her foot out under the desk so that it lightly touched his. It hit him in the gut, almost hurt.

They were in the first phase of love, a state of illness.

Lightning quick she withdrew her foot again when Sjö-berg came clumping into the office without warning. Hamad remained sitting in the same position, without turning his face toward him.

Sjöberg looked tired too, and a little worried.

"We need to talk a little, all of us," he said. "Can you come into my office for a moment?"

"I won't be able to be there," said Wallin. "I have a checkup at the hospital and just have to finish one little thing before I leave. Can we discuss it tomorrow?"

"Sure," said Sjöberg. "No problem. We're so grateful you're here at all."

He quietly left her office and left her in peace. For now the storm clouds were gathering in earnest. Suddenly she found something.

She had quickly thrown together the report that morning and then turned off the computer, shut the door, and leaned back in the chair with her hands clasped behind her neck to think through everything. And decided that the investigation was not up to standards. That there were too many loose threads. In the excitement during and after the arrest of Simon Tampler, they had left too much to chance.

But no damage done, it was never too late to do it right. Tampler was the murderer, there was no doubt about that. But all the rest? There were several question marks that needed to be straightened out.

Why had someone placed a collection of playing cards in Erlandsson's pocket? For this person could not reasonably be Erlandssom himself, they lacked fingerprints. And the murderer, Tampler, categorically denied it. Could anyone else have slipped them into the pocket? In that case, who and why? Or perhaps our friend Tampler was lying? Why in the world would he do that—confess to a murder, but deny that he had put four playing cards in the victim's pocket? Dead man's hand besides.

But perhaps her thinking was following too narrow a train of thought. *Those cards must fulfill a function.*

For that reason she sat down at the computer again and tried to expand her view, and now it started to come loose. While she scrolled down the screen and browsed through the pages of hits, suddenly something completely different than Wild Bill Hickok's fatal poker hand showed up. Something apparently as far from violent, sudden death as could be imagined. Namely a type of coral.

"Dead man's hand, finger coral, *Alcyonium digitatum*, species in the subclass eight-legged coral animals. Dead man's hand forms long, pale, branching colonies that may resemble a swollen human hand. The species is common on rocky seabeds from Bohuslän to Halland." All according to the Web version of the Swedish National Encyclopedia.

She continued searching on the internet, eager to find out as much as possible about this colony of small coral animals, but without finding anything of great interest. Until she started searching for "Alcyonium digitatum." And suddenly was back on Flashback again.

"Before we begin, I want Petra and Jamal to listen to this song too," said Sjöberg. "A bit unorthodox perhaps, but still. Take it seriously and see it as pure inspiration before ongoing work."

Westman and Hamad exchanged surprised glances as Andersson gave them each a set of earphones, but they listened. At first with a smile on their lips, but then with greater seriousness. Sjöberg observed Hamad visibly swallow. Which tallied with other observations he had made during recent days, that Hamad was not really in balance after the gunfire. But the song's message certainly sat like a lump in Sjöberg's throat too. In all of them, he assumed.

"Cod," said Sjöberg. "Where do we go from here?"

"We search for the runaway, Rebecka Magnusson," Andersson answered with a determination in his voice that was unlike him. "And we'll search until we find her."

"Petra?"

"We find out what happened to Larissa Sotnikova," Westman answered.

"And Dewi Kusamasari," Sjöberg added. "We have three missing girls. It's clear we have to find them."

"All these girls should be considered particularly vulnerable," Sandén pointed out. "One is disabled, one is a runaway, Lara, is a Russian orphan, very young at the time of the kidnapping and no language skills to speak of."

"We also have a number of other unanswered questions," Hamad started. "Who was the younger girl who borrowed Lara's bicycle? The playing cards—why did they lack fingerprints? Who put them in Erlandsson's pocket, and why?"

"And the coordinates," said Sandén. "What was that scrap of paper doing in the pocket, and were they coordinates at all? You almost start to think we should pick up on that position again, now that ELO has spoken from Cod's spiritual hiding place."

Everyone in the room smiled in agreement. But no one laughed. Now it was in earnest.

Then suddenly Wallin showed up in the doorway.

"Sorry, I have to leave right away," she said excitedly. "But I have important news. Something for those so inclined to bite into."

Everyone stared at her with tense expectation. None of them doubted any more that it was important if Wallin said it was. Sjöberg smiled to himself.

"Dead man's hand is a so-called finger coral, a colony of small coral animals. In Latin they're called *Alcyonium digitatum*. *Alcyonium digitatum* is also the name of a user on Flashback. A user who was only registered on the twenty-second of June and has a single entry recorded. A question concerning how large the margin of error is on a handheld GPS of a certain brand."

Sandén whistled.

"All who answered the question were in agreement that it could be a matter of a radius of fifty to sixty meters. Which was exactly what Jens and I assumed. This entry is dated the twenty-fifth of June. It takes three days from when you are registered as a user until the account is activated. This I interpret as that Alcyonium digitatum's purpose in registering on Flashback secondhand was to get an answer to this very question."

"Secondhand?" Hamad asked doubtfully.

"Yes. Listen, and you'll hear. Another interesting observation is that The Saint's last entry on his own thread, 'I want to kill someone. I'm going to kill someone,' is dated the twenty-fifth of June. The debate on the thread is still going on, but The Saint himself had already withdrawn by then. Why? I'm guessing he got a bite."

Everyone was listening attentively to what Wallin had to tell.

"Someone made contact with him via PM, that is, sent him a personal message. You can only do this if you're registered on Flashback, so not if you're just hanging out there without being a member, because then you don't have access to that function. I believe this was Alcyonium digitatum's primary purpose with the membership registration. To make contact with the serious-minded Saint."

"A contract murder, that is?" said Sjöberg.

"Exactly. And that's also why Tampler admits the murder, but not the playing cards and the coordinates. He has presumably been paid to keep quiet about that. He's prepared to take his punishment for the murder, but wants the money to be there when he gets out again."

"But," said Hamad, scratching his head, "why does the instigator give the killer the task of putting the playing cards and the coordinates in the victim's pocket, if it doesn't then come out that this has to do with the murder?"

"It wasn't the idea that Tampler should go to prison for murder. Then we would have unraveled the coordinates anyway, and by and by perhaps found what the instigator is after."

"And the cards, dead man's hand?" asked Westman.

"For one thing, it's evidently a signature. But I think it's a lead besides to what all of this is really about. Namely Larissa Sotnikova.

"The murder of Erlandsson took place early in the morning of August second. Wild Bill Hickok was shot on August second. Larissa Sotnikova disappeared on August second. It was important that we notice that August second is an important date."

"But who ordered it?" Sjöberg asked thoughtfully, and directed mainly to himself.

"That remains to be seen," Wallin answered with a cryptic smile.

"So now the next step is to pump Tampler, go through his computer, and follow the money," Sjöberg stated, and a concurring murmur was heard from the others.

"Damn, now I'll be late!" Wallin exclaimed with a quick glance at her watch. "See you tomorrow!"

And then she disappeared from the room, leaving behind the odor of a rather sickly-sweet perfume.

"You didn't play the song for Walleye, did you?" Sandén asked.

"No, I didn't actually," Andersson answered. "She got her inspiration from somewhere else. Strange person!"

Now Ida was gone too, even if no farther than Uppsala, to be with her siblings. But in only a few weeks she would go off on her long journey to the other side of the globe. Adrianti was left alone in the big house. Alone with the sorrow, alone with the memories of the life that definitely was now over. All the children had more or less moved away, and Svempa was dead.

Murdered. By a crazy drug addict who did it for the fun of it. The funeral would not take place for three weeks, this sort of thing took time in Sweden. Until then she had to maintain the facade that everything was normal. Keep the house clean and tidy, bake for the funeral reception. Do laundry. The little there was now to launder, when everyone was gone. But then? What would happen then?

She had nothing. No job, no knowledge about anything other than running the household. And no money, it appeared. When she contacted the insurance companies, she got the impression that everything belonged to the children. They had managed that poorly, she and Svempa. Neither of them of course had counted on the fact that he would die so soon. But that was the small problem. She was used to living in straitened circumstances from her previous life, so she would probably survive this too. Purely physically.

The bigger problem was she longed so incredibly for Dewi, her little nestling, her own little angel. *Angel*—that's what the name meant back home, in Indonesia. And when she thought about Dewi, all the anxiety settled like an aching clump in her belly. Because Dewi could not be gone for all time, she could not be dead.

Why hadn't Adrianti stuck to her guns long ago and raised a fuss when Dewi never came home? Swedish young people travel, but they stay in touch, write long letters, call home occasionally. And they can be gone for a year in the worst case, never for four. She shouldn't have listened to Svempa, not let herself be convinced by his carefree view of the matter. She ought to have gone to the police, made sure a missing persons report was sent out.

The silence was suffocating. She had to have people around her, voices. Someone to talk with and cry her heart out with. That was why at last she decided to breach their silent agreement and go see Staffan. Despite everything. But was stopped at the door by that policeman, Sjöberg.

He was extremely sympathetic, a good listener too. It felt good to talk with him, although he held her accountable for what happened with Staffan. And opened old wounds. Got her to talk about Dewi's crushed foot, pumped her for facts about the Roskilde festival, and went over Dewi's journey, Dewi's brief, vacuous messages. But he understood. He grasped how it must feel, grasped how much she missed her daughter and realized that perhaps there was reason to worry. For real. He even made a promise that he would find out where Dewi was. And he seemed believable when he said it.

But that was last Wednesday. Now almost a whole week had passed and nothing had happened, she had heard nothing about how the search for Dewi was going. Adrianti began to feel desperate. She was climbing the walls in this amazingly beautiful, well-appointed prison. For that reason she plucked up her courage once again, cast a final resigned glance at the quickly aging face in the mirror, and locked the door on what for the past thirteen years she had called her home. She had to speak with Staffan.

―᳝᳝᳝᳐―

Sjöberg had put his colleagues in the finance division to work on investigating Simon Tampler's monetary activities, especially with respect to deposits and withdrawals of five- and six-figure amounts. If it was as it seemed, that the kid had been hired to take the life of Sven-Gunnar Erlandsson, the money ought to be seen somewhere. And he had clearly stated that 100,000 kronor was what he required to carry out a murder.

Now Sjöberg really should have been in an interrogation with Tampler, in the presence of legal counsel, but Tampler was understandably in poor shape and the medical assessment had been made that the interrogation would have to be postponed for the time being. Sjöberg had a feeling that they would not get much more out of him anyway, especially if it was as Wallin thought, that more money awaited if he kept his mouth shut.

Instead he was now sitting in Andersson's office going through Tampler's computer. Without finding any traces of an email conversation with "Alcyonium digitatum."

"We'll have to put someone who understands computers on this job," Andersson sighed. "The kid has apparently been careful and deleted everything of interest. Besides it wouldn't surprise me if all the communication occurred via temporary email accounts, proxy servers located outside the country, and other things that make it almost impossible to trace."

Sjöberg moaned, he didn't understand enough to even bear to ask.

"Okay, call in a technician," he said.

Andersson did as he was told and just then Sandén entered the room.

"I'm wondering about what Walleye said about dead man's hand and the date, the second of August," he started. "If it really is the case that the one who instigated the murder of Erlandsson wanted to show the police that the murder had to do with the Russian summer child's disappearance—isn't it reasonable to believe that Erlandsson would be responsible for the disappearance?"

Sjöberg nodded.

"Who would have reason to murder him for that?" Sandén asked rhetorically.

"Staffan Jenner, naturally. Who has lost Lara, his wife, and his reputation to boot."

"But then why have the guy murdered? Why not simply go to the police?"

"Revenge? Hatred?" suggested Andersson, who had now finished the call to the tech squad.

"Yes, maybe," said Sjöberg. "But why right now? It's been eight years since it happened."

"Maybe he found something out quite recently. Maybe a witness has shown up?" said Andersson.

"Or else," Sandén continued his line of reasoning, "maybe it's the other way around. *Erlandsson* perhaps quite recently found something out. Held Jenner accountable for the girl's disappear-ance, and was taken out for that reason. And Jenner now directs the suspicions for the disappearance at Erlandsson. In both cases, Staffan Jenner is guilty of serious crimes."

Now Westman also showed up in the room with an eager look in her eye, but she let the ongoing discussion continue without interrupting.

"I see it as more likely that the same person committed both crimes than two different murderers," Sandén continued. "Seems a little far-fetched, I think, that people murder each other left and right in a circle of acquaintances."

"Yes, that's a little too much like *Midsomer Murders*," Andersson observed.

"Besides," said Sandén, "it was actually the case that Lara was Jenner's summer child, that Jenner went with Erlandsson when he visited that trailer encampment where Rebecka Magnusson was last seen, and—"

"That Jenner was along in Roskilde to bring home Dewi," Sjöberg filled in. "And ever since then, she's been missing."

"Exactly."

"May I poke my nose in the conversation?" said Westman. "I was thinking about that girl on the bicycle. The one who according to the witness on Murgrönsvägen was seen with Lara right before the disappearance. Lara, easily recognizable in her orange raincoat, had loaned the bicycle to a smaller girl who is said to have been blonde. A girl they were never able to locate. According to the witness statements from Mälarhöjden athletic field, the whole Erlandsson family had talked with Lara at about twenty to eleven when she made her stop there. Except Ida, who was at home sick. And Dewi, for some reason, who actually was there."

Sjöberg listened with great interest, without really grasping where she was going.

"What if we've gotten everything turned around?" Westman continued. "What if it were so simple that Lara didn't loan out her bicycle to a younger girl, but instead she loaned out her raincoat to a bigger girl? For example, Dewi."

"Brilliant, Petra," said Sandén.

"The little blonde girl on the bicycle was still Lara," Andersson clarified, presumably mostly for his own sake, "and the bigger girl was walking next to her in the raincoat. Who had coal-black hair, but the witness couldn't see that because the hood was on."

"But what was Dewi doing there, wasn't she at the soccer camp?" Sjöberg asked.

"She must have been on her way home for some reason," Petra answered. "But how did it happen that no one noticed that?"

"Perhaps she didn't *want* anyone to notice it," Sjöberg mumbled. "Maybe that was why she borrowed Lara's raincoat, even though it was no longer raining."

"That means that Dewi is our most important witness in the search for whoever kidnapped Larissa Sotnikova," Andersson said.

"Or that something happened," said Sjöberg. "An accident, perhaps."

A new thought suddenly struck him.

"Adrianti Erlandsson said that Dewi was fifteen when she had that accident. When a washing machine fell on her that crushed her foot. She had just gotten a moped as a birthday present. Dewi was born in July of '86, which means she turned fifteen in July of

2001. That is, right before Lara disappeared. But during the day before the disappearance she was at the soccer camp, so Dewi's accident had evidently not happened yet. What if Dewi happened to kill Lara? And right after that had an accident—perhaps she was punishing herself? Dewi was never the same again, fled the country as soon as she finished school."

"We have to find Larissa Sotnikova," Westman stated.

"We have to find Dewi Kusamasari," said Sjöberg.

"Then maybe we'll find Rebecka Magnusson in the process," Andersson hoped.

"Conny, we have to search that forest area in Huddinge again," said Sandén with a voice that was almost commanding. "We may have missed something, maybe we weren't at our best, either of us . . ."

"You're right," Sjöberg said firmly. "We'll go there with dogs tomorrow. Now let's bring in Staffan Jenner and Adrianti Erlandsson."

The phone rang in his pants pocket. Unlisted number.

"I don't know if you remember me," said the voice at the other end, "but I worked at SEB at Kungsträdgården with Sven-Gunnar Erlandsson. Kristina Wintherfalck—we spoke last week."

"Sure," said Sjöberg, "thanks for taking the time."

"I'm calling because I'm a little worried. An exaggerated reaction perhaps, but—"

"It's no problem," said Sjöberg patiently. "Better one time too many than one time too few. What's happened?"

"Well, it's like this. After our last conversation I sent a condolence bouquet to Adrianti—Svempa's wife, that is. Then I called to find out how she was doing. We don't really know each other all that well, only met a time or two a year, at the Christmas dinner and that. But I thought that . . . Well, that perhaps she doesn't have so many . . . and Svempa and I were close. Purely work-related."

"Yes?"

"Adri sounded extremely depressed on the phone. She was frightfully sad about what had happened, didn't know what she should do with her life. And the children are as good as moved out, and one thing and another. So I said a few comforting words, it felt like that was better than nothing. Then I've called her every day at the same time, about four approximately. The last few days she has sounded more and more desperate, and to a greater extent the conversations have revolved around Dewi, her biological daughter. She has evidently been out traveling for a number of years, but Adri recently started to think she was no longer alive."

Sjöberg felt a twinge of discomfort and started to wonder seriously where this conversation was heading.

"I felt so terribly sorry for her, so I considered driving out to Älvsjö and sitting down with her one evening. That hasn't happened yet. However, today I had news that I hoped would cheer her up. But now she's not answering the phone. I've tried to reach her for over an hour, both on her cell phone and her home phone without getting an answer. And she knew I would call, we talked about it yesterday. To be frank, I'm worried that she might harm herself."

"It's good that you called," said Sjöberg. "We'll go there right away. Thanks."

"No problem. Hope she is okay."

"By the way," Sjöberg remembered, "what was the good news you had?"

"That Dewi is alive," Kristina Wintherfalck answered.

Sjöberg felt his heart skip a beat.

"Where did you get this information?" he asked.

"A couple of friends of mine who have been working at SEB in Singapore for many years told me that Dewi lives in the same building as them. They saw her the other day."

"You're joking," said Sjöberg, without believing that for a moment. "Are you sure of that?"

"Dead certain. They knew her from a long time ago."

"Kristina, I want you to text me as soon as possible all the details about where in Singapore this residence is and the exact address, telephone number for your friends, and so on. What are their names?"

"Ingrid and Calle. Håborg."

"And do not utter a word to them about this conversation. And to no one else either. Okay?"

"No problem."

"Many thanks. I'll be in touch."

Sjöberg ended the call and met three curious looks.

"Dewi is alive," he said with a crooked smile.

"The hell she is," Andersson exclaimed. "And living in Singapore?"

"Exactly," Sjöberg nodded. "And you, Cod, are going there with me."

"Sure," said Andersson, "I'm in. When do we leave?"

"As soon as possible. As soon as this evening, if possible. You go and arrange airline tickets and hotel."

"In a jiffy," said Andersson, hurrying out of there with a smile on his lips.

"And us?" Westman asked. "Should we drive out to Älvsjö and cut down Adrianti Erlandsson?"

"Quick as a wink. If she doesn't open, then go in. Without orders for house search, it's an emergency case. Then we'll go in and pick up Staffan Jenner for questioning. Where the hell is Hamad?"

"He . . . must have had an important errand to perform," Westman answered. "Shall I call him in?"

Sjöberg thought a moment before he answered. "Uh, let him be so he's rested tomorrow."

"What do we do with Jenner?" Sandén asked. "Do we enter his place too if he doesn't open?"

"Absolutely not. We have nothing on him so far."

"Suspicion of murder and/or instigation to murder?" Sandén proposed.

"Pure speculation," Sjöberg snorted.

"So what we do tomorrow?" Westman asked.

"Search the area around the position in the Huddinge forest with dogs."

"Cadaver dogs?"

"That too. Sandén will take the lead there. I'm not sending Wallin out in the woods again for a while, so you'll go along instead, Petra. And a bunch of crime technicians, in case you find something. Hamad and Wallin will hold down the fort here."

Andersson came back into the room out of breath.

"The plane leaves in an hour and a half. 6:50 with Lufthansa to Frankfurt. We land in Singapore at 4:55 p.m. tomorrow, 10:55 a.m. Swedish time."

"Good. Then we should each get a taxi and ride home to fetch our toothbrushes. And no jeans now, Cod, this is business."

I see a pretty, friendly, and innocent girl. Like they always are. That's how I've imagined she should be too, just like all girls, all women should be. Every day. But if I were a hunter—which I am sometimes—I would not hunt tame animals. I don't shoot cows peacefully grazing on the meadow. Or a dog with her pups. I don't shoot the hen patiently pecking on the farmyard, and not the sow either. No, when I go hunting I want them wild, unbridled, snorting, furious. I want resistance, otherwise it doesn't do anything for me. They shall flee or fight, run, claw, hit, and howl. I want a roaring lion, or a frothing buffalo. A gazelle, perhaps?

A gazelle she is, the little one. Long, slender, fast legs that move like drumsticks on that bicycle. She turns toward me as I come up behind her, casting a frightened look to the side. Why? She isn't afraid of me, is she? Girls are never afraid of me. To start with.

TUESDAY

T he heat hit them as soon as they stepped on the street, a damp heat in sharp contrast to the cooled air inside the hotel. The temperature was around 30 degrees Celsius, just like during the rest of the year. Never much lower, never much higher. They were more or less right on the equator.

The hotel where they were staying was a small, charming boutique hotel with a pool on the roof, in the middle of the "business district" on a comparatively quiet street, across from the considerably more renowned Raffles. Nothing could have been more agreeable than just sitting down with a Singapore Sling after a long night's journey. But even though the sun had already vanished somewhere behind the skyscrapers, the workday had just started back home.

Åsa was not beside herself with happiness when Sjöberg came rushing into the apartment yesterday afternoon just to grab a few shirts, some underwear, and his passport. It was her first workday after a long, magnificent summer vacation. The step from the summer paradise in Bergslagen to a full workweek as a high school teacher was perhaps a little too big, Sjöberg agreed with that. But that was the way it was, and Åsa bit the bullet. Plus Singapore was a shopping paradise, so she and the children would all probably get something out of it.

Right next to the hotel was a cheap Chinese restaurant, with simple tables and chairs out on the street. They sat there awhile and soaked up the atmosphere with a beer and a bowl of heavenly noodles, not the least bit reminiscent of anything you could order at a Chinese restaurant at home.

Sjöberg studied the map he got at the reception desk and determined—which the concierge had already told him—that a taxi was probably the most suitable mode of transportation for freshly showered European tourists. It was cheap besides, by Swedish standards.

Andersson had his thoughts concerning whether they were now eating breakfast, lunch, or dinner, and jointly they decided to consider it lunch for the time being. Whether there would be any question of dinner, the future would reveal. They both felt reasonably alert after managing to scrape together almost eight hours of sleep during the flight. Presumably they would be able to force down another meal without any problem before it was time to go to bed.

When mealtime was concluded, they walked along Seah Street at a leisurely pace—in a fruitless attempt to keep their shirts dry—to the heavily trafficked North Bridge Road.

After successfully defending themselves in a tough exchange of words with several sinewy cyclists, who wanted them to ride a rickshaw, they were finally able to squeeze into an ordinary taxi.

The drive went to a less central area that was still in the city itself. Just as much as the city center, this part of the city also consisted of skyscrapers, with low white colonial buildings scattered among all the modern ones, and even an occasional small green area. Singaporeans seemed to treasure their parks.

Balmoral Crescent was a complex of elegant twenty-seven-story buildings, framed by tasteful flowerbeds, beautiful stone paving, and small rippling waterfalls. The inner courtyard was a small park with lawns, bushes, and pruned trees, swimming pools and tennis courts, groupings of chairs, loungers, and parasols—solely for those fotunate enough to live here.

Sjöberg and Andersson took the elevator up to the twelfth floor where they were received by Ingrid Håborg, a woman in her fifties with light-red curly hair, a youthful body that seemed made to hang fashionable clothes on, and a natural suntan granted only to those who spent a long time in the tropics. A few hours earlier she had been warned they would be coming, without being told why. She asked with some worry in her eyes whether she could offer them anything, but they declined politely and remained standing in the hall.

"It was nice of you to see us," said Sjöberg with a disarming smile. "And you don't need to be worried, nothing has happened. We're not here for your sake whatsoever."

She looked with some doubt from the one to the other, but when Sjöberg explained his errand, she relaxed.

"We've received information that Dewi Kusamasari is living here in the vicinity. What can you tell us about her?"

"Oh, I haven't talked with her in years. I worked with her step-father here in Singapore, at the time when he met her mother. Back then we socialized a good deal, wonderful kid. I . . . I heard about Svempa, a terrible story . . ."

"So you haven't seen her for thirteen years?"

"Well, Calle and I visited them at their house in Älvsjö when we were in Sweden . . . five or six years ago. Dewi was in high school then."

"And now you're neighbors—for how long?"

"I don't really know," Ingrid Håborg said. "For several years, anyway."

"But you haven't spoken with her?"

"The thing is, she's a bit reclusive. We call her Greta Garbo, a little jokingly. She always has a big sunhat on when she goes out, and big dark sunglasses. We thought she was Korean or Japanese. Until I saw her in the pool one day. Without either hat or sunglasses."

"But you didn't talk with her?"

"No, I was on the balcony when I caught sight of Dewi. I didn't want to stand there shouting. I thought I would talk with her next time we saw her."

"Where does she live, do you know that?"

"On the top floor. I was thinking about going to see her, actually, but . . ."

"But?" said Sjöberg encouragingly.

Ingrid Håborg shifted foot.

"Well, we've run into her many times and she hasn't said anything. So apparently she doesn't remember us. Then I guess it seems a little forward to go to her door. And it's always a little awkward to say hello to someone when you're not recognized . . ."

"Do you know anything more about her?" asked Andersson. "Does she work? Is she living with anyone?"

Ingrid Håborg threw out her arms and shook her head.

"We don't know anything about her, that's what's so peculiar. It says Yuan on the mailbox, so it's possible she's married. But I haven't seen any man. And I work during the day, so I have no idea what kind of hours she keeps."

"But you're absolutely sure it's her?" Sjöberg asked to be on the safe side.

"Yes, good Lord, you see that by the foot if nothing else. It looks . . . a little different."

It was drizzling rain as they forced their way ahead through the forest, but Sandén had a whole drove of people ahead of him, so in any event he avoided doing the heavy work. He was walking along what almost seemed to be a path, on the heels of Hansson and two of her men from the tech squad, Westman, four uniformed constables, and a K-9 patrol.

When they passed the rock where he and Wallin sat a while and rested, he felt a shiver go through his body. He ought to have reacted immediately—in retrospect it was obvious that she had been feeling lousy even then. Pale and feeble, uninspired and without any trace of that gleam in her eye that normally never left her. Considering how much blood she lost, it was a marvel she could even stand up. But what surprised him most was his own determination and stamina. He did not recognize himself in that way of taking hold of the situation, moving mountains when it was required. Hoped he would never have reason to do so again either.

When they arrived at the point from which Wallin proceeded when she drew her imaginary circle, a tense mood settled on all involved. So now here they were. With mixed emotions about what they would really accomplish. Apart from the dogs, who pulled on their leashes. They wanted results.

It was thundering somewhere in the distance. It was a quiet summer rain; rain gear was actually quite unnecessary, but it protected against the whiplash of the branches. And against ticks in the best case. But it was like a sauna inside the rainsuit.

"This is the indicated position," said Sandén. "From what I've been told, the margin of error may be about fifty or sixty meters. So we measure up a circular area with a diameter of one hundred and twenty and search inside that. If we don't find anything, we'll expand the area. I have no idea what we're looking for really, or even if we're at the right place. It might be drugs, weapons, hiding places, or dead bodies. But seek and ye shall find. In the best case. Or the worst. Now let's go."

They took off in their various directions, paced out their sixty meters, with the dogs evenly dispersed across the sectors of the circle. Sandén had a metal detector. He started at the outer edge of the circle and worked his way in, sweeping meticulously across the ground to right and left before taking another step in the direction of the middle of the circle. Studied everything he passed energetically.

Could someone have dug here? He crawled under tree trunks, lifted fallen branches, pushed aside smaller stones, and plowed his way ahead through dense thickets. Nothing. And then the same thing out again, with a few degrees shift in direction. The instrument did not let out a peep.

When on his second turn he had arrived almost halfway to the center of the circle and was working only twenty meters or so from one of the K-9 handlers, the metal detector suddenly registered something. The dog became eager, tearing and pulling on the leash.

"Yes, come on now, Biscuit, is there something over there? Shall we go and look? Keep an eye out," said the K-9 handler encouragingly to the springer spaniel, letting himself be pulled over to Sandén, who was scraping at the moss with his foot.

The dog was running in half-circles around Sandén, barking and whipping his tail.

"There's something here, is there?" Sandén asked stupidly. "Does he react like that to metals?"

"Nope," the K-9 handler answered. "He's indicating a corpse."

—⁓—

I myself am more like an elephant. Calm, secure, loyal, responsible. I can go for months, years, and not devote myself to anything other than the hunt for food and the care of my dear ones. And the females I surround myself with are capable creatures. I'm careful when I make my choices. They know what I require of them and they do their part, it's part of the deal so to speak. It's good. A little boring, but good.

Then comes the mating season. Then something happens in my body, in my head. That frenzy comes over me, desperation that it can never be the way I want it to be. Then I have to have something that's not offered. So I see to it that I get it. I have planned for a long time, know exactly which one is the weakest animal in the flock, the easiest to bring down. She is the one who is the most afraid, who screams the loudest with terror painted on her face. She's the one I want.

And there she sat on the bicycle and looked at me with her big, frightened eyes. She had left the flock, cycling around completely unprotected from everything and everyone. And why should she say no? You can trust me. *Because I radiate security. Love.*

So I set her bike in the trunk and put the girl child in the front seat. She only thought that was nice.

"I'm going to show you a place where it's a lot more fun to bicycle," I said. "There aren't any cars, no hazards. But it will be an exciting adventure."

I drove her over to the forest where I played as a child, parked a good distance from the houses, and then we followed the power line road a little into the forest, and after that we cleared the way ourselves. I carried the bicycle and she ran ahead of me jabbering.

Until we were almost there. Out of view of the surrounding world's distrustful eyes.

I didn't want her like that any longer, now I wanted to hunt. It was simple, just hitting. I struck her in the face, she was sad at first and cried. I roared and struck harder, held onto her so she would claw herself loose, howl and scream. Then I let her run a little. She was so little, I caught up with her in no time at all. But I let her run in the belief that there was a possibility that she would succeed in getting away. She fell down, scraped her knees, tore her clothes, but that was how I wanted her, like a wild animal.

At last she couldn't bear it any longer, gave up. Simply lay there crying on the ground, inconsolable. Her whole being begged me to take her, do what I wanted with her.

So I did.

She asked for it, the little whore.

I threw her over my shoulder and carried her to the earth cellar. She no longer made any resistance, let herself be thrown into the darkness and the cold. Then I kept her there, to return to when the spirit moved me.

In my own treasure chamber.

They thanked Ingrid Håborg for the help and took the elevator all the way to the top floor, the twenty-seventh.

"Is this a skyscraper?" Andersson asked in his knowing way. "Or just a regular high-rise? Twenty-seven stories is a real joke in Singapore."

They rang the doorbell, but not a sound was heard from inside. It was a gamble, they were well aware of that. Nothing indicated she should be at home. It was seven thirty, she could hardly have gone to bed. But she might work nights, or she might be out partying at one of the piers—like all the other Westerners, according to the taxi driver. It might also be the case that she was watching them through the peephole and decided not to let them in. The young woman seemed rather light-averse, if they could believe Ingrid Håborg.

But suddenly a peeping noise was heard from within, whatever that might mean. Several peeps and then a rustling like from a chain. And then the door opened.

"Hi, Dewi," said Sjöberg with a friendly smile. "My name is Conny Sjöberg, and I come from the Hammarby police in Stockholm."

A pair of alert, dark-brown eyes met him with curiosity. She glanced at the police identification in his hand and then looked at Andersson. Just as he opened his mouth to introduce himself, she anticipated him.

"And you must be Odd Andersson, from *Idol 2008*."

Andersson lost his train of thought and looked quite foolish as he stood with mouth half-open without getting a sound out.

"So you follow the Swedish news from the other side of the globe?" Sjöberg said, amused.

"Only the most important news," Dewi replied, now with a broad smile on her face. "TV4 Play, you know. Come in."

Then she took a step to the side and let them in with a welcoming gesture. In one hand she had a crutch she was leaning on.

Sjöberg did not dare lower his gaze.

"Should we take off our shoes?" Andersson asked with a doubtful look in Sjöberg's direction.

"Make yourselves at home," Dewi answered, closing the door behind them, applying the double security chains, and entering a six-digit code on a panel in the wall. Then she limped off into the apartment, which was very reminiscent of the one they had just visited.

"Do you feel nervous?" Sjöberg ventured to ask.

"Are you referring to all the locks?" Dewi replied, sounding anything but nervous. "Just an old habit."

They followed her up to a railing, and before and below them an amazing room—or rather a hall—opened up, with an approximately seven-meter-high ceiling. The room was taken up by an elegant lounge suite that looked particularly comfortable, with tasteful Indonesian art hanging behind it and on the facing wall was enthroned a sixty-inch flat-screen TV. Straight ahead, seen from where they were standing, sliding glass doors opened out onto a large balcony with resplendent plants, rattan furniture, and a breathtaking view.

"Shall we sit down?" Dewi suggested.

"That sounds like a good idea," Sjöberg said, who had a strange feeling they'd been expected.

She led them past a modern kitchen that Sjöberg estimated cost a small fortune, through a dining room with stylish furniture in scaled-down Indonesian fashion, and down a stairway of the same parquet as the other floors on the top floor.

"Outside or inside?"

"Outside seems quite fantastic," said Sjöberg. "What a view."

"What may I offer you? Tea? Or perhaps a glass of wine?"

"Mineral water is fine," Sjöberg replied. "We're here on official duty."

"Oh, that sound serious," said Dewi with an attractive little laugh.

All of her was attractive. With a gentle, lovely voice, shoulder-length, glistening black hair, and lively, intelligent eyes.

They followed her out to the balcony. The large candles on the table were already lit, so Sjöberg drew the conclusion that she must have been here when they rang the doorbell. From a refrigerator on the balcony she took out a bottle of carbonated water for each of them, three chilled glasses, and a bowl of ice, before she sank down on an armchair across from them with a radiant smile on her lips.

"Do you live alone here?" Andersson asked.

Dewi nodded in response.

"You must have plenty of money."

"I can't complain," she admitted.

"How do you support yourself?"

"Is this an interrogation, or what's this really all about?" Dewi asked, still smiling.

"Well, we'll probably have to call it an interview," Sjöberg started. "How do you support yourself?"

"Poker," Dewi Kusamasari replied. "I play internet poker."

—₩—

The wind had picked up. While the K-9 handlers continued to search for additional signs from their well-trained animals, the other police officers were digging. It was not an uncomplicated job. The ground was hard, and the roots of trees and bushes had pressed their way through the layers of earth they had to get past. It must have been years since anyone had last dug here.

Hopefully at least eight years ago, thought Westman. But whoever had done it had done a solid job.

After they had dug one and a half meters into the ground, a bicycle handlebar appeared. This did not bode well. Her stomach turned, but the only thing to do was continue.

In ominous silence, nine police officers dug further down into the underworld until the bicycle was up. It was a red cycle in a size that appeared to fit an eleven-year-old. And the helmet was there too.

Carefully they continued to do what had to be done. A few of them dug deeper, while the others worked on the side to expand the hole. The rain became heavier and the sky above the treetop suddenly lit up with lightning. Westman counted to eight before she heard the thunder rumble. Hansson ordered an investigation tent set up over the area where they were digging.

Ten minutes later it was flashing all around them. The rain pattered against the tent, making an almost deafening noise for those working inside. But no one complained, they worked doggedly on with small, sensitive spadefuls to be able to stop in mid-motion at any moment if anyone struck something fragile. *When* someone struck something fragile.

And then they did, after another few minutes. About half a meter from the bicycle, at approximately the same depth.

He wasn't able to dig deeper than that, thought Westman. He was digging a wider grave instead. It was simpler than standing down in the hole and digging.

But when Hansson had dug out a good portion of the body with her bare hands, and brushed away the final remnants of earth from what was left of the face of the dead person, it was clear to them that this could not be Larissa Sotnikova. It was a woman. Judging by the size of the skeleton and what was left of her clothing it was possibly a very young woman, but not a slender eleven-year-old.

Rebecka Magnusson, Westman thought dejectedly.

But Lara must be somewhere too. So they continued to dig. Right below where the bicycle had been, the remains of another body were soon revealed. This time it was definitely a small girl. It sounded as if the lightning were striking somewhere right in the vicinity.

And now all the dogs started barking a little farther away.

More bodies, thought Westman. "We're in a fucking graveyard," she said to Sandén.

She was an amazing plaything. Wonderful little Lara. But good times never last. I didn't realize how little they can take, such little ones. I went there with food for her, made sure she didn't get cold. She was lying softly on the mattress and I emptied the bucket when I visited. When I hit her, I did it with great care. I even let her out a few times, but then she wasn't able to run any longer, was hardly able to stand up.

It was then I realized it was time to start digging. When that day came, it was best to be prepared. And it came quicker than you might have guessed. For two weeks I was able to have her, my little gazelle. Then the fun was over.

Until then I enjoyed myself to the fullest. As often as I had the opportunity I made my way out there, to my treasure chamber. The blood rushed in my veins when I lifted away the pile of twigs, unlocked the padlock, and climbed down to where she was lying, pressed against the wall with eyes wide open. In the beginning she screamed, resisted, but the more time passed, the more I had to torment her to get her to protest.

The last days I could hardly see any life in her at all. She didn't fight, didn't even open her eyes. For that reason it was just as well what happened. I thought she still had that wild animal left inside her, pretended she was struggling against me. I shook her, threw her down on the mattress, and took what I wanted.

When I was finished, she was no longer breathing.

The grave was ready to receive her and I felt empty inside. A little melancholy.

Hamad was rested. True, Petra had chased him back into service the previous afternoon—despite Sjöberg's apparently explicit orders—but the whole thing was soon cleared up. After knocking on Jenner's door at Blåklintsvägen in Herrängen, he and Petra went home together to his apartment in Årsta, devoted a few hours to each other, and slept. And then devoted a couple of hours to each other again. But he got enough sleep. Enough energy for a whole regiment.

Adrianti Erlandsson and Staffan Jenner were both adults, and neither of them had any specific threats or suspicions of crime directed at them. For that reason they had every right to be where they wanted, when they wanted. And personally he had a hard time believing that Adrianti would take her life before they got to the bottom of what had happened with Dewi.

Quite different matters occupied Hamad's thoughts. He was sitting with Sven-Gunnar Erlandsson's iPhone in hand, going entry by entry through the entire contact list. Somewhere here he would find what he had been looking for the past year and a half, he was convinced of that. He would build his case on that.

He browsed down among the contacts and compared with the notes he made the previous week, when he looked over Erlandsson's outgoing and incoming calls. Here were internal SEB numbers, cell phone and home numbers for coworkers, soccer parents, soccer girls, family members. Often the entries included telephone numbers, street addresses, and email addresses. Staffan Jenner was there of course, Lennart Wiklund and Jan Siem likewise. He also found contact information for workmen, piano tuner, dentist, car repair shop, and others that now and then needed to be engaged. All with names, numbers, email address, and possibly also a street address.

Except . . . "The Contractor"? Who in the hell was the contractor who had neither name nor address? Or the "Schoolmaster"? "IT Wizard"? And who was the "Municipal Commissioner"?

Hamad picked up the phone and called his contact at Telia, who gave him the information that the number for the "Contractor" number belonged to a prepaid card account. He had not expected anything else. The "Schoolmaster" and "IT Wizard" also called from untraceable prepaid cards. *Obviously.*

And then there was the "Municipal Commissioner." His name was Lars Karlsson and resided in Huddinge. And was obviously a complete idiot, if it was as Hamad suspected. It was soon confirmed that sure enough he was as named, a municipal commissioner. Unfortunately, he also proved to be chairman of the school board.

When a few minutes later he had logged into the suspect registry, he could only establish that the municipal commissioner was more idiotic than Hamad ever could have wished for. He was namely suspected on good grounds for attempted sex with a minor. Along with a middle school teacher—could that be the "Schoolmaster," perhaps? Fifteen hundred kronor was what the municipal commissioner had been prepared to pay so that his political career wouldn't be only a memory, so that his family and friends wouldn't turn their backs on him.

"A forest cemetery," Sandén muttered as he and Westman slipped out of the tent, out into the pouring rain to find the dog that was barking.

It was twilight out there, raining like hell, but the thunder seemed to have gone past.

"It's the Flood," said Westman. "Letting loose on the wrong people."

It sounded like several dogs were barking now, but further away, outside the search area. They followed the angry sound, fought their way through the dense vegetation, climbed over a fallen tree, crawled under another. When it was possible, they jogged between the trees, stumbling in blueberry bushes. Sometimes they had to take detours past large boulders cast out by primeval forces.

What was the K-9 patrol doing so far away? Had they let the dogs loose?

At last, they caught sight of them. They were in an opening, a forest glade where the trees had drawn back. They were all standing in a circle, gathered around something on the ground. The dogs had calmed down now and were prowling around expectantly with ears perked up, watching one of the handlers who was crouching, working with something. In his hand he had a tool of some kind, and as Westman and Sandén came closer they saw that he was trying to cut a thick chain with a bolt cutter.

The springer spaniel's handler informed them that the dogs indicated at a large pile of brush, which they then moved. Under the branches two overlapping metal hatches had been revealed, which they were now trying to get open. The chain was linked to a sizeable padlock and had been drawn between two loops that were part of the hatches. Knocking on it made it echo from below.

"This must be an old smugglers' hiding place," one of the police officers observed.

"Maybe here we'll find the reason for the bodies over there," said Sandén hopefully.

"Or something better," said the crouching policeman, who at the same moment with a grimace managed to divide the chain into two parts, pull it out of the loops, and tear open the hatches. Up against them came a frightful stench, but he swung himself gracefully down through the opening and landed with a thud on the earth floor.

"But what the hell . . ." was heard from below.

A disillusioned murmur. A few seconds of silence, then a completely different tone of voice.

"There's a person down here!" he called. "A young girl! I don't know if she's alive, but I'm coming up with her, get ready up there!"

Then they heard a moan and soon he was in the opening with the girl in his arms. Two pairs of hands were extended down toward him, took the loose-limbed body under their arms, and lifted. She seemed light as a feather as they pulled her up out of the underworld and placed her on the ground to the side of the place where she had spent the last five months of her young life. For this was definitely Rebecka Magnusson. Emaciated and battered. But she was alive.

Half an hour later Sandén and Westman went over the earth cellar in the company of two of Hansson's technicians. An ambulance had quickly been arranged, and for the second time in a brief period Sandén had succeeded in the enterprise of delivering a seemingly lifeless body to the ambulance EMTs in Glömsta. This time, however, he was not alone; instead the whole K-9 patrol helped out, and they reached the ambulance in only ten minutes.

The earth cellar was a pigsty. The bucket that the girl used as a toilet was full, and excrement had flowed out onto the floor. The stench was nauseating. Sandén imagined how she had finally given up. For five months she was regularly visited by a man who abused and, in all likelihood, also raped her. Without hope of release. A punishment that had no time limit. Now he had left her to die. There was no longer any reason to eat. There was still some water left in a ten-liter container, but of what she had been given to eat, only empty packages remained. She was worn out. She was letting herself die on her own. It would have been less inhumane to shoot her.

And the other victims of this man's desires, how long had it taken for them before it was over? Little Lara, only eleven years old? He could not bear to think what it was like for her during her last months of life. Or was it only a matter of weeks, perhaps even days?

On a mattress on the floor was where they had spent their last days. There were plenty of blankets and covers. In a corner, someone had thrown a knit sweater. It had evidently been enough to keep Rebecka Magnusson alive.

The intent appeared to be to keep them alive as long as possible, in any case as long as he had use for them. Alongside the mattress was a flashlight. That was the little light they had. And if the batteries died, they had to do without. It must have been frightful. Frightful and lonely.

There was a flash of light from time to time as the technicians took photographs. The others worked to gather evidence. Hair, blood, body fluids, fingerprints. They had already found blood all over. The question was simply whose. How many were there? Who had lost their lives here? Was it only the two whose remains had been found, or were there more? And who was the unknown woman who shared a grave with Larissa Sotnikova? Was she missed by anyone? Perhaps they would never find out.

For the one who did this knew what he was doing. He specialized in the weakest, most vulnerable in society, those who lacked a protective network, those who were not missed by anyone. Or not that much. Those who were of no use and whose absence wouldn't really matter. He was a real cynic, in other words. A cowardly cynic with one thing in mind: satisfying his own perverse needs.

"Come here and let me show you something," said Westman.

She had pulled the mattress away from the wall and was on her knees studying a wooden molding at floor level.

Sandén crouched down at her side. Even though they had set up powerful lamps in the room, he did not see what she was referring to until she aimed an LED flashlight straight toward the molding.

"I drew my fingers across the molding," said Westman. "Otherwise I never would have discovered it. It's extremely small and extremely shallow. Someone has carved something here."

"It's just a few lines," said Sandén.

"I think they're letters. Cyrillic letters."

Sandén looked at Westman, perplexed. Then the lightbulb came on.

"Russian letters, you mean? Did little Lara do the carving?"

Westman nodded pensively and looked around. Ran her gaze over walls and floor, bedclothes and trash. Then shook her head.

"Nothing," she said. "There's nothing here she could have used. I think she did it with her nails."

"It must have hurt like hell," Sandén sighed.

"It must have been important as hell," said Westman.

That's the way I am once and for all. I want to rape, I need to rape so that life will feel meaningful. And what does it matter? Any whore will do. Women are whores by nature, only camouflage it in more or less obvious ways.

And that Russian girl, my little gazelle, what would have become of her? She would've grown into a whore, naturally. An orphanage child with no parents, and from Russia besides. Now she no longer exists, will no longer be a burden to society. I miss her of course, in my own way, but it was unavoidable that things turned out the way they did.

But when you lose one, there are thousands more. She wasn't the only one. The earth is full of women and girls who beg to be used. You can even pay for it, and some are worth it if needed. But the pleasure is not really the same as when you lure your prey into a trap.

Larissa Sotnikova. She gave me everything I could ever dream of.

But Adrianti, that experienced old hooker. Did everything you asked for. It hurt and she cried and moaned, but still let it happen again. And afterward that meddlesome smile, that pleading look that begs for confirmation. I'm fed up with it. I can hardly bear to see the person, feel only contempt. Nausea.

Sooner or later I'm going to kill her. It's unavoidable.

"Poker?" Sjöberg said in amazement, exchanging a quick glance with Andersson, who looked just as surprised. "You support yourself by playing poker?"

Dewi Kusamasari nodded frankly and placed a piece of ice at the bottom of her glass.

"And you finance all this with that?" Sjöberg continued with a gesture in the direction of the apartment.

She nodded again and poured water in the glass.

"I thought there were very rigorous regulations about residency permits and long-term visas in this country. Such as, for example, that you have to have permanent employment."

"There are," Dewi answered, "but citizenship is the simplest way, of course."

"Do you mean you're a citizen of Singapore? So you're married to a Singaporean?"

"No," laughed Dewi. "It's not certain even then that you get citizenship, and besides it takes many years in that case. I became a citizen of this country when my biological father acknowledged paternity."

"Oh. And he did it just like that?" Sjöberg asked, snapping his fingers.

"I can be pretty convincing when I put my mind to it. I 'made him an offer he couldn't refuse.' He's a finance man, involved in various types of investments. He acknowledged paternity and loaned me a sum of money. Which I compensated him well for when I had saved up enough on my own."

"I'll be damned," exclaimed Andersson, who had a hard time concealing his delight.

"Do you know why we're here?" Sjöberg asked.

"I think I have an idea, yes."

Sjöberg studied her in the glow of the wax candle for a few seconds, hoping she would present that idea. The cicadas were singing intensely down in the garden, not even the big city traffic could drown them out. With eyes that gleamed in the darkness, Dewi looked back at him without saying anything. He was struck by a feeling that she was a step ahead in some way, that he was at a mental disadvantage.

"Your stepfather, Sven-Gunnar Erlandsson, was found dead in the Herrängen forest a little over a week ago," said Sjöberg. "But you already know about that?"

"I read about it in the newspaper. On the internet."

"You have no contact with them at home? In Sweden?"

"No, it's been a little skimpy on that front lately."

Sjöberg took a gulp of water from the glass. Andersson did the same.

"Ice?" said Dewi, extending the ice bucket.

"Thanks, I'm okay. You couldn't tell us what happened, could you?"

Her gaze wandered from Sjöberg to Andersson and back again. A slight smile was playing on her face the whole time. Sjöberg did not know how he should interpret it, but had no hope that the question he had asked would actually give rise to an interesting response. He was seriously mistaken.

"Where do you want me to begin?" she asked surprisingly.

Sjöberg immediately recovered.

"Why not start at the beginning," he suggested.

And Dewi Kusamasari told them:

It was a morning in early August 2001. Dewi was fifteen years old, had just had a birthday and it was a big one. As a birthday present she got a moped from her dad and was overjoyed. That day the whole family was at the soccer camp at Mälarhöjden athletic field. Except Ida, who was sick in bed at home. But Mom, Dad, Rasmus, Anna, and Dewi were at the athletic field. Due to the rain, the whole family packed into the car even though they wouldn't be driving far. It had been raining the whole morning. Visibility was poor and it might be slippery, so the gleaming new moped had to stay behind in the garage at home on Vaktelstigen. Still, it didn't matter if it was pouring down rain. Dewi loved playing soccer, regardless of the weather.

But at quarter to eleven something happened that Dewi had not counted on. She got her period. It was a fairly new experience for Dewi, and the bleeding was copious and irregular. She was not at all prepared and had no protection with her. What should she do? Sneak into the dressing room and root around in the other girls' bags to see if she found anything? No, that wasn't a possibility; she might get caught, exposed as a thief. She could have talked with a teammate, her mother, or one of the female officials, but she felt uncomfortable doing that. The situation was terribly awkward, and she was ashamed to bring it up with anyone, didn't want anyone to know.

She took a look at the clock and realized that it was only fifteen minutes until lunch break. Perhaps she should try to endure those fifteen minutes and then run home? But no, that wouldn't work, during those fifteen minutes she was guaranteed to bleed through. She wavered a while between the various alternatives, but that could not go on. She had to make a decision quickly, and at last she decided to sneak away. Immediately. If anyone asked where she had been she could say she had to go to the restroom, that she had to wait awhile because it was occupied. During lunch no one would miss her, there were so many people being fed hot dogs. She would have vanished in the crowd.

With a last glance over her shoulder, she left the athletic field without anyone noticing her—she hoped, anyway—and then jogged on Vantörs-vägen over toward Herrängen. With each step, she felt how the blood was pumping. She cast a glance down at her shorts and saw how a dark stain was starting to take shape in the blue fabric. Turned her face away as soon as a car passed and hoped that no one would see her. If she made her way in among the side streets, she would probably avoid the curious glances of the general public. In the residential area presumably people would stay indoors on a rainy day like this.

Just as she was about to turn onto Isbergavägen, the Jenners' summer child showed up on her new bicycle. Poor little Lara, who had been so sad the last few days because the return trip to Russia was quickly approaching. And it was completely understandable, Lara had no parents and lived with a lot of other children in a children's home. Dewi could well imagine what it was like to grow up in a Russian orphanage, and she shivered at the thought of it. Lara would be pale and skinny when she showed up in Älvsjö in June, of course she was sad when she was forced to go back a few months later. And she didn't really dare believe that perhaps she would get to live with the Jenners for real, that they would adopt her. But now Staffan had given her a bicycle so she would understand how welcome she was, Marie had called and told that to Mom.

And here she was now on her fine red bicycle, sweet little Lara. Even though it had stopped raining she still had her raincoat on, the one she got at Gröna Lund earlier in the summer. She seemed much happier now.

"Hi, Dewi!" she called, long before Dewi caught sight of her.

Dewi was startled and made a quarter turn. Did not want to be observed from behind at any price. Or from the front.

"Hi, Lara. What a nice bicycle you got."

"Papa Staffan," said Lara in her characteristic way. She understood Swedish without problems, but made it easy on herself when she talked.

Now she slowed down so she could cycle alongside Dewi, who started walking again.

"You bleed," Lara then said and pointed at Dewi's soccer shorts, where the spot had now become so large that it was visible from all directions. "Hurt yourself?"

So now Dewi was in a situation where she had to choose between using the world's lamest white lie or simply saying what was going on. How hard could that be, really? What could happen? Nothing. So she chose the latter.

"It's the kind of thing girls get sometimes," she answered. "You know that, huh?"

Lara nodded, big-eyed.

"I have to go home and change pants. Do you want to go with and see how Ida is?"

"I go to Ida," said Lara. "Raincoat?"

Dewi looked at the girl, who was pointing at her orange raincoat and then at Dewi with a question on her face.

"May I borrow it? God, how sweet you are!"

So Lara stopped, got off the bicycle, and pushed down the kickstand with her foot. Wriggled out of the raincoat and handed it to Dewi, who gratefully took it and pulled it over her head. She kept the hood on, so as not to be recognized, to avoid explaining.

"You're the best, Lara!" she said, giving her a big hug before they continued their journey home.

They followed Isbergavägen, Murgrönsvägen, and then Konvaljestigen, in the direction down toward the school and the woods. A big girl in an orange raincoat and a slightly smaller one on a brand-new red bicycle. Her blonde ponytail peeked out from under the helmet.

When Dewi first noticed the engine noise, she turned around to make sure it was not anyone she knew. But she only needed to see the front of the car as it turned the corner in their direction to realize that luck was not with her. By reflex, she threw herself into the hedge that happened to be between her and the lot they were just passing. She squeezed through it, and to Lara who watched her, surprised and almost terrified, she hissed, "Don't say I'm here! Don't tell anyone you saw me!"

Through the branches she witnessed how the car drove up to Lara, who stopped and got off the bicycle. Then how the familiar figure got out of *the car and with a warm smile went up to the girl and stroked her across the cheek.*

"Hi honey, so you're out with your new bike? Hop in the car so I can drive you."

"Only to Ida," Lara answered. "Bicycle. Not car."

"Ida's sick, she can't play today. I'm going to show you a place where it's a lot more fun to ride your bicycle. There aren't any cars, no hazards. But it will be an exciting adventure."

Little Lara lit up, perhaps forgetting Dewi, who was hiding in the bushes. Happily, she jumped into the front seat while he put her bicycle into the trunk. And then they rolled off, disappeared from there.

Larissa Sotnikova had disappeared. For all time.

—◦—

"A few hours later, when Lara still had not been found, he winked at me. He winked during the search party, winked too when he answered one of the police's questions: 'No, the last time I saw her was twenty to eleven at Mälarhöjden athletic field.' I guess it was an expression of solidarity in general, with the same content as a pat on the shoulder maybe. But I drew the conclusion that this wink held a secret promise. To me and to all the others who liked Lara. He was making sure she would not have to go back to Russia. He was hiding her until the adoption papers were signed, made sure she was okay in the meantime.

"If I had only understood better, grasped that you don't lie to the police if you have nothing to hide. I was fifteen years old, too young to realize that people can be completely different than what they present themselves to be."

"So in your secret understanding, you chose not to say anything to the police, either," Sjöberg summarized.

"Then," Dewi answered. "To start with."

———

When Adrianti opened her eyes, she didn't know at first where she was. How had she ended up here, and why? It was pitch-black and completely silent. Not a ray of light anywhere; the room she was in had no windows at all.

Thoughts were whirling in her head. What time was it? What day of the week? Where were the children? Ida? And then there was something about Dewi. Where was she? And Svempa, something had happened.

Then it all came back. Svempa was dead. He had been shot, murdered. She would have to move out of the house, leave everything she ever had in her new country. And then the worst of all: Dewi was gone. That policeman, Sjöberg, had insinuated that maybe Dewi had disappeared for real. A thought she had already had, but dismissed. Her beloved little Dewi. How could she live without her?

Then she smelled the scent of a man. A tangible, insistent odor that filled the whole room. It was stifling. The more she thought about it, the greater her need to breathe became, the need to get out. She moved, let out a faint sound that was reminiscent of a sigh. Even though it was so warm in the room, she felt how the hairs rose on her arms. But she had to try to get out of there without waking him.

But where was the door? She did not remember in which direction she should search and could not even see her hand in front of her. Slowly she slid up into a sitting position, reaching for the floor with her foot. It was closer than she recalled, had completely forgotten that they were on a mattress on the floor. She pushed off with one hand and stood up. The darkness made her dizzy. She held her hands in front of her in the air without touching anything, placed one foot ahead of the other, and was about to take another step when she reacted to a movement beside her.

A hand wrapped itself around her ankle.

During the days that followed, Dewi kept her eyes on him. Out of pure curiosity and in secret. He could not very likely know she had seen him that morning, she should have been at Mälarhöjden athletic field. But she made herself invisible and spied on him when he least suspected it. And sure enough, he disappeared in the wrong direction on a few occasions when by his own account he should have been doing something else. Such as being at work. And always in the same direction.

Dewi respected his decision to keep the whole thing to himself. In her innocence, she thought it seemed reasonable not to initiate anyone else in such an important, decisive secret. For what would happen to poor Lara if the truth came out? And not least to him? So it was just as well to keep silent. And laugh up your sleeve that everything would be so much better for Lara than was thought to begin with.

But after a few weeks, the curiosity became too great. It was still summer vacation, so she had all the time in the world. And a moped that she was more than happy to ride for long distances. For that reason she decided to lie in wait for him at the crossing where she had previously seen him go in that mysterious direction. Hoped that he would do it this time too. And he did.

She followed him at a safe distance, took cover behind other vehicles so that he would not discover her and hoped that he didn't intend to take a major highway, leaving her behind. He did not do that either. He neither discovered her nor pulled away from her.

When he finally parked the car, they were out in the Huddinge forests. Dewi was fairly familiar with the area, because Lake Gömmaren was not far from there where she had been swimming a few times with friends. She pulled the moped a short distance from the road, laid it down in the moss, and covered it with spruce branches. Then she sneaked after him into the forest, leaving space and being careful not to be heard or seen. And she managed to shadow him all the way to the earth cellar without him suspecting anything. He glanced over his shoulder a few times, but it did not seem to have to do with Dewi. She felt a little exalted, the whole thing was a titillating adventure. That was how she saw it then.

Once there, she took cover behind a few trees that stood close together. Crouched down, she observed him as he used the spade he had carried from the car to remove a pile of brush. It concealed a door. The tension was excruciating as she saw him remove the padlock to make his way down into the underworld.

But when she saw his head disappear below ground level, it struck her that this could not have anything to do with Lara. He wouldn't let her spend weeks—perhaps even months, if the adoption process dragged on—underground. It was an inhuman way to treat a child. A person. Even if it was to do good. No, Lara would have been better off at the orphanage, Dewi was convinced of that. He was up to something else down there. In that case, what had happened to Lara?

But now a sound was heard from below. Screams and moaning, and she recognized his voice very well. What was going on? Had he hurt himself? Should she make herself known, run up and offer her help? Not quite yet, she didn't dare. She waited a while and hoped the noise would die away, that she had only imagined it all.

And maybe she had too, because now nothing more was heard. He reappeared in the opening. Now with something big and heavy in his arms. She heard how he swore to himself as he pushed the strange object up through the hole and set it in a heap on the ground above him. Dewi could not make out what it was, perhaps it was clothing. Then he looked around again before he took a sturdy hold under the bundle with both arms and carried it away.

It was a body. Dewi now saw that it was a little girl with blonde hair and the clothes Lara had been wearing when she had last seen her. Dewi was still not able to take in what she saw. What had happened with Lara? Was she sick? Wounded? Where did he intend to carry her?

When he had gone off a short distance with Lara in his arms, Dewi ventured up to the opening of the earth cellar. Carefully she climbed down the ladder and looked around.

The first thing she noticed was the bicycle. A completely new red bicycle, which she immediately recognized. And the helmet hanging on the handlebars. Then she saw the mattress on the floor, the covers and food. The bucket that apparently served as a toilet. So Lara had spent the time since the disappearance here.

Dewi couldn't understand what she was looking at. Something was really wrong. She made her way up the ladder again, spied for movement in the direction he had gone, and sneaked off in the same direction.

Now it really got awful. From her position behind a large boulder, she saw him let go of Lara. He let her simply fall, without taking into account that this was a human being. If he had set her down, carefully lowered her, there would still have been some form of respect, but this . . . Lara was only a package, garbage, something he was getting rid of.

Dewi saw Lara's body disappear down into a hole—a grave. Along-side it there was a large pile of dirt. She felt how her gaze turned blurry, drew her hand under her nose, and sank down in the moss, not capable of doing anything.

He went off again. After a while she heard at a distance as the heavy hatches closed with a metallic bang that echoed between the trees. A few minutes later he was back with the bicycle, the helmet still on the handle-bars. The man she no longer knew, whom she realized she had never known, threw the bicycle on top of the girl with a sound that would never leave Dewi. A muted thud and something as innocent as the rattling of bike pedals. Then he filled in the hole and left.

It felt very unsatisfying not to be out there searching in the Huddinge forests, Wallin thought. At the same time, this was a logical decision for Sjöberg to make. Her doctor had warned her in no uncertain terms not to go to work at all. That was just silly, she could just as well sit here as at home. But okay, run-ning around in that damned seven-league forest was maybe not the smartest thing to do, she agreed with that. And it did ache at the incision—or incisions, there were evidently a number of layers that had been cut and sewn up—which did have to heal properly before she engaged in overly physical activities. Such as digging.

The morning—and yesterday evening as well—she had spent in Älvsjö. When Westman called her yesterday after the doctor's appoint-ment and all four of them had taken off to Herrängen, fearing the worst. While Hamad and Westman searched for life in the Jenner residence without success, she and Sandén broke into the Erlandsson home. Thankfully without finding anything unwanted there.

Unfortunately, Adrianti was still missing. They did not succeed in making contact with any of them this morning either. This gnawed at her. Adrianti seemed so vulnerable. Alone and fragile. And if it now turned out that Dewi was alive, it would be a great tragedy if Adrianti took her own life just as her beloved daughter rose up from the dead.

But there was another conceivable scenario, and it was just as frightening. That Adrianti at last decided to resume contact with her old lover and opened her heart to him, aired her apprehensions about what might have happened to Dewi, what Dewi might have seen or heard and the conclusions she might have drawn. If it was as Sandén said—that Staffan Jenner was either behind the murder of Erlandsson or else the murder of Erlandsson as well as a handful of vulnerable girls, young women. Yes, then it was logical that in that situation, Adrianti was next in line. A woman without a protective network who talked too much, speculated too much, and who was extremely vulnerable. Adrianti Erlandsson was easy prey for a misogynist.

Once every fifteen minutes, Wallin phoned both Adrianti and Jenner in the hope that one of them would answer their phone, so that they could bring them in for questioning. But still without result. Instead she had to attend to other things; she skipped lunch. She was too restless to eat anyway, too many interesting things were going on all at once in this investigation. And it irritated her no end that she was not in the center of events.

So she did her own digging. At the computer, that is.

Because the technician had just been there to retrieve Simon Tampler's computer, it would be a while before they would find out how the communication between him and his client unfolded. If ever. It seemed unlikely that the exchange of such sensitive information would have happened in a way that could easily be discovered and that would get both of them convicted. Consequently, Wallin harbored no great hopes that the technician's analysis of Tampler's computer would lead anywhere. So she took hold of the case in her own way, and instead tried to understand how the person behind the murder of Erlandsson had *found* Simon Tampler.

Once again, she went through all the threads where there was talk of hit men and murder for hire, but nothing popped out. Once again she went through all the threads where Simon Tampler had been active or even the one taking the initiative. Now she sat with the thread she had already scrutinized many times before her, which first brought her attention to Tampler. "I want to kill someone. I'm going to kill someone."

Then her phone rang. It was her colleague from the financial crimes police, who only had bad news. No, no large amounts had been deposited in any of Simon Tampler's accounts, and no, no small amounts had been deposited from unexpected quarters that might combine to add up to a large amount either. In brief, Tampler had no money.

How, she asked herself, had the person who commissioned the murder of Erlandsson paid Simon Tampler? Most likely cash in hand. When? Well, why not immediately before and immediately after the assignment was completed? Which even more clearly pointed to Staffan Jenner. He was the one who had walked with Erlandsson the farthest on the way home from Långbro Inn.

Jenner could have met Tampler without any great difficulty in the darkness in the Herräng forest, handed him fifty thousand, and stayed there waiting until it was over, when the rest of the amount changed ownership. And surely with the promise of more money if Tampler kept his lips sealed. In case his luck ran out and he was sent to prison. Wallin had heard Hamad and Westman describe how Jenner rattled off one street after the other during the first interview as he was describing how he made his way home after the dinner at Långbro Inn. Cried out as being rehearsed.

On the other hand, Jenner had seemed to be somewhat of a nervous wreck. It did not seem all that probable that he would have arranged a meeting with a man who was unquestionably out to kill just about anything on two legs. So perhaps not.

Then it suddenly struck her that there actually was a way for less well-off people to transfer money from one corner of the world to another. How did that work? With eager fingers she clicked her way to Western Union's Swedish website and found the text: "Fast—your money is there in a few minutes. Easy—more than 370,000 agents in more than 200 countries, and no bank account required." It was no more difficult than that. With fake identification and so on. No problem at all. She shook her head that she hadn't thought of it before. Perhaps because it was so un-Swedish in some way. And un-Swiss.

She backed up to the murder thread she had been staring at before FiPo called. Fastened her gaze on the screen before her:

> The Saint: You can keep making fun of me, I'll grant you that.
> I know what I'm about and that I'll make it happen.

Spitfire: How much do you have to pay to have someone "eliminated"?

The Saint: I would do it for 100K.

Yo Gurt: I wouldn't even crush someone's foot for so little money.

Goyz: Do you even have a gun?

The Saint: I have a Glock 38.

Goyz: I think it's time for a diaper change now, Saint.

The Saint: I'm going to do it even if no one will pay me. That's just how it is. You can think what you want. I'm strong in my conviction.

And suddenly it was crystal clear to Wallin what had gone on when the person who ordered the murder of Sven-Gunnar Erlandsson found the lost Simon Tampler. The word "un-Swedish" came back to her.

The phone rang again. This time it was Westman. She sounded agitated.

"We've dug up two bodies," she reported. "One of them is without a doubt Larissa Sotnikova's."

Wallin let out a deep sigh. Commentary was superfluous.

"He threw the bicycle on top of her," Westman continued. "The other is the body of an unknown woman, presumably young, maybe a teenager."

"Rebecka Magnusson?" Wallin suggested.

"No. We found her alive in an earth cellar not far from there."

"Amazing! So she's alive after such a long time?"

"Barely. You can't guess how horrible it's been for her. Five months underground. Cold as hell, a flashlight as the only source of light. And apart from the fact that she'd been left to starve to death, she was badly treated in all conceivable ways. He beat her almost to a pulp."

"And presumably raped her," Wallin added. "Was it possible to talk with her?"

"No, she was unconscious. But Lara has something to tell."

"Lara?"

"We found something we think are Russian letters carved in wood. Can you find out what they mean?"

"Sure. Can you text them to me?"

"They're on their way. Talk to you later."

Right then her cell phone peeped and Wallin scrambled to find herself the unusual, for her, tools of paper and pen, in an attempt to write out the Russian characters.

For an amateur it was almost impossible to imagine how the words should be pronounced or what they might conceivably mean. But it seemed to be two words. Which in itself could become more, or fewer, when they were translated to another language.

She started by searching for a translation program between Russian and Swedish on the internet and found various options without difficulty. The problem was that she had not found any way to enter Russian characters on the keyboard. After a Google search she found a number of interesting tips concerning ASCII conversion in Windows, but suddenly realized that perhaps she didn't need to turn herself into a full-fledged computer programmer specializing in character tables just to solve this reasonably simple problem. Instead she entered "translation, Russian" into the search field on Google, whereupon the first thing she caught sight of was an article in *Dagens Nyheter* about a woman who was employed at Swedish Television to translate Russian TV programs to Swedish.

And that was really all she needed. She called the Swedish Television switchboard and was transferred to the translator in question.

"Malin Westfeldt."

"Hedvig Wallin is my name, and I'm a police inspector with the Hammarby police. I need your help, if that's all right?"

"Sure, no problem. What's it about?"

"Translation. From Russian to Swedish."

"I do know a little about that."

"It only concerns two words. Can I send them to you on your cell phone?"

"Absolutely," said Malin Westfeldt, giving her cell phone number without being asked.

Her voice sounded very nice. *Maybe she moonlights as a weather reporter occasionally,* Wallin thought as she forwarded the message she had just received from Westman. There was a ring in the receiver when the Cyrillic characters reached their recipient.

"Here it is," said Malin Westfeldt, and it took a few seconds before she continued.

"This is simple," she said happily. "Very simple."

—⁓—

For a long, long time she remained sitting out there in the woods before she collected herself and stood up. With tears running down her cheeks, Dewi made her way back out to the road where she had left her moped. Threw aside the spruce branches she had covered it with and put on her helmet.

Actually, she could just as well forget about that. What did it matter if something happened to her? Life would never be the same anyway. Everything was destroyed. And if she hadn't had the moped she never could have followed him here, never could have witnessed this horrible thing. Then she could have lived the rest of her life not knowing what really happened to poor Lara.

What should she do? Stir the duck pond in Herrängen and go to the police? Destroy the lives of a lot of people by revealing everything? Because it was not just him who would be drawn into perdition, but everyone in his immediate vicinity.

She drove toward home. At first she was just sad. Desperate when she thought about what little Lara had been subjected to, what it had been like for her during the two weeks that had passed since she disappeared. Then she became angry. At him at first, but then at herself. Because she was so naive and always believed the best about everyone. Evil apparently had many faces, she had learned that today. Why hadn't she simply said what happened when the police asked her? Then Lara would have been found immediately; she would be alive today, wouldn't have to suffer.

During the ride she decided. She might have to choose between plague and cholera, but she had to be able to live with herself, even as the world collapsed around her. And when at last she opened the garage door and rolled the moped in, she was so angry she wanted to break things. With tears flowing, she lowered the kickstand and hung the helmet on the handlebars, sniffling and swearing.

She knew what she had to do. It was hard, but she would do it, just had to calm herself down first. Breathe, wash up. Before she called the police.

Suddenly he was simply standing there. Smiling in the doorway. She wasn't prepared for this at all, this was not what she had imagined.

"What's going on?" he asked gently, taking a step toward her. "You look completely wrecked."

Another step, he was right next to her now.

"What happened to you, little lady?"

Then something burst inside Dewi. She became . . . hysterical. In the proper sense of the word. Like a wild animal she threw herself over him, struck and struck with clenched fists against his chest and body. He was pressed against the wall, reached out a hand to the switch, and managed to get the garage door to lower.

"Close the door now, you sick bastard!" Dewi screamed. "You think that will help? But it won't, because I'm going to see to it that you go to jail for the rest of your life! I know what you've done! I know you murdered Lara! And I know you've buried her! How could you do that? To Lara? To us? You're out of your mind!"

Even though she struck him incessantly he looked mildly amused standing there, taking one blow after the other without hitting back. At last she gave up, turned around, and rushed off toward the door that led into the house. It was always locked; he knew it would take her a while to wriggle the keys out of her pocket and unlock the door.

So with calm steps he went after her, but not all the way. Because to the left of Dewi was the pile of duckboards, with the old washing machine on top. To the right was the car.

If she had only turned around she would have seen what was coming, but instead she stood fumbling at the lock with trembling hands.

Suddenly she saw in the corner of her eye that something was moving to her left, right above her. And then it was too late. He had managed to overturn the washing machine and it was on its way right toward her.

She pressed herself against the car, tried to squeeze into the small space between the front of the car and the inside wall. It was a hairbreadth that she almost managed, but her foot was caught. It ended up under one of the corners of the washing machine, and then everything turned black.

When, despite the severe pain, she gradually came around, he was leaning over her. And he had not moved the great weight from her foot. What was left of her foot.

When he opened his mouth to speak, it was with a gentle voice. Lightning was flashing from his eyes, but the voice was smooth as velvet.

"Next time I'll do it the right way," he explained. "But I'll start with your mom. Never forget that, Dewi. I'll start with your mom. When I'm through with her, it will be your turn. And I'm going to take my time."

She could not recall anything that happened until she woke up at the hospital. Blurred images, pain medication, IVs, and operations. She was told that it was Anna who came home and found her in the garage. The family was devastated, kept watch at her side day and night. She herself was completely void of feelings.

Sjöberg sat for a long time, looking out over the city's glittering lights without saying a word. He was captivated by Dewi's story. Felt a light breeze flutter past his face, odors of curry from somewhere. No one else said anything either. Andersson was presumably in the same mood as he was. Dewi perhaps felt relieved at having been able to tell someone this horrible thing for the first time. That was what Sjöberg hoped, in any case.

Then he was interrupted in his musings by an incoming text message on his phone. It was from Wallin:

"The bodies of Lara and an unknown woman have now been excavated. Rebecka Magnusson was found alive in an earth cellar in the vicinity. Lara left a message in the earth cellar, carved with her nails in wood: 'Ida's dad.' Dewi ordered the murder of Erlandsson (no evidence)."

With a sorrowful smile, Sjöberg handed the cell phone over to Andersson. It was time to move on.

"So you kept silent," he said gently. "For all these years. For your mother's sake. And perhaps a little for your own, too?"

Dewi shrugged her shoulders. Sjöberg thought he saw a flash in her eyes that had not been there earlier.

"Are you happy here? In Singapore?"

"I think so. Yes. Now I am."

"Since he's gone?"

She nodded.

"Do you want to tell about the time afterward? When you were still living at home?"

She did not answer, but instead sat looking into the lights a while. Sjöberg observed her in silence, gave a thought to the code lock in the hall.

"My mother was a whore," she said unexpectedly.

Sjöberg and Andersson exchanged a quick glance.

"She lived in great poverty and did what she had to in order to survive. Rich Singaporeans go to Batam and play golf when they have free time, hire a mandatory caddie, and then get a more or less mandatory blow job afterwards. I found this out during my time here. That's probably how she met my real dad. He already had a family in Singapore, acquired another one on Batam. A lot of men do that. But when they get tired there are no papers, it's just over. So Mom had to start working again. And that was when she met . . . him. To everyone's great delight. Including mine."

"A real win-win situation," Sjöberg interjected.

Dewi nodded with a joyless smile.

"But after what happened with Lara, I saw everything with new eyes. Suddenly I understood what those muffled screams from the bedroom meant. Why Mom sometimes had a hard time walking in the morning. It was not about loving caresses and problems with joints, but something completely different. Namely that he regularly during those thirteen years subjected her to brutal rapes. That was what he went in for, that was why he dragged her along with him to Sweden. Us. She was pleasant, good with the children, nice to look at, and was prepared to do go along with anything at all. Including rape. You don't find that kind of wife in a hurry. But it wasn't enough for him. Muffled shrieks and a little pain weren't enough for it to be fun, he wanted more. Then little Lara crossed his path, and he took the opportunity."

"She wasn't the only one," Sjöberg revealed. "Our colleagues have just found the body of another person, a young woman. And in an earth cellar a fifteen-year-old girl was found who had been missing for five months. Alive."

Dewi's eyes filled with tears. She put her hands to her mouth.

"What could I do?" she said. "Whatever I would have done, it would have been wrong."

"You can console yourself that the fifteen-year-old girl presumably never would have been found if you hadn't taken the life of Sven-Gunnar Erlandsson."

Sjöberg felt Andersson's gaze. Perhaps he was worried about how the situation might unfold. But he made no efforts to intervene, kept in the background, and let Sjöberg run this his way. Which he was grateful for.

Dewi laughed, and suddenly she was the same as when she first received them. Self-confident, invincible.

"I'm not capable of such a thing, of course," she answered frankly.

"We found some interesting things on Erlandsson," Sjöberg continued. "Among other things, position coordinates for the place where the bodies were buried."

"What luck, then," Dewi said, without a trace of the gentle side that had emerged as she told her story.

"It is interesting, considering you were the only one who knew what was there."

"And him of course. Maybe he was worried he wouldn't find his way back."

Intelligent.

"We also found a set of playing cards. More exactly a dead man's hand, if that means anything to you?"

"Sure," Dewi answered. "The cards Wild Bill Hickok had in his hand when he was shot in a saloon in Deadwood in 1876. The second of August," she added with a derisive smile.

Sjöberg smiled back. Restrained. The young woman was a murderer, you could not get away from that. But she had her reasons. And she was impressive, he had to begrudgingly admit. He was torn.

"So it has nothing to do with you?" Sjöberg attempted, without hope of success. "You, who seem to know a bit about poker?"

"No," Dewi answered, breathing out.

"Okay," said Sjöberg. "We'll leave that. Tell us what happened in Denmark. At the Roskilde festival."

"Nothing happened. Lina and I were there for a couple of days, then she went home. I kept going. Was out traveling for a while, then I decided it was time for me to settle down. Here. Which was the plan from the start."

"So you never saw Jenner and Erlandsson when they were down looking for you?"

Dewi looked at him with the deepest seriousness in her eyes.

"I thought I'd made it clear how things stood. If he had found me, he would have killed me. As long as I was living at home and kept up the facade, he was no threat to me or my mother, and I was no threat to him. On the contrary, I was needed for the family's well-being. But as soon as I flew the nest, I was in danger. As I said: if he had found me, he would have killed me."

Naturally. That was how it hung together.

"That was why you never said goodbye," said Sjöberg, mostly to himself. "That was why you never revealed anything about where you were. But why did you wait so long?"

"To move away from home? I needed to get an education. How would I manage all alone out in the world if I hadn't even finished elementary school?"

"No," Sjöberg said coldly, "that's not what I meant. Why did you want so long to take the life of Sven-Gunnar Erlandsson?"

He saw how she steeled herself again. Vacillated between sincerity and hard-boiled defiance without the slightest sign of fear.

"I am not involved in the murder," she said, smiling. "But if I had been, then I would have chosen an occasion when all the children had moved away. So they would be spared standing there in shame in front of the whole neighborhood when who he really was came out. Like now, for example. I would have been far from there, made sure not to be drawn into the case myself. I would have put some lost soul on the job, who otherwise would have murdered some other wretch, someone who perhaps wasn't guilty of anything."

Sjöberg poured more water in his glass. What should he do now? He had all he needed from Dewi Kusamasari. *Except a confession.* And he was not sure that was what he wanted.

"Ice?" she asked again, still smiling.

She was truly beautiful. With a charisma like a whole crazy nebula. *Don't let yourself be enchanted by that,* Sjöberg told himself.

"Sure. Thanks."

"Idol-Odd?"

"Thanks, sure," Andersson answered embarrassed.

"You must miss them," said Sjöberg. "Your family."

"Incredibly," Dewi answered. The smile had evaporated. She looked mournful.

"I thought about suggesting that you come with us back to Sweden. Your mother is beside herself with worry. She started suspecting that you had met the same fate as Lara."

Dewi looked at him with uncertainty.

"Now you're joking with me?"

"I would never dream of that," Sjöberg said honestly.

"I'm staying here," said Dewi firmly.

"We need you as a witness."

"You intend to put me away for incitement to murder. You won't succeed in that."

"We also need you as a witness. Your testimony is indispensable where Lara Sotnikova is concerned. There are also people who for private reasons need to find out the truth. The Jenner family, for example, not least Staffan."

"You'll get my testimony. And a detailed one besides. It's in a desk drawer, fifty typewritten pages. And if you're interested, I've also made a psychological analysis of Sven-Gunnar Erlandsson. Tried to put myself in his head, discover what drove him. Amateurish of course, but still. No one knew him better than me."

"Come with us," Sjöberg said encouragingly. "For Adrianti's sake."

Dewi shook her head sorrowfully.

"You'll have to tell her I'm doing fine. And how things are. Am I wrong?"

Sjöberg thought about it. Swept his gaze across the skyscrapers, the illuminated city which in the darkness was reminiscent of an enormous carnival. She was not wrong. He could tell Adrianti Erlandsson that Dewi was doing fine, that she was free and successful. And certainly he would also tell her what she had done. And why.

He observed Dewi, her dark glistening eyes that had seen so much that no person ought to have to see. And a feeling came over him: the feeling that this really was what she wanted. That what she had just said was an appeal that he should tell the truth, exactly as it was: that it was Dewi who had ordered the murder of her stepfather. And that it would then not be a given that Adrianti or the siblings would want to see her after that.

"No," Sjöberg answered. "Of course you're completely right."

"So they can choose themselves," said Dewi. "But please tell them there are bedrooms for all of them. And how much I love them."

"I'll do that," said Sjöberg. "I promise."

Then she got up and opened one of the glass doors to the living room. Limped away, was gone awhile, and then came back with a file folder filled to the bursting point.

They followed her up the stairs, saw how she lifted off the security chains and entered the six-digit code. Sjöberg had never for a moment thought she meant to hold them there. Regardless of how the conversation had developed.

Might she live happily for all her days, he thought as they left Dewi Kusamasari and her amazing apartment at Balmoral Crescent. Somewhat empty-handed.

———

Adrianti felt how the warmth from his hand spread into her body. The touch was gentle and sensitive, a question rather than a command, and it caused the hairs to rise on her arms. She became soft and compliant, let herself be drawn back down in the bed. Suddenly the air was perhaps not so thin, the darkness perhaps not so frightening.

"Stay with me," Staffan whispered, stroking her across the back.

"It's stuffy in here," Adrianti answered. "Dark."

"I'll open the door, so we let in a little air."

"That's just what I was going to do."

"I'll do it. You'll only knock something down. The drum set, for example. Lina wouldn't like that."

Adrianti smiled. It was true, she didn't even remember in which direction the door out of Lina's studio was. They had withdrawn back here to be in peace. In peace from lights and sounds and all the demands of the outside world: telephones and doorbells, the eyes of the neighbors, passing cars. Here it was absolutely silent.

They had devoted the whole evening and a large part of the night to talking. And making love. They had talked about all that had happened, about their feelings about what had happened, about life and about each other. In the darkness and the silence, it was possible to talk about everything.

Staffan got up out of the bed, supporting himself against her shoulder.

"What time is it?" she asked. "What do you think?"

"I was up for a while at about seven. That feels like a long time ago. Eleven?"

"I can't sleep that long," Adrianti said definitely. "It can't be more than nine."

Then the door opened and daylight flooded into the room.

"Quarter past three!" Staffan laughed with a glance at his watch. "It's quarter past three!"

"You're joking! I haven't slept so long in years."

Presumably she never had. When would she have had the opportunity to sleep away half a day?

Staffan crept down by her again.

"This was probably exactly what we needed."

Then he got serious. Not in that stern, authoritative, demanding way she was used to, but in his own slightly mournful way.

"I love you, Adri," he said, stroking away a wisp of her hair that had found its way into her mouth. "You do know that I love you?"

She nodded. Was not sure that she knew it. But she loved him, too. Always had.

"But we'll take it easy, Adri. We'll take it at your pace. At the pace that's best for all concerned."

She kissed him on the forehead. Looked into his amazing blue eyes, which were always completely sincere. Adrianti could really not bear to wait, wanted him now and forever.

"I need you," she said. "You make me feel . . . important."

He caressed her across the cheek, across the hair. Kissed her.

"You are," he said then. "You are very important. Otherwise I would have moved away from here years ago. I want to be with you."

"Staffan, I have no house, no money. I'm an extremely bad situation."

"I have a big house. I have a little money, too. And I would really like to have a situation. Even if it's a bad one."

Adrianti laughed. It felt like it was a very long time since she had.

"We don't need to broadcast it," Staffan continued. "We'll take it a little easy with the children. But we can be together anyway, can't we?"

"The children," said Adrianti. "I've got to turn on my phone. They may have tried to reach me."

She reached for her handbag and took out the phone.

Turned on the power and entered the PIN code.

"Do you think I'm irresponsible?" she asked.

He made a deprecating gesture with his hand, shook his head.

"Fifteen years ago, nobody had a cell phone. When did it become irresponsible to want to be by yourself for a while?"

The phone peeped. Text message. And then another. Another. And yet another. Adrianti entered the speed dial to voice mail and listened attentively to the messages. A delight that could not be put in words spread inside her, and she felt tears welling up in her eyes.

Staffan looked at her, presumably not grasping what was happening. But it didn't matter to him, he took her free hand in his and squeezed it hard. Showed clearly that whatever was playing out inside her, he was there for her. As support, as someone to share happiness and sorrow with.

When it was done, she dropped the cell phone to the floor, set her head on the pillow, and simply cried. A very peculiar reaction that did not at all reflect how happy she was. But there was something inside her that burst. It simply had to come out, and she could not stop it. Life had taken a whole new turn, and only now did it occur to Adrianti how much the uncertainty had tormented her.

Staffan asked no questions, simply lay by her side and held her. Caressed her carefully across the face, dried her tears with the edge of the sheet.

"It's Dewi," said Adrianti finally. "She's not dead. Dewi is alive and living in Singapore."

Staffan's face cracked into a big smile.

"He did what he promised," Adrianti continued. "Inspector Sjöberg kept his promise, and he's seen her."

Staffan took her head between his hands, kissed her on the forehead, and looked her long in the eyes before he spoke.

"That's amazing, Adri. Wonderful, beloved little Dewi. We'll go there. We'll pack our bags and go there."

"She has many rooms and many beds," Adrianti laughed, even as the tears ran. "But he wants to see me before I go. Conny Sjöberg wants to speak with me first."

"So when is he coming home?" Staffan asked eagerly.

"Friday morning."

"Then we'll leave on Friday evening."

"Regardless of what it is he wants to tell me," Adrianti added.

Staffan Jenner nodded in agreement, got up and pulled her to her feet, caught her in an embrace.

———

And then, last but not least . . . Hamad was now up to the fifth, and last, unidentified entry among Sven-Gunnar Erlandsson's telephone contacts. Someone who, as in the case of the "Contractor," the "Schoolmaster," the "IT Wizard," and the "Municipal Commissioner," lacked both name and address. Someone who, in contrast to the idiotic municipal commissioner, had an untraceable prepaid phone account. Namely, the "Police Chief." And Hamad felt reasonably convinced of who that was.

To be on the safe side, he verified the number one more time. And sure enough, the "Police Chief's" number was identical to the one from which the triumphant call had been made to Gunnar Malmberg's official cell phone. Which was the same as the number called from Erlandsson's cell phone via the Södertälje tower at exactly the same time. In brief, it was a matter of one and the same call.

When Simon Tampler had been investigating his new plaything as he sat on the train and caught sight of the "Police Chief" on the contact list, he could not refrain from making a little crank call.

Pumped up as he was after the murder, with adrenaline and God knows what. So he made the call to the "Police Chief" and ended up, lo and behold, with Acting Police Commissioner Gunnar Malmberg. However, via a number that was forwarded to Malmberg's official cell phone. Namely Malmberg's secret prepaid card number. Which remained to be proven. But who other than Malmberg himself would forward their calls to Malmberg? No one, of course.

And what was more, the nightly calls to Petra after her unmasking of the rapist Peder Fryhk had come from this very number. So it was Malmberg who was behind those threatening calls with no words, which for almost a year's time had disturbed Petra's sleep and mental well-being.

This was not particularly surprising. Hamad had known for a long time that Gunnar Malmberg was the Other Man. But now he had the telephone number. The secret, untraceable number Malmberg used only in his contacts with other men who also had secrets, who were also living double lives. For example, the former anesthesiologist at Karolinska Hospital, Peder Fryhk.

Perhaps the "Chief Physician" had previously had a separate entry in Sven-Gunnar Erlandsson's contact list. Perhaps that entry had been deleted in connection with Fryhk ending up at the Norrtälje prison. For Hamad was completely convinced of what this was about. These gentlemen were part of a closed society with a very particular interest, namely the violent assault of women. It was a question of something as repugnant as a rape ring. For even such differently constituted creatures needed playmates. Even though they required one hundred percent secrecy about their doings, they were also in need of like-minded companions, same as normally put-together people.

We humans are so much alike, thought Hamad, *and yet so different.*

Gunnar Malmberg could be new to the rape ring. Perhaps what he and Fryhk had done together was sufficient to satisfy Malmberg's needs. Perhaps a longing for the forbidden had become unbearable after Fryhk ended up in prison. But it could also be the case that Malmberg and Erlandsson had been together longer than that. It was not easy to know. What was quite clear, on the other hand, was that Malmberg needed company.

According to what had emerged so far, the interests of the ring partially diverged. Fryhk and Malmberg seemed to be content with raping adult women from time to time, while Municipal Commissioner Lars Karlsson apparently had an attraction to younger ones too. Perhaps Sven-Gunnar Erlandsson needed to break things up on occasion with something really brutal, something he could not even share with the others in the rape ring?

The question was: How did they find each other, these perverted swine? What happened when Acting Police Commissioner Gunnar Malmberg one day decided to take action, prepared to sacrifice his career, his family, and his honor to rape defenseless women? Did they meet on the internet? At Haga Video?

Perhaps you started on a modest scale, and then continued on riskier paths?

But perhaps the risk was not all that great, if the network included men in high positions in society, men with power. If politicians, corporate executives, and high-ranking officials in the legal system supported each other, how much evidence might then simply disappear in the mills of bureaucracy? Who knew how many perpetrators had gone free with the help of the thoroughly corrupt Gunnar Malmberg? The champion of women. Falseness personified. It made him dizzy to think about it.

When Hamad got access to the telephone lists, he put two and two together and drew his own conclusions about the connection between Erlandsson and Malmberg. Suddenly it was clear to him that in one way or another it was about rape. Once that insight had been reached, there were two conceivable scenarios: Either Erlandsson was—like Malmberg—a rapist, or else he was on the trail of a rape ring. A society where not only the "Police Chief," but also Lennart Wiklund, Jan Siem, or Staffan Jenner might be a member. Both alternatives could serve as a motive for murder.

Hamad had done what he could to drive the investigation in that direction, to open his colleagues' eyes to the fact that it apparently was about rape. But for Petra's sake, it was extremely important that what he knew about that telephone call not be revealed. Something that was compromising for himself, for his contribution to this investigation, Hamad was aware of that. But he was prepared to take the blows. Because it simply could not come out that it was Malmberg who, together with Fryhk, had raped Petra. Not until the time was ripe for Malmberg's arrest. And it would be, sooner or later. Hamad would see to that.

With the good help of Sjöberg, he thought as he carefully placed all the telephone lists from the Erlandsson case in the so-called sink.

—⁓—

"What a racket! Where are you, anyway?" Hamad asked, when he managed to figure out the conference call equipment.

"You wouldn't believe your eyes if you saw us," Andersson replied. "Conny's in a wheelchair. I'm in a hospital bed. Just refused an IV."

Hamad wrinkled his brow and exchanged glances with the others in the blue oval room. Sandén, Westman, Wallin, Rosén, and Hamad had gathered around the conference table to summarize the day's events. Gunnar Malmberg had also announced that he intended to participate in the meeting, but for the present he was conspicuous in his absence.

"Are you in the hospital?"

"Well, no. Not exactly. We're at a bar. Doctors and nurses are serving drinks from IV stands. But we're content with a good old-fashioned beer. From a glass."

"Ha, ha. So you're not drinking out of a bedpan?" Sandén teased.

"Not yet. I guess we'll have to see what happens later."

"Is he conscious, Sjöberg?" Rosén asked, who, like the other meeting participants, had a smile on his face.

"I'm here," Sjöberg replied laconically.

Hamad could hear how Sjöberg came to attention when he realized the prosecutor was also at the meeting.

"Thanks for the message, Walleye," Sjöberg said then. "Tell us what happened."

Sandén made a gesture to Westman to start.

"To start with, I can report that Rebecka Magnusson is on the road to recovery. She has still not regained consciousness, but they are keeping her anesthetized for the time being. The situation is stable and she's going to be fine. The family is with her and her mother sends greetings to you, Cod, in particular, and thanks you for caring. Rebecka was severely mistreated for a long time, but ironically enough it was the lack of food after Sven-Gunnar

Erlandsson's death that was killing her. The whole thing is too awful."

"As you heard, we also found two buried bodies," Sandén continued. "One was Larissa Sotnikova. She too was severely mistreated, according to Hansson. There are only bones left of her, but a number of them were evidently broken. The other body has been there longer. We have no leads about who she might be."

"I read in the newspaper this morning," Wallin interjected, "that four hundred ninety-four children seeking asylum have disappeared in Sweden since the beginning of the year. They are at risk of being exploited in the sex trade and as slaves. If you specialize, like Erlandsson, in particularly vulnerable children and women, you only have to pick and choose. That's the vulgar reality."

"So little Lara pointed us to Erlandsson," Westman continued. "She carved 'Ida's dad' in Russian on a piece of wooden molding that was hidden from Erlandsson behind the mattress on the floor. With her fingernails. And Rebecka will have a few things to say too, when she regains consciousness."

"And the evidence in the earth cellar speaks for itself," Rosén commented.

"Dewi Kusamasari will also identify him," said Sjöberg. "We've seen her, just came from there. A very agreeable acquaintance, I must say. Despite the horrifying experiences she has as baggage."

"Despite the fact that she's behind the murder of Erlandsson?" Wallin provoked.

"Despite that," Sjöberg replied. "She has provided a written account of what happened in connection with Larissa Sotnikova's disappearance. We'll fax it over when we get back to the hotel. How did you figure out it was her, Walleye?"

"I think she was searching the internet about crush injuries. Specifically in the feet. Then she happened to end up on Flashback, in Simon Tampler's murder thread, and then the idea was planted of how she might get rid of Erlandsson. You didn't get her to confess?"

"No," said Sjöberg. "But in a hypothetical conversation, she accounted for how she could have proceeded *if* she were to have instigated the murder. I tried to convince her to come along to Sweden, but she was not interested in that. And I understand. We have absolutely nothing on her, really. And I have no idea what the extradition treaty with Singapore looks like."

"Not so good," Rosén replied. "Especially if evidence of a crime is lacking."

"And we're damned happy about that." Sandén summarized in his unconventional, politically incorrect manner what everyone else was thinking deep down. "The murder of Erlandsson is the best thing that has happened in Älvsjö in this millennium, I think. Everyone's happy."

"A real win-win situation," Hamad thought he heard someone murmur off in Southeast Asia. He could not tell which of them.

"So celebrate, lads," Sandén continued. "Imbibe a few intravenous Singapore Slings until you become human again!"

And then suddenly he was standing there in the doorway, Acting Police Commissioner Gunnar Malmberg, who at long last showed up.

Hamad was prepared, had been sitting with his finger on the switch during the entire meeting. So. The call was made. The call to the "Police Chief" from Erlandsson's cell phone.

And there it was. Eric Clapton's "Layla." Unplugged.

"Excuse me, I simply must take this call," said Malmberg.

The thumbscrews were starting to be turned. Hamad could not stop the smile that spread across his entire face. His gaze met Petra's and she smiled back. A wave of warmth passed through him.